Praise for the Dave Cubiak Door County Mystery series

DEATH STALKS DOOR COUNTY

Finalist, Traditional Fiction Book of the Year, Chicago Writers Association

"Can a big-city cop solve a series of murders whose only witnesses may be the hemlocks? An atmospheric debut."
Kirkus Reviews

"A tight, lyrical first novel."
Publishers Weekly

"The characters are well drawn, the dialogue realistic, and the puzzle is a difficult one to solve, with suspicion continually shifting as more evidence is uncovered. . . . Impressive."
Mystery Scene

"Murder seems unseemly in Door County, a peninsula covered in forests, lined by beaches, and filled with summer cabins and tourist resorts. That's the hook for murder-thriller *Death Stalks Door County*, the first in a series involving ranger Dave Cubiak, a former Chicago homicide detective."
Milwaukee Shepherd Express

"A satisfyingly complex plot . . . showcasing one of the main characters, Wisconsin's beautiful Door County. A great match for Nevada Barr fans."
Library Journal

"Skalka's descriptions of the atmosphere of the villages and spectacular scenery will resonate with readers who have spent time on the Door Peninsula. . . . [She] plans to continue disturbing the peace in Door County for quite a while, which should be a good thing for readers."
Chicago Book Review

DEATH AT GILLS ROCK

"In her atmospheric, tightly written sequel, Skalka vividly captures the beauty of a remote Wisconsin peninsula." *Library Journal,* **starred review**

"The second installment of this first-rate series provides plenty of challenges for both the detective and the reader." *Kirkus Reviews*

"A well-wrought, tightly plotted police procedural with a nuanced, brooding detective, set on the gorgeous lakefront of a frigid Wisconsin peninsula."
Hallie Ephron, author of ***Night Night, Sleep Tight***

"A compelling, complex whodunit saturated with long-ago sins and festering hatreds." **Robert Goldsborough, author of** ***Archie in the Crosshairs***

DEATH IN COLD WATER

Winner, Edna Ferber Fiction Book Award, Council for Wisconsin Writers

"When philanthropist and major donor to the Green Bay Packers football team Gerald Sneider is kidnapped, the FBI wants to pin it on either terrorists who have been threatening the NFL or the millionaire's debt-ridden son. . . . Starring a tenacious cop who earns every ounce of respect he receives." *Booklist*

"A fast-paced story [with] a final, satisfying conclusion." *Mystery Scene*

"Sheriff Dave Cubiak is the kind of decent protagonist too seldom seen in modern mystery novels, a hero well worth rooting for. And the icing on the cake is the stunning backdrop of Door County."
William Kent Krueger, author of ***Windigo Island***

"A haunting depiction of heartbreaking crime."
Sara Paretsky, author of ***Brush Back***

DEATH RIDES THE FERRY

A DAVE CUBIAK DOOR COUNTY MYSTERY

PATRICIA SKALKA

THE UNIVERSITY OF WISCONSIN PRESS

The University of Wisconsin Press
1930 Monroe Street, 3rd Floor
Madison, Wisconsin 53711-2059
uwpress.wisc.edu

3 Henrietta Street, Covent Garden
London WCE 8LU, United Kingdom
eurospanbookstore.com

Printed in the United States of America

This book may be available in a digital edition.

Library of Congress Cataloging-in-Publication Data

Names: Skalka, Patricia, author. | Skalka, Patricia. Dave Cubiak Door County mystery.
Title: Death rides the ferry / Patricia Skalka.
Description: Madison, Wisconsin: The University of Wisconsin Press, [2018]
| Series: A Dave Cubiak Door County mystery
Identifiers: LCCN 2017044542 | ISBN 9780299318000 (cloth: alk. paper)
Subjects: LCSH: Door County (Wis.)—Fiction. | LCGFT: Detective and mystery fiction.
Classification: LCC PS3619.K34 D426 2018 | DDC 813/.6—dc23
LC record available at https://lccn.loc.gov/2017044542

Map by Julia Padvoiskis

Door County is real. While I used the peninsula as the framework for the book, I also altered some details and added others to fit the story. The spirit of this majestic place remains unchanged.

To

Barbara . . .

With joy and gratitude for our many years of friendship

Music is indeed the most beautiful of all Heaven's gifts to humanity wandering in the darkness. Alone it calms, enlightens and stills our souls.

Pyotr Ilyich Tchaikovsky

DEATH RIDES THE FERRY

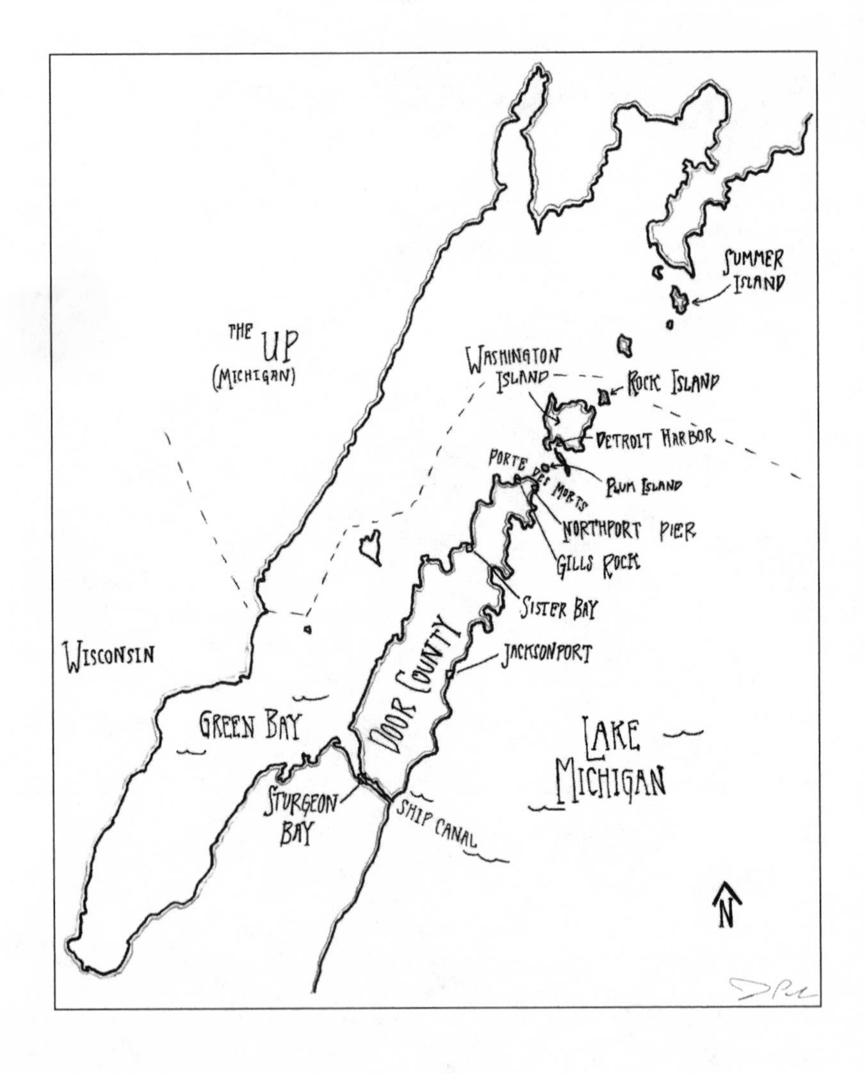

Summer Island
Washington Island
Rock Island
Detroit Harbor
Porte des Morts
Plum Island
Northport Pier
Gills Rock
Sister Bay
Jacksonport
The UP (Michigan)
Wisconsin
Green Bay
Door County
Lake Michigan
Sturgeon Bay
Ship Canal
N

BUSMAN'S HOLIDAY

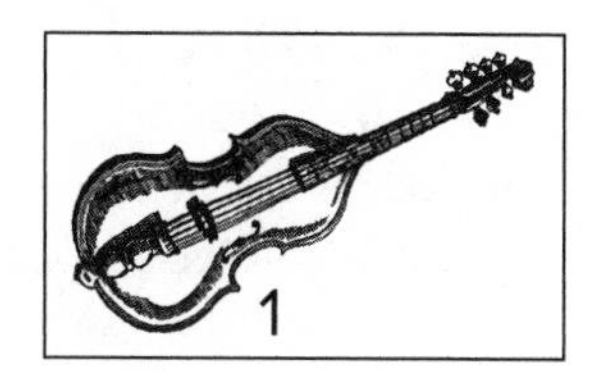
1

He had never been on a movie set and shouldn't have been on that one. Ignoring the Authorized Personnel Only signs, Dave Cubiak wandered the grounds of the Viola da Gamba Music Festival. Nobody stopped him. So much for security, he thought as he strolled past a pair of youthful guards hired to patrol the premises during the four-day event, known as Dixan V. Despite their crisp uniforms, they were just kids, more interested in their cell phones than in their jobs. He could lecture them about their responsibilities, but he didn't—partly because it was his day off, and partly because he understood the reason for their lack of concern. They were on Washington Island, off the tip of the Door County peninsula. Given the remote location, the perfect summer weather on that Wednesday afternoon, and the genteel nature of the event, they could conceive of no threat.

Cubiak wasn't interested in the performances. He came to watch the documentary film crew and to spend time with Cate, who was photographing the fest for a major music magazine. So far, he had found neither. Landing the assignment was a big deal, Cate had told him, because this was the first time that Wisconsin was chosen to host the show since a prized musical instrument vanished from the island forty years ago during the first festival, Dixan I.

A whistle blew, and a crowd of people costumed in a gaudy array of tie-dyed shirts, outlandish bell-bottoms, and pastel, polyester leisure suits paraded past. They were the extras who had been hired for the day's filming of the Dixan I reenactment. Groovy, the sheriff thought. Then he laughed. Had people really dressed like that?

Well, it was a different time back then, some would say a simpler time, although he would disagree.

As the extras settled on the lawn with their white box lunches, Cubiak realized that he was hungry. He glanced at his wristwatch, a habit that amused his youthful deputies. They teased him about being old-fashioned, but he didn't care. Whenever one of them needed to know the correct time, he would look at his wrist and respond while they fumbled for their cell phones. "If this was high noon in Dodge, you'd be dead," he told them.

The timepiece, a high school graduation gift from his parents and the only item of value they had ever given him, remained uncannily accurate. It was 2:12 p.m.—later than he thought, and late enough that the toast he had eaten hours earlier was mere memory. If he was lucky, the food service was still operating and he could grab a bite. But he had miscalculated and reached the food truck just as it was closing.

Cubiak pulled a long-forgotten power bar from his pocket and tore open the worn label. The emergency snack must have been in his jacket for weeks because it had disintegrated into an unappetizing mess of nuts and seeds. He sighed. He could make do with what he had and continue searching for Cate and the film crew or drive off-site for a sandwich and then come back later. Half-heartedly, he bit down. While he ate, he studied the faux audience that lounged on the lawn. There were women and men of all ages in the group, and they all looked so happy, he thought.

It was a short break. A second whistle blew, summoning the extras back to work. The crowd parted to reveal a shabby woman sitting alone on a boulder. She was alarmingly thin and dressed in dirty ragged jeans and a torn cotton top. Her Cinderella look contrasted sharply with the cheerful, time-warp attire of the extras. A faded patchwork bag hung across her sunken chest, and tangles of brown hair dangled to her stooped shoulders, obscuring part of her face and making it impossible to guess her age. Was she one of those youthful nomads who dotted America's landscape searching for adventure or a place to sleep, or was she an old-fashioned hippie who stubbornly clung to the vestiges of a lost dream?

The woman lifted a box lunch to her chin and pushed the crumbling remnants of a sandwich into her mouth. There was something pathetic and desperate about her. He didn't think she was on the staff, but the fact that she was eating food from the catering truck implied that she had some connection to the event. Maybe he could ask her to tell him about early music and then repay her for her time with a highly caloric, supersized milkshake or a giant piece of custard pie.

Cubiak was starting toward her when his phone vibrated.

"Sir, sorry to intrude, I know it's your afternoon off, but there's been an incident at Detroit Harbor and since you're on the island . . ." The communications deputy left the rest unsaid amid the background chatter of the 911 dispatch center some fifty miles away in Sturgeon Bay.

The sheriff tossed the rest of the half-eaten power bar. "Sure, no problem. What is it?" he said. An announcement blared from a loudspeaker pointed in his direction, and he turned away to hear better.

"Shoplifting at the new gift shop. The owner claims that she caught a customer with three hundred dollars' worth of goods in her purse."

Again, he thought. There had been a rash of thefts that summer. The most outrageous episode involved a two-thousand-dollar, carved wooden bench being hoisted into the back of a van from outside a gift shop while the stunned manager watched from inside. Luckily, Cubiak had been down the road when the call came in and arrived in time to catch the perp in the act. A local, no less.

Like many resort areas, Door County was a magnet for thieves. The professionals preferred small, pricey objects, like gold rings and jeweled bracelets, while sticky-fingered tourists favored the less expensive souvenir items: silver earrings, plaster-cast seagulls, and decorative mugs. But every snatched item hurt the bottom line of the merchants, whose profit margins were painfully narrow.

“On my way,” Cubiak said. He hung up and looked back at the cluster of white boulders. The derelict woman was gone, as if he had only imagined her.

The harbor gift shop occupied a restored log cabin, one of the island’s first structures. It sat a few yards back from the main road near the ferry launch. The bell over the door jangled when he went in. The owner was waiting for him. She wore a slim-fitting denim dress and had several rings on each hand.

“Thank goodness, you’re here,” she said.

Although she addressed the sheriff, she kept her eyes pinned on the alleged thief, who was blonde, around the same age, and equally well put together, in a black tunic and leggings.

The store owner was strident in her accusations, while the shopper, a Meryl Gregory, was equally insistent that she was just an innocent tourist. She had put the assortment of turquoise jewelry and handwoven silk scarves into her canvas tote after they became too numerous to hold, she said, and had every intention of paying for them.

Cubiak suggested that the visitor prove her good intentions.

While the two women completed the sales transaction, he looked out at the marina. The temperature had climbed steadily since morning, and in the late afternoon heat, there was little activity. Two grandmotherly types fanned themselves in the shade of the park gazebo as a family of three slowly pedaled away on rented bicycles. Along the shore, a half-dozen young boys leaned over their fishing poles and baited the hooks, while a young couple launched a tomato red kayak into the bay. Out on the water, the ferry that had just departed Washington Island passed one coming from Northport. Like children’s toys being pulled in opposite directions between the island and the mainland, the ferries traveled back and forth across Death’s Door, the strait that separated the two. It was all part of summer’s relaxed rhythm in Wisconsin’s vacationland.

A mint green convertible headed the line of cars and SUVs that had queued up for the next ferry. The string of vehicles wound past the gift shop. There were more than the sheriff imagined could fit on the ferry, although he knew from experience that most would squeeze on and those that didn't would take the next boat over. A cluster of bicyclists and pedestrians gathered as well. Among them was the downtrodden woman Cubiak had seen near the performance center. As before, she was alone and kept off to the side. She had pulled a wide-brimmed hat over her head and leaned against a fence post, clutching the faded bag that still hung from her coat-wire shoulders. How had she gotten here? he wondered. Then: What was in the bag?

He hoped it wasn't a stash of stolen goods.

The thought that the disheveled woman might be a common thief pained him, although he couldn't say why.

"That's the kind you watch like a hawk," the shopkeeper said. She had the alleged shoplifter by the elbow and had come up behind him, where she paused and followed his gaze out the window.

Oddly, the cruel remark gave Cubiak some relief. The pathetic vagabond waiting for the ferry wouldn't have half a chance to steal anything, not like the well-heeled and scowling woman in the grip of the shopkeeper.

"She seems harmless," he said, hoping without reason that the bulk in the bag was a ration of food for later.

The store owner harrumphed. "For a sheriff, you're an awfully trusting soul," she said. She gave him a warning smile and then turned a stony but polite face to the woman she had caught stealing. "Good day," she said.

Cubiak followed Ms. Gregory to her car.

"It would be best if you didn't come back," he said as she settled into the driver's seat.

He waited until she pulled into the line, and then he watched until her luxury sedan rolled onto the ferry and both sailed toward the peninsula.

As long as he was at the marina, he decided to get something to eat before returning to the festival grounds to look for Cate and the movie people. It was late in the day and there were only a few people in the harbor restaurant. "Anywhere's fine," said the waitress behind the counter.

He folded his six-foot frame into a checkered vinyl booth in the rear and greeted the two elderly gentlemen in the adjoining booth and the couple with the two toddlers sitting across from him. He had learned that's what folks did in Door County, Wisconsin. While he waited for his food, he listened to the retrospective of Beatles music that played in the background. He had few quiet moments on the job and enjoyed the rare opportunities he had to sit and relax. He had finished eating and was on a second cup of coffee when a lanky teenager in long, baggy shorts and a neon blue T-shirt slammed through the door. The boy had the look of someone who spent the summer outdoors. His face and arms were deeply tanned, and his hair and eyebrows had been bleached nearly white by the sun. All eyes turned to the teen, and the waitress smiled and said hi. The boy was too busy scanning the clientele to notice. When he spotted Cubiak, he hurried over.

"Sheriff?" The young man leaned in and lowered his voice. "Captain Norling radioed and told me to find you and ask you to come with me."

"Why?"

"Something's happened. He wouldn't tell me what, just that I had to get you. Please," he added, biting his lower lip.

"Oskar Norling, the ferryboat captain?" Cubiak had met the captain twice before and pegged him as a serious man, not the kind to send anyone on a fool's errand.

"Yes."

"Who are you?"

"Kevin, his grandson."

Once out the door, Kevin set off at a brisk pace for the water. Nearly running, he led the way past the loading area to a small, blue motorboat that was tied up farther down the dock.

"Please." Kevin indicated the boat. "I need to take you across."

"We're going to Northport in that?"

Kevin was already onboard starting the engine. His reply was lost in the roar.

Cubiak hesitated. Kevin looked all of fifteen, and the boat more like a soap dish than something able to safely cross the infamously treacherous waters of Porte des Morts. Reluctantly, he climbed in and took a seat.

"You do this often?" He had to yell to be heard.

"All the time."

It was cold on the water, and the motorboat offered little protection from the waves that smacked the prow. Cubiak gripped the narrow gunwale and pinned his gaze to the dark shadow of mainland on the far side of the passage, willing the dense forest to pull them forward out of the clutch of the whitecaps that churned the surface. Every year, a half-dozen locals swam across the four-and-a-half-mile strait to prove it could be done, but he couldn't imagine such an undertaking. He was a mediocre swimmer who liked knowing he could touch bottom whenever he needed to.

"There's a life vest under the seat," Kevin said, as if sensing his passenger's unease.

"Thanks," he said and glanced at the boy.

A bounty of human bones and sunken ships lay scattered across the lake bed beneath them, but Kevin seemed oblivious to the proximity of death.

"You're making me nervous, standing like that. Shouldn't you sit down?" the sheriff said.

"I can see better from up here."

Cubiak tried to relax.

"How'd you know where to find me?" he said finally.

"The lady at nine-one-one said you were on the island. When I saw your jeep in the marina, I figured you couldn't be far and asked around."

The sheriff couldn't help but smile to himself. Small-town policing was a far cry from what he had known in his other life as a Chicago cop.

Suddenly, the little boat roared past the breakwater that protected the ferry landing from the angry lashes of the deadly channel and entered the gentle waters of the harbor. Kevin slowed to a crawl and brought them round smartly alongside a long concrete dock not far from where the ferries were loaded.

"Over there," he said and pointed to one of the bigger boats moored off to the side. To Cubiak it looked like the ferry he had seen leave the island earlier that afternoon. He couldn't be sure. To him the boats were all the same, and he found it almost impossible to distinguish their names. He was accustomed to the Eastern European alphabetic jumble of letters—the *s*'s and *z*'s and *ch*'s—that were liberally sprinkled through the names of his childhood neighbors and friends. The Washington Island ferries were christened with long Scandinavian names that combined consonants and vowels in ways that stumped him.

Again, Kevin led the way. When they reached the *Ledstjarna*, he stopped. "My gran—the captain is waiting for you," he said, with an awkward bow.

Cubiak's footfalls sounded loud and out of place on the metal loading ramp and the deserted bottom deck. He was halfway to the second level when Captain Norling appeared at the top of the stairs.

"You're here," he said, staring past the lawman. "This way."

Norling was tall and barrel chested. He had a closely trimmed burnt-orange beard and a black watch cap smashed down tight on hair that was graying but still brushed with color. Cubiak remembered him as reserved, and he kept his own counsel as he followed the ferry captain past the rows of empty benches on the port side to the lounge entrance on the rear deck. Norling pushed the door open, and they stepped in. *Lounge* was too grand a word for the spartan room. The lighting was harsh, and the furnishings, although spotless, were designed for function, not comfort. It was a place to escape a too-hot sun or a too-strong wind and nothing more.

Cubiak took in the scene. A woman sat at the middle table along the inside wall, her back toward the entrance. Her chair was pulled in tight and she was bent forward, her head resting on her arms, as if she had fallen asleep during the short crossing. He couldn't see her face but from her slight frame and tattered clothing he recognized her as the woman he had seen earlier on the island, the misfit he had noticed sitting on the boulder outside the festival hall and again waiting at the ferry dock.

"Is she sick?" he said, hopefully.

Norling pursed his mouth. "Dead. I checked her pulse."

The sheriff did the same. The body was warm but he couldn't detect a heartbeat. Out of habit, he slipped his hand beneath the dull hair that fanned out over the woman's shoulders and pressed his fingers to the side of her neck. Again nothing, except the gritty feel of dirt on her skin that complemented the musty, unwashed aroma that perfumed the air. There was another strong scent in the air.

He looked at the captain. "Did you notice that?"

"Can hardly miss it. Smells like garlic to me," Norling said.

Cubiak knelt and peered at the victim's face. In death she looked younger but sadder than she had in life.

He had a detailed mental image of the woman and the surroundings, but, following procedure, he used the camera on his cell to take several photos.

"Who found her?"

"The senior deckhand. We'd finished unloading, and he was checking for lost items and stray children when he saw her."

"Where were you?"

"I was in the pilothouse finishing up the usual paperwork."

"Did you call for an ambulance?"

"No. I sent for you. I never had anybody die on one of my runs and figured it was best to get you here. It's too bad, you know, not just for her."

"What do you mean?"

Norling scowled. "Brings back memories of the first festival. A young woman died then, too. Not up here. She'd already left, but she'd been on the island with her husband, one of the musicians. It was a bad business all around."

"That was forty years ago."

"Yep, it was."

Cubiak glanced around the empty salon. He was concerned with what had happened earlier that afternoon, not four decades prior. "Do people usually come in here during the ride?"

"Only if the weather is bad or they're locals who don't care about the view. Most people like to ride outside, especially the tourists."

"How about on this trip?"

"I was on the bridge the whole time. The crew would know better."

"I'll need to talk to them. They're all still here?"

Norling nodded.

"And the passengers?"

"Oh, they're all gone. Scattered. Tourists mostly, I reckon." The ferry captain paused and then, as if anticipating the next question, he went on. "In the summers it's generally visitors who ride out for a few hours and then come back the same day. We don't keep track of people, if that's what you're wondering. We never have. There's never been a reason to."

"What about surveillance cameras?"

Norling laughed. "Cameras? This ain't the big city, Sheriff."

"You don't remember seeing anyone you knew?"

The boatman pulled at his chin. "Come to think of it, there were a couple of locals on board. Two retired schoolteachers. Nice as they come. I can give you their numbers if you want."

"I'd appreciate it. At least, it's a start," Cubiak said.

He bent and looked under the table. "The deceased was carrying a bag, one of those big cloth things women like. She had it when she got on the ferry."

Norling frowned. "Now how the hell would you know that? No offense meant."

"I saw her standing with the other pedestrians waiting to board. The bag was slung over her shoulder then."

"Maybe it's in her lap. Whenever we go out, my wife always puts her purse in her lap. Like she's afraid someone's gonna steal it if she puts it down."

They studied the still figure.

"No, the bag's not here," Cubiak said. It was gone, along with everything the dead woman carried in it, he thought. Her identification, her money if she had any, and whatever it was that she was holding onto so fiercely—all vanished.

THE WOMAN IN THE LOUNGE

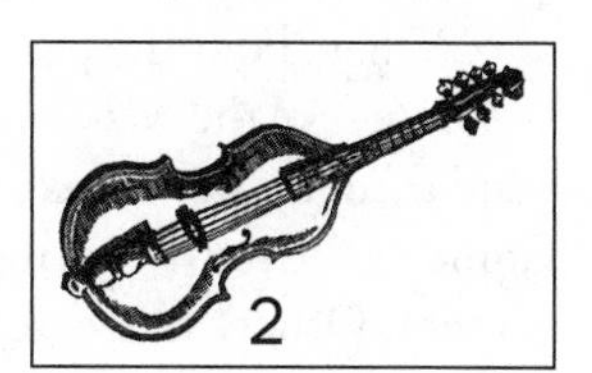

The crew of the *Ledstjarna* stood in the shadows near the front loading ramp. From the upper deck, Cubiak took their measure. It was a four-person team: two adults and two adolescents, all male. The men had the heft and muscle that come with age and hard work. Like a matched pair, they leaned against the side wall, standing with their arms crossed and one foot resting against the metal bulwark. The teenage boys looked to be around sixteen and were probably working their first summer jobs. They were lanky and twitched with nervous energy. As he crossed the deck, the sheriff noted that all four were suntanned, blue eyed, and Scandinavian. Norling said Tim Vultan, the senior deckhand, discovered the dead woman but the others had probably seen her too. For the boys, the experience would have been especially upsetting. Better to work up to it, Cubiak thought.

He stepped up to Vultan, the tallest of the lot. He had a stoic, tired face and wild eyebrows that seemed to be waving at the world.

"Let's start by having you walk me through the procedure you followed on the island," he said.

At the question, Vultan uncrossed his thick arms and relaxed. This was familiar territory. "It was the same as always. We loaded the vehicles first. There were twenty-three this trip. I collected tickets while the others directed traffic and got everybody lined up. We gotta get as many on as possible in precise rows that can unload quickly." The deckhand squinted despite the dimming light. "'Course we also gotta make sure nobody's crammed in so tight they can't open their doors. Worst thing is to have some idiot back into somebody else. Nobody likes that. People get real protective of their vehicles, and we respect that."

"What about the passengers?"

"We take the walk-ons last. Once they cross the ramp, the boys here send them upstairs where they're free to sit or stand wherever they please. Some of the tourists bring bikes, and if they want to stay with them we let 'em. Otherwise we secure the bikes in a corner and send the riders upstairs just like the others."

"And do you collect their tickets as well?"

"It's part of my job."

"What was Norling doing all this time?"

"The captain was in the pilothouse going through his checklist. Engines, pressure gauges, weather, and such. It's a short jaunt but he doesn't want any surprises out there."

"As far as any of you recall, was there anything unusual about this crossing?"

"Nothing at all, Sheriff, and I've been doing this for nearly thirty years." The other man spoke up. He had a gray Santa mustache and he took his time with his words. "There's usually not. Mostly it's tourists going back and forth. They're not here to talk to us. If it's regulars, we might say hello but even then most people keep to themselves. They've got business to take care of and aren't looking to chat."

"Do you remember seeing the woman board the ferry?"

"No, sorry."

The two teens shook their heads.

Vultan grimaced. "I do, but only because I caught a whiff of her when she gave me her ticket. She smelled like she could have used a bath and some good mouthwash."

"What about during the crossing? Did any of you notice her, see what she was doing?"

Again they shook their heads.

"So you don't know if she talked to anyone or where she was before she sat down in the lounge?"

The teens shuffled their feet and shrugged. "Sorry," they said in unison.

"We were all here on the main deck, like always. It's a short trip and we've got plenty to do both before and after. Those few minutes on the water is our little bit of downtime. When we dock at Northport, it's another rush, except that everything is in reverse," Vultan said.

"Normally, once the ferry is empty you'd start loading up again, right?"

"After a few minutes, yes. First we check the boat. I go around making sure all the passengers are off. My helper here"—he indicated the other man—"looks for stuff they might have left behind and the boys go around too, picking up papers and trash."

"And that's when you found her."

He pulled at his lip. "Yes."

"It didn't strike you as odd to see the woman at the table like that?"

"Odd, yes, but not unheard of. People are out in the sun all day and then, on the trip back, the sound of the engines and the rocking on the water can lull them to sleep. I let her be until I finished my rounds and then I came back. I said, 'Miss, you gotta get up,' real loud a couple of times. When she didn't respond, I shook her shoulder and when that didn't do nothing, I got this queer feeling that something bad had happened and I right away went and got the captain."

"Who was on the ferry at the time?"

"Just the four of us and the captain."

Cubiak felt a sharp pain over his right eye and rubbed his forehead to ease the pressure. "The passenger had a bag with her. A tote or a big shoulder purse. Did you see that?"

The senior deckhand shook his head. "If she was carrying it when she came aboard, I didn't notice. And I didn't see it when I found her in the lounge, but I wasn't looking either."

"What about the rest of you?" the sheriff said.

None of the other three remembered seeing the missing bag either.

"Do you work the same shifts all summer?"

"No. It varies, depending on the day of the week and what's going on up on the island," Vultan said.

"So you've been on different boats the past week or so."

"Yeah, mostly."

"Do any of you remember seeing this woman make the trip to the island?"

The boys and the old man shrugged.

"We're going back and forth all day during the summer. In July and August alone, we'll handle twenty thousand or more folks. Unless it was the queen of England, I don't think we'd remember any one person," Vultan said.

His small joke evoked a laugh from the rest of the crew.

"Besides, our ferry's not the only way to get there," he went on. "She could have taken the passenger ferry from Gills Rock or hitched a ride with someone who had a boat. Hell, I've even seen people kayak across the strait. Crazy as all get out, but if you live long enough you see people do some pretty strange stuff."

It was nearly seven, but still light out. The ambulance idled near a stand of dark green pines. Dr. Emma Pardy waited nearby in her car. When Cubiak dismissed the crew, she approached the ferry. The medical examiner wore striped leggings and a loose flowing top. With a cup of coffee in one hand, she looked like another tourist. It was the black bag she carried that gave her away.

"Sorry to have to end your day this way," the sheriff said as he offered her a hand and helped her aboard. Pardy was a triathlete and in better shape than he, but she never refused his small gestures of courtesy.

"What have you got?" she said.

"Victim is female. Age uncertain but looks to be fairly young. No visible signs of trauma. I saw her waiting to board the ferry, and the senior deckhand remembers collecting her ticket, so she was alive when they left Washington Island and then was found dead about ten minutes after they unloaded at this end," Cubiak said on the way up the stairs.

"And the trip is how long, thirty minutes?"

"Just about, from the time the boat leaves one harbor and ties up at the other."

"That's a pretty narrow window. Anything else?"

"Nothing. None of the crew remember seeing her onboard, and I haven't had a chance to talk to any other passengers. I know she had a tote bag with her but that's missing, so no ID."

"A Jane Doe then," Pardy said with a touch of sadness.

At the lounge door, she pulled on her gloves. "You've taken all the photos you need?"

"Yes."

"Right then. Give me a few minutes."

Cubiak waited for Pardy to inspect the scene. Then he helped her lay the body on the floor.

"I'll give you what I can," the medical examiner said.

Temporarily dismissed, he retraced his steps to the pilothouse where Norling was waiting. The room was square and lined with windows on all four sides. The radio was mounted in one corner and an alarm panel in another. A radar screen and a series of gauges filled the instrument panel.

"How much longer is this going to take?" the captain asked, his hand resting on the silver wheel that steered the boat.

"As long as Doctor Pardy needs. She's generally pretty quick with the preliminaries."

"Good. Then I can have my vessel back."

"I'm afraid not. Until we know how the victim died, I have to treat the death as suspicious and keep the ferry out of commission."

"Here?"

"Yeah, here."

Norling looked up from his paperwork. "You can't do that. The boats get docked on the island overnight. It's a safer harbor." He pointed toward the Northport landing. "If a strong south wind comes up, that breakwater doesn't offer much protection."

"I have no choice."

"Look, Sheriff, I'm sorry the woman is dead, but I have a business to run. It's obvious she had a heart attack. I've seen it before."

"You could be right, but Doctor Pardy has to determine cause of death. Until we can rule out anything suspicious, the ferry is a potential crime scene and it stays put."

Norling scowled. "This is going to make my life difficult and maybe scare people away."

Actually, it might be a draw, Cubiak thought, but he kept the notion to himself. "We'll be as quick as we can."

Several shouts came from shore, and both men turned to see a trio of noisy tourists piling into a car.

Cubiak waited for them to drive off.

"Did another boat go back after you docked?"

"Sure. That's how we run them."

"Was it full?"

"I wasn't paying attention, but it seemed like there were a half-dozen cars and a couple of walk-ons."

"Did you notice if anyone made the round trip?"

"You mean take one ferry here and then go back on the next trip? Now why would somebody want to do that?" Norling stared out the window again and was quiet a moment. "I have seen it happen. Once because some idiot left his car here and a couple times with young lovers who couldn't stand to be parted for longer than necessary, you know what I mean. But today, no, I don't think so."

The sheriff laid his card next to the logbook. "That's my direct number. Call me if you think of anything."

Pardy was still bent over the victim when he returned. "Twenty minutes," she said at the sound of his footsteps.

Cubiak backed away from the door and continued down the stairs. Seven years prior, when he made his first crossing, he had been as anxious as a kid strapped in a rocket ship. Despite growing up in Chicago not twenty minutes from Lake Michigan, he was skittish around water and leery of boats. He remembered standing on the upper deck and getting more nervous each time a car thudded over the ramp and the boat trembled. He was convinced they would sink in the deepest part of the strait. Over time, he learned to sail and to pilot a powerboat and made several dozen trips on the ferry back and forth to Washington Island. Experience and knowledge tamped down his fears and gave him a deep respect for those who made their living from the water. Still, in a storm, he would stay onshore if given the option. Not even the lumbering comfort of the sturdy ferry would entice him to test his luck when marine warnings were issued.

From the main deck he looked out at the small harbor. The moon was more than half full, and beneath its glow, a gentle stillness had settled over Northport. Like the boat, the landing was empty, and almost ghostly in the silver light. Cubiak figured that the two cars in the lot belonged to the last of the restaurant staff. He couldn't imagine that the dead woman had visited the café, but he had time to fill before checking back with Pardy and so he headed across to the diner.

"We're closed," a strong female voice rang out as he pushed through the door. From behind the cash register, a tall, hefty woman looked up. "I said we're closed." Her voice was gruff and lines of fatigue were etched in her face. Then she noticed Cubiak's badge. "Oh, sorry, Sheriff. I didn't realize it was you. If you want something, I'll get Bruce to rustle up a bite."

She was being polite, trying not to look past him at the ambulance and the ferry moored to the side dock.

"Just a couple questions, if you don't mind," he said.

"About that woman they found dead on the ferry?"

"You heard?"

She shrugged. "Word travels."

He gave them a verbal picture of the deceased. "Do you remember seeing a woman who fits that description? Or maybe notice anything unusual?"

Bruce, the cook, replied first. "I been in the kitchen all day. Don't see any of the customers from back there. Only breaks I had was once to eat something myself and twice for a smoke and then I was out back in the woods. Didn't see anything I don't normally see," he said.

The waitress was equally unhelpful. "Probably a couple hundred people here today, but all of them pretty much fit the standard tourist mold. I'd have remembered if I'd seen one of those hippie types. We used to get them all the time. But not anymore. Not for years."

Cubiak took down the names of the staff on the earlier shift. "Call me if you think of anything," he said. He gave his card to the waitress and another to Bruce, like so many bread crumbs dropped in the sand.

Outside, the ambulance had pulled up alongside the ferry. He walked over and waited with Pardy as the EMTs maneuvered the gurney down the stairs and onto the dock.

"Anything?" he said.

"There was a strong odor of garlic, which might not mean anything. But beyond that, nothing. No obvious sign of trauma or injury."

"The captain thinks she had a heart attack."

"She's fairly young but it could be. I'll know more tomorrow after the autopsy."

The sheriff walked the medical examiner back to her car. From the edge of the dark forest, he watched her taillights disappear down the road. A few minutes later, the ambulance pulled away with Jane Doe inside.

Who are you? he wondered. What were you doing here?

TRACE AMOUNTS

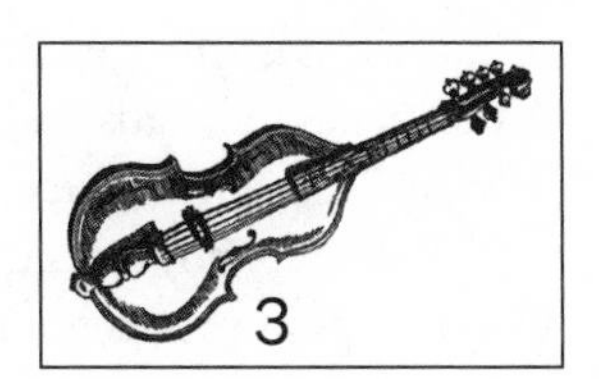

Emma Pardy called the sheriff's office early Thursday morning.

"Looks like Norling was partly right about Jane Doe. The victim suffered cardiac arrest."

Cubiak put down the traffic report he had been reading. "She had a heart attack?"

"Yes, but it's what caused her heart to stop that's of more interest. There are indications she was poisoned."

He picked up his coffee. "Go on."

"You noticed the garlicky odor?" Pardy said.

"It was hard to miss."

"At first I thought it was from something she'd eaten, but when I did the autopsy I realized it was a result of a toxin. Besides the aroma, there's a range of indicators: dilated blood vessels, severe burns to the lining of the mouth and the lungs, as well as edema and swelling of the brain. She had all the symptoms."

"What kind of poison would do that?"

"At this point I don't know. I can't pinpoint the exact cause until the toxicology results are in, and that could take a couple of weeks."

"But if you had to take a guess?"

The medical examiner didn't hesitate. "I'd put my money on selenium."

"Never heard of it."

"Most people haven't. It's a nonmetallic element, part of the sulfur and polonium family. It's found in gun bluing—the stuff collectors and antique dealers use to darken metal. But selenium also occurs naturally in some foods and even in water, and we need trace amounts in our diet. A deficiency can cause several medical issues, but too much can kill."

"Assuming it was selenium, what's too much?"

"That depends on the situation. I've seen only one case and that was when I was in med school. The victim was a physically fit, middle-aged professional photographer who processed his own prints and 'toned' them with selenium dioxide to make the images more permanent. In his case, the poisoning occurred over many years and resulted from inhaling the fumes in his darkroom."

Cubiak recalled the scene on the ferry. "There was nothing else found with the body. Nothing she could have inhaled." Unless someone took it, he thought.

Pardy seemed to be following his train of thought. "Inhalation is just one way to administer the poison. Whatever it was, the victim could have ingested it before she got on board. A toxin like selenium would take a bit of time to work. How long depends on the amount."

"More than a few minutes?"

"Absolutely. I found only a small amount of the poison in her system, so death wouldn't occur for at least a couple of hours."

"Sounds like it's pretty easy to get hold of this selenium stuff," he said.

"Well, digital cameras pretty much eliminated the toning process, so photographers aren't in the market for it anymore. But like I said, it's used in gun bluing so it's available anywhere guns are sold, including the internet. And people take selenium supplements, too, thinking they're good for them," Pardy said.

"Which means there'd be nothing suspicious about a person buying it," Cubiak said.

"Exactly. Including the victim." Pardy paused. "She could have done it herself, Dave."

The sheriff remembered seeing Jane Doe outside the performance center the previous day. She was gobbling down a sandwich like she was starving. But if she had laced the food with poison in order to kill herself, maybe she was eating fast to be done with it.

Cubiak had endured enough dark nights of the soul to realize that Pardy's suggestion had to be considered. Everything he had seen of the victim implied that she was in desperate straits. From her perspective, perhaps the universe was tinted black, and all hope had drained away. Why come to Door County, then? Why travel from the place she called home to take her own life? And what about the bag he had seen her holding? What had happened to it?

"Maybe, but I don't think so," he said finally.

At 10 a.m., Cubiak pinned Jane Doe's photo to the wall of the incident room and filled in the staff on the circumstances surrounding the discovery of her body. He described the missing bag and shared the medical examiner's theories about the woman's death.

"We've got an unknown victim, a suspicious death, and no leads," he said. He assigned one deputy to file a report with the Department of Justice's missing persons database and another to contact law enforcement in the neighboring counties to inquire whether they had any information on a woman fitting the victim's profile. Mike Rowe, another of Cubiak's deputies, was to ask the local radio stations to report news of the woman's death and to urge anyone who recognized the description or who saw or heard someone talking with her to get in touch with the sheriff's office immediately. Then the deputy was to head up Highway 57 and nose around the lakeshore communities. The sheriff said he would do the same on the bay side.

"Maybe we'll get lucky. Our victim didn't materialize out of thin air. It's nearly forty-five miles from Sturgeon Bay to the ferry dock. Unless she had a car, which I doubt, she had to have some way of getting from place to place. Somebody had to have seen her."

Once he dismissed his deputies, Cubiak contacted the state evidence team. Finally, he called Norling.

"The state boys are on their way but the *Ledstjarna* is going to have to remain out of commission until they finish." He stumbled over the name of the ferry and silently apologized. "This evening is probably the soonest you'll have the boat back on the water."

The ferryboat captain responded with an impressive range of salty verbiage. "We don't even know how many people walked through that room before Tim discovered that woman. You're not going to find anything."

"Maybe not."

"I have a job to do," Norling said at full volume.

And I don't? The sheriff kept the thought to himself. "I told the evidence crew to expedite things. That's the best I can do," he said.

Cubiak's first stop north of Sturgeon Bay was Carlsville. If Jane Doe had come through the crossroads community, she hadn't stopped. From there, he headed to the village of Egg Harbor. The community's year-round population of 291 swelled to several thousand during the summer, and on that sunny afternoon a good number of locals and tourists vied for space on the sloping lawn of the waterfront park. There had been a kids' puppet show in the park that morning, and the weekly afternoon bluegrass concert was about to start. He circled through the swarm of folding chairs and coolers with Jane Doe's photo. No one remembered having seen the woman. He tried the local bars and the food store as well. Nothing.

He went on to Fish Creek. The town was hosting an art fair, and white-tented booths filled the old square and lined the neighboring lanes. Many of the exhibitors had spent the previous two weeks in Door County, moving from place to place. But none of them recognized the victim. Nine miles farther up, he walked a long stretch of the Ephraim shoreline and talked to vacationers who were enjoying time on the beach or waiting to rent kayaks and canoes. Again, nothing.

He hoped to have better luck at the passenger ferry in Gills Rock. The ticket seller took her time inspecting the photo but finally shook her head. "No, sorry, Sheriff. I've never seen her before."

He spent another hour talking to the day staff at the Northport restaurant but struck out again. How could a woman so distinctively attired travel incognito up the entire length of the peninsula?

Cubiak called Rowe. "Any luck?"

"Nada. I tried Institute and Valmy as well as Jacksonport and Baileys Harbor, but nobody remembers seeing her."

"Well, we're not done yet. There's still Sister Bay and Ellison Bay and two islanders that I have to question," the sheriff said.

In the middle of the afternoon, Cubiak boarded the ferry at Northport. The vessel was filled with tourists who were reveling in the start of the long weekend, and their happy mood was infectious. By the time the boat docked at Detroit Harbor, he wondered if he was on the wrong track. What if Pardy was mistaken about the cause of death? What if Jane Doe's death wasn't a case of suicide or murder? If she had worked for an antiques dealer or a gun seller, she might have had routine contact with selenium, which could have resulted in her death, just like Pardy's example of the med-school photographer.

Earlier that morning, Captain Norling had emailed him the contact numbers for Grace Abernathy and Loretta Cummings, the local women he recalled seeing on the same ferry as Jane Doe. The women had agreed to meet Cubiak at Grace's house. From the harbor, it was a short hop to the road where the two had been next-door neighbors for more than a half century. The moment the door to the cottage opened, he understood that they had prepared for his visit. A large bouquet of lilies scented the air, a collection of throws was neatly folded, and the row of sofa pillows was plumped and neatly arranged. There were traces of rouge on the women's faces, and, by Door County standards, both were quasi-formally dressed in navy blue slacks and pastel twinsets.

"We've never talked to the sheriff before, not in any official capacity," Grace said as she led the way through the uncluttered living room to the red brick patio. Cookies and lemonade had been set out on a small pink table, more evidence of their planning. Cubiak admired the view of the water and waited for the women to complete the ritual of pouring and serving before he spoke.

"You were both on the four o'clock ferry to the mainland yesterday?"
They smiled and nodded.
"Do you mind if I ask why?"
Grace tucked a loose strand of gray hair behind her ear and answered for the pair. "Not at all, Sheriff. Loretta and I are ladies of leisure, now that we're retired, and every two weeks we treat ourselves to an outing. Yesterday we went to the movies in Sturgeon Bay. We always go for the senior discount day. Then we have dinner with my sister. She's widowed, and with the kids all gone her house is empty. So we stay over at her place and take the ferry back in the morning."
"You drove, then."
"Of course."
"During the crossing, did you stay in the car or get out?"
"Oh, we got out. I can't tolerate being cooped up in the car. We always get out and go up on the deck."
Cubiak laid the photo of Jane Doe on the table. "Did you see this woman onboard?"
Grace held the photo up for a close look and studied it for several moments. Then she shook her head. "No, sorry. I didn't see her."
When it was her turn, Loretta glanced at the picture and then pushed it across the table as if it were toxic. "I saw her, and I have to tell you that it was quite unpleasant. I had to walk through the lounge to get to the ladies' room and went right past her. She was sitting there at the table, and she smelled awful. I'm sorry to have to say that but it's true."
"Do you remember what she was doing?"
"She was reading a book. At least, it looked like she was reading it. She was holding it and staring at it intently."
"What kind of book was it?"
Loretta furrowed her brow. "I'm not sure. It had a blue cover but it wasn't a regular book, not like a novel or something from the library. It was bigger, like a scrapbook. I was too focused on my own business to pay that much attention. Anyway I'm allergic to garlic. I can't stand the smell, and the room reeked of it."
"Did you see anyone talking to her?"
"No, she was alone."

"How far into the ride were you then?"

"About halfway across. I remember looking to the west and seeing nothing but water."

"And was she still there when you came back?"

Loretta blushed. "I just saw her the one time. When I finished, I went back the long way, down the other side, to avoid having to walk through the lounge again."

"But the woman was alive when you saw her?"

"Absolutely. She was very much alive." Loretta hesitated. "To be honest, I felt a little sorry for her. She seemed so sad, as if something was very wrong. Maybe I should have said something to her."

Grace clasped her friend's hand. "Now, Loretta, don't you go blaming yourself. You didn't do anything wrong."

Loretta picked at her napkin.

Cubiak let the moment pass. Then he said, "You're an observant woman, and that's very helpful. But tell me, what makes you think that woman on the ferry was sad?"

Loretta opened her eyes wide. "Oh, Sheriff, it's because of the way she was crying."

THE YELLOW VIOL

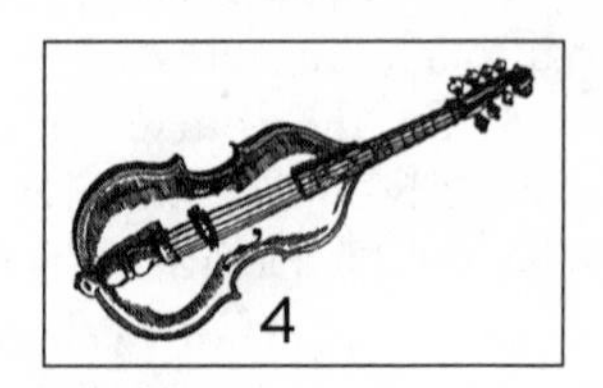

Grace Abernathy insisted that Cubiak have more cookies and lemonade before he left. He was happy to comply, and not just because the homemade refreshments were tasty. He felt indebted to her friend Loretta for the information she had provided. She was the first person who remembered seeing Jane Doe on the *Ledstjarna*, and from her he learned that the victim was alive when the ferry was still ten minutes from Northport. Even more important was her eyewitness account of the victim's actions and frame of mind. When he saw the young woman earlier, she seemed pensive and preoccupied but not unhappy. Something had happened during the interlude to bring her to tears.

After meeting with the ladies, the sheriff drove to the festival. The next series of concerts started in ten minutes and the grounds were filled with people hurrying to reach their seats. As he pushed through the cheerful throngs, he pictured Jane Doe sitting on the ferry and wondered what went through her mind before she died. Had she been crying because of something that had happened at the festival? Or because she had taken the poison, as Pardy suggested, and then had a change of heart and realized too late that she wanted to live?

A ridge of cold sweat trickled down Cubiak's neck. After his wife and daughter were killed, he had come close to ending his life on more than one occasion. But each time, he imagined the terror he would feel if he changed his mind when he had reached the point of no return. What happened if you had committed yourself to death and then decided you wanted to live? Had the horror of such a moment led Jane Doe to desperate tears? Or had some other matter driven her to this state? Perhaps something she saw in the scrapbook had made her cry. Or had she met with bitter disappointment on Washington Island? A breakup with a lover would do it. Perhaps she had followed someone to the Dixan V festival and then been rejected. Or she had other dreams that were trampled on and destroyed? Jane Doe died after she left the island, but why had she come here in the first place?

Cubiak swiped at his brow. The sun was high and the heat was building. As he looked around for shade, he was struck by the transformation on the festival grounds. With the filming of the reenactment completed, the extras had discarded their vintage clothing. A middle-aged couple in khaki shorts and T-shirts leaned against the boulder where the dead woman had sat the day before. They were drinking white wine and arguing about music.

The program listed nightly concerts in the hall, but the afternoons were given over to smaller performances by groups of three, four, and six musicians. The sheriff knew little about classical music beyond what his friend Evelyn Bathard had taught him about opera while they worked on the coroner's dilapidated wooden sailboat. From the bits and pieces that he overheard as he wandered the grounds, he knew the musicians were playing stringed instruments, but the music was different from anything he had ever heard. It seemed to have a simpler, cleaner sound than the more familiar music of Mozart and Beethoven. He wished he could sit in on a performance, but he had little time for music that day.

A poster on the front wall of the performance center identified the festival organizers as James Frost, Veronica Winslow, and Mitchell L. Stone III. He found the trio huddled around a small table in a cramped office at the rear of the building. The blinds were drawn but the room faced west, and on that sunny afternoon the window air-conditioner did little to cool the space.

Cubiak knocked. "Sorry to interrupt," he said.

The three looked up startled.

"I hope this is important, Sheriff. We have a busy schedule," Frost said after introductions were made. He was short and stout and patted his forehead with a white handkerchief as he spoke.

"I'm sure you do." There wasn't an empty chair, so Cubiak stood and told them about the woman who was found dead on the ferry.

"I heard about that. It's too bad, of course, but what does it have to do with us?" Winslow said. She was tall and slim and wore a tailored navy suit topped with a flowered shawl. In the heat, the layers seemed incongruous.

"She was here during the enactment, and I hoped that one of you could identify her," Cubiak said. He showed them the photo.

Winslow replied first. "I never saw this woman before. She isn't one of our musicians, that's for certain."

"Could she have been part of the crew?"

Frost dismissed the notion with a wave. "No. No way."

"You're sure?"

"Absolutely. I vetted the whole lot."

"She was seen on the grounds yesterday, and I'm trying to learn what brought her here. It's possible someone involved with the event knew her or knew why she was here."

"And?"

"And I need the names of everyone involved with the festival—extras, film crew, musicians, whatever."

The AC momentarily clicked off and in the hard silence that followed, the organizers exchanged somber glances.

"Sheriff, you have to realize that we can't have a dead woman associated with Dixan V. It would ruin everything. Not just this year's event, which so many people have worked for so hard, but"—Winslow gestured toward the grounds outside the center—"everything."

"Why? Because four decades ago, a woman died after the first Dixan festival?"

The three stirred uneasily.

"It's more than that. You don't understand because you're not from here," Frost said, his tone harsh. "Sorry, no offense meant."

That was the second time in two days that a local had said that. Cubiak nodded to indicate that none was taken. He had lived in Door County for nearly seven years and had served as the top law enforcement officer during most of that tenure, but he knew that the longtime residents still considered him a newcomer.

"I don't mean to sound insensitive to the poor woman on the ferry, but it's just that we are trying to live down our own sorry history with the public and the Dixan sponsors. This year's festival is our chance to salvage the island's reputation. If we don't succeed, as Veronica just said, then it's over for us. Finito. Poof." Frost blew a puff of air at his empty palm like a child would at the fuzzy head of a dandelion.

Winslow pushed a small brochure across the table. Her nails were neatly manicured, and it was clear from her posture and manner that she was the kind of person who took appearances seriously. "This is from the first—the only—Dixan Festival ever held on Washington Island before now."

Cubiak skimmed the headline. "I've heard a little about it. But that was forty years ago."

"That is correct."

"During which a rare violin disappeared."

Winslow sighed and exchanged frustrated looks with her colleagues.

Mitchell Stone stretched his elongated neck and spoke for the first time. "Not a violin, Sheriff. A viola da gamba," he said as he adjusted his striped tie. "Shall I assume you don't know the difference?"

Cubiak ignored the dig. He was out of his league and they all knew it. What had Sister Mary Nicholas told his class of fourth graders: true humility is acknowledging what you know as well as what you don't know. "You may," he said.

Stone cleared his throat. With his bald pate and the tortoiseshell glasses perched on his arched nose, he looked like a man who should have a couple of roman numerals after his name, the sheriff thought.

"Stringed instruments have been plucked and bowed since ancient times. I won't bore you with the ancestral lineage, but for our purposes let us just say that they eventually evolved into two separate families or categories. The newer, more modern family includes the violin, viola, cello, and bass. The other, older family is called viola da gamba, which includes a number of different instruments, from the high-pitched, five-string pardessus to the deeper viola bastarda."

Stone was showing off, and Cubiak let him.

"Many people argue that the gamba was the precursor of the violin family, but it's not. What is indisputable is that by the early seventeenth century, the violin had overtaken the viola da gamba as the preferred string instrument in classical music and has maintained a firm grasp on that claim. Meanwhile the viola da gamba faded into the shadows, only to enjoy a revival of sorts over the past hundred years, to the point where it has cultivated its own following and devotees."

Frost pointed to the picture on the front fold of the pamphlet. The black-and-white photo depicted a rigid and unsmiling man holding an odd-looking instrument.

"That is a viola da gamba. To the uneducated eye it looks like a large violin but there are important differences in size, tenor, material, and just so much more. The sounds are different as well. Even playing is different. A violin is held *en braccio*, in the arms like this." Frost swept his up to demonstrate. "And the bow is grasped from above, like so." He arched his hand with the fingers pointing down. "But a gamba is held with the legs. In fact, gamba means leg in Italian," he said, leaning over and opening his knees to show how this would be done. "And the bow is held with an underhand grip." This time the tips of his fingers pointed up.

Cubiak glanced at the pamphlet. "Is that the instrument that disappeared?"

"Sadly yes. This is the renowned yellow viol, a rare sixteenth-century instrument fashioned by Augusto Fiorrelli. Not quite in the league of a Strad—a Stradivarius—but worth close to a quarter million even back then. It vanished from Washington Island in the midst of the first Dixan festival. The man holding it is Franz Acker, who at the time was among the world's premier gambists."

Winslow took up the rest of the story. "The Europeans resented the fact that the Gamba Association picked America to host the festival and then were even more appalled that such a remote location was selected. Ultimately, they consented to attend and perform with our American gambists only because Acker agreed to be the headliner, and he came only because he was assured that the isolated nature of the island enhanced and even guaranteed security. When the viol disappeared, there was plenty of finger-pointing. A chorus of 'I told you so' and 'never again' erupted, and our reputation was in shreds. In the rarefied world of the gamba, Door County became a pariah, and for four decades the threat or promise, depending on how you look at it, of 'never again' held sway."

"Until now," Cubiak said.

"Yes, until now." Stone looked over his glasses at the sheriff. "In one of life's sweet ironies, George Peter Payette, one of the world's foremost gambists and the only one to participate in every Dixan festival, lives on the peninsula. It was because of his reputation and his involvement in the festival that the association agreed to return. You understand," he went on quickly, "that the festival is held only once every ten years—hence the name—making this only the fifth in the history of the society."

"What became of the stolen viol?"

Stone lost some of his starch. "It was never found. The island was searched immediately and again several times later but with nothing to show. There was a horrific storm the night the instrument went missing, and one theory is that whoever took it slipped away from the island on a private boat that sank in the strait on the way to the mainland."

"Is there any proof to that story?"

"Absolutely none," Frost said. "If it's true, then the viol is lost forever. But if by some means the yellow viol made it to the peninsula and out into the world, I'd say it's tucked away in the private collection of a discriminating financier or someone of that ilk."

"It's worth how much now? A million, maybe?"

Stone gave a rueful smile. "Oh, indeed. That much and perhaps more. Some musicologists would even say it's priceless. You see, it's really unique. Most early viols were made of mahogany, but Fiorrelli made the yellow viol from a plank of South American wood that was unknown in Europe. Some historians think it was the kind of wood the Cubans used to make cigar boxes. In any case, it was considered quite exotic on the continent, and the sound it produced was very special."

"The wood was yellow?"

"A logical assumption for anyone to make, but no, it was not. All the great masters developed their own secret varnishes. Stradivari's was red in tone and Fiorrelli's yellow. The finishes provided a mere hint of coloration; they did not actually distinguish the hue of the wood. In the case of the yellow viol, the name comes from the strings. Fiorrelli created the instrument as a gift for his wife, whose favorite color was yellow. To please her, he soaked the strings, which were made of sheep gut, in a solution made from the vermilion flowers that grew in her garden. According to old texts, which may be hyperbole, the strings glowed as if they'd been kissed by the sun. Eventually, of course, they were replaced with ordinary strings, but the name stuck."

"You've all seen it, then?"

"Of course. We were all here for the first festival. We've all seen the yellow viol."

"Did any of you play it?"

Stone regarded Cubiak as if he were a philistine. "Certainly not. Acker was the only person who was allowed to touch it."

Except for the thief, the sheriff thought. "I still need the lists," he said.

Frost crossed to a bank of metal file cabinets and tugged at a drawer that refused to open. "And you shall have them, sir. We are not obstructionists. But I hope you understand our position." He yanked again and the drawer sprang toward him, throwing him off balance. When he recovered his footing, he rummaged through the contents. "Music, like so much in life, consists of tangibles, notes on a page as it were. But musicians, again like so many, are a superstitious lot. Beethoven's music is monumentally great, but beyond the power of the notes on the page, his compositions are imbued with the tragedy of his deafness. Even though he didn't lose his hearing until later in life, we are still intrigued by the idea that a man who could not hear could create such magnificent sounds. How? How, we ask ourselves? So there is the man, the music, and in the case of Beethoven the truth of his deafness. And the mythology that arises because of it. It is a good myth. But this story of a woman who dies after leaving the island on the day of the reenactment of Dixan I is a very different matter. It has all the earmarks of a bad myth. If it takes hold and her death is associated with the festival, then it becomes a curse."

The organizer handed a sheaf of papers to Cubiak. "We can't allow that to happen."

There were more than one hundred names on the lists that Frost provided: fifty-six musicians; fourteen staff; thirty-seven extras, all of whom were island residents; eleven people on the security force; and a three-person film crew—producer, soundman, and cameraman. Surely it takes more than three people to make a movie? the sheriff thought.

"What about food service?" he said.

"I have no idea. We contracted out with a local company." Frost scribbled the contact information on a piece of paper. "You'll have to talk to them about their employees."

Cubiak stopped at the door. "By the way, how's the festival going?"

"What do you mean?"

"Did you get the musicians you wanted? How are ticket sales going?"

"Yes, we've got the top names here, and tickets are selling well. You've seen the crowds."

"It's a success, then."

"Indeed."

"Congratulations."

The musicians were in rehearsal, so the sheriff questioned the support team first. No one recognized the dead woman in the photo.

He struck out again with the security team. None of the men and women on detail remembered seeing the victim or noticing anything unusual.

"Nothing, huh? I could've told you that before you started," the head boss said when Cubiak stopped at the security tent. "These classical music fans are a pretty sedate crowd. Anyway we're really not that focused on the people."

"Then why are you here?"

"Mainly, we're guarding the instruments. You wouldn't believe what some of them go for. A musician from Missouri told me she had to take out a second mortgage to buy her violin."

"Viol," Cubiak said.

"Whatever. The guy who's doing the master workshop? His *viol* is insured for more than two hundred grand. All told, there's a couple million dollars' worth of stuff up here."

"What happens at night?"

"They got a choice. Some of them leave their instruments in the performance center, where we keep them under lock and key. Others take them with. If they do that, they're responsible. We only look out for items on the festival grounds."

Cubiak held out higher hopes for the members of the film crew, professionals who would be focused on filming people. He fancied himself a bit of a movie buff. From his Chicago life, he remembered when it seemed as if entire neighborhoods were taken over by Hollywood film crews. The streets were lined with convoys of unmarked trucks with black cables spilling out the back doors, and generators pumping electricity into forests of blinding lights.

After considerable searching for the Dixan V film crew, he was directed to the producer, a slender, fortysomething woman who was unloading lights and tripods from a beige minivan.

"This is it?" he said, trying to keep the disappointment from his voice.

She laughed. "We've got a cameraman, he's our cowboy, and a nerd working the sound board and mixer. As the producer, I'm the 'mom,' the person who makes sure that what needs to get done gets done, tells people where the toilets are, and has a pocket full of candy."

She pointed to the small assemblage of equipment. "We're shooting a fifty-minute PBS documentary, Sheriff, not a major motion picture. Combining our footage with stills and video clips from the first fest, we'll have more than enough to capture the essence of the story."

He showed her Jane Doe's photo.

"Sorry, no. I never saw her but if you leave that with me I'll show it to my colleagues when they're done working. We shot all day yesterday so it's possible we caught her on some of our footage. It's all digitalized, and I'll upload it tonight. If I send you the password, you can go through it."

"How much do you have?"

"Six or seven hours' worth, maybe more."

There went his evenings. "Thanks," he said. Again he handed out his card.

The musicians were still in rehearsal when he got back to the performance center, so he headed to the food service.

The tent was closing when he got there. Again he missed lunch—croissant sandwiches, judging from the discards on the tables. He showed the photo to the two cooks. Cubiak didn't expect any positive results and wasn't surprised when they didn't recognize her, though he was grateful for the sandwich they gave him. He ate and waited another fifteen minutes for the three servers to wrap things up. When they went off duty, he met them outside the tent.

The servers were a cheerful lot, two women and one man, whose bright smiles dimmed only momentarily when he identified himself.

He talked to the women first. They were blonde and fair skinned, and both were second-generation Polish from central Wisconsin and seniors at UW–Madison.

"Sorry, I don't recall seeing her," the first helper said, looking at the photo.

The second woman was only slightly more helpful. "I think I saw her the other day, but I can't be certain. There are so many people here. After a while, it's all a blur."

The man had stepped back and waited until Cubiak finished with his coworkers before he introduced himself. Eric Fielder was darker and had the high cheekbones of someone whose ancestors hadn't escaped the marauding Mongolian hordes seven centuries ago. He also had the toned body of a twentysomething athlete, but the creased forehead and the faint lines around his eyes told a different story. He had done many things, including a stint in the merchant marine, he told the sheriff, and, yes, he had seen the woman. "She was loitering over there"—he indicated a stand of maple trees at the edge of the meadow—"yesterday at lunch."

"You fed her even though she wasn't crew."

Fielder shrugged. "She looked starved, and I didn't think it was right that she go hungry. By then everyone else had been served, and I knew the leftovers would be thrown out. It seemed a shame to waste food, and giving it to her did no harm."

"You're not from here," Cubiak said.

"No. Germany. I was hired for the summer. The businesses are always short-staffed during the tourist season, and they like Europeans like me. We work hard and our accents add an exotic touch to the scenery."

"Did you talk with the woman, before or after you gave her lunch?"

"Not really. We may have exchanged a few words—enjoy, thank you—but nothing beyond that."

"Had you ever seen her before?"

"No."

"She didn't say who she was or what she was doing here?"

"When I saw her the only thing she seemed interested in was food." Fielder hesitated and then looked out at the crowd that lingered in the area. "If you want to talk to somebody who might be able to help you, talk to him," he said and pointed to a tall, skeletal man in a wrinkled khaki suit who was loping along the periphery of the gathering. "I saw the two of them arguing."

"Who is he?"

"I don't know, but he must be someone important because he's always around."

The man Fielder had singled out was Richard Mayes, and according to the credential hanging around his neck he was Management. Up close, Mayes was even more gaunt than he appeared at a distance.

"What exactly is your job at the festival?" Cubiak said.

"A little of this, a little of that. Basically I grease the wheels, keep things going," he said, glaring at his inquisitor with sunken eyes.

"Sounds important."

Mayes was in the middle of making a harrumph sound that was either an affirmation or a laugh when the sheriff held up the victim's photo. The man recoiled.

"Do you know this woman?"

"No."

"You were seen talking with her," Cubiak said.

"I talk with a lot of people. That doesn't mean I know them."

"Do you argue with all of them?"

Mayes bit his lower lip. "A festival like this draws a lot of people. Most of them are pure music lovers but some are just wanderers, crazy people, and she was one of those. She came up to me and demanded to be hired as an extra. I told her we were almost finished filming and didn't need anyone but she kept insisting. So, yes, I lost my patience."

"Why did she talk to you?"

Mayes gave an exasperated lift to his bony shoulders. "I don't know. Because she was crazy? Because I was here? Because of this?" He held up his credential. "Why don't you ask her?"

"I can't. She was found dead on the ferry yesterday."

Mayes blanched. "Oh, my God, I am so sorry."

He seemed about to say more when his phone chimed. Mayes glanced at the screen and threw a panicked look at Cubiak. "Another emergency. Excuse me, but I have to deal with this," he said.

After the last afternoon rehearsal, the sheriff finally met with the musicians. He had heard bits and pieces of their music over the past two days and wanted to know more about them as people: How old were they when they started playing? Who were their favorite musicians? What did they listen to when they weren't performing? But there was only time for the matter at hand. It took nearly two hours for him to question the players about Jane Doe, and again he came up with nothing. Everyone was polite, but sorry they hadn't seen the victim.

Afterward, he asked around for Richard Mayes but was told he had left the island. Cubiak checked in with the station. The deputies had nothing to report, and there had been no leads from the public. Earlier Cate told him she would be shooting into the evening, so there was no reason to wait for her. With nothing else to do, he headed to the ferry dock. He had forgotten sunblock and it had been hours since he had drunk any water. The tinge of a headache appeared at his temples, and as he waited to board, he rubbed his forehead. Something had to give, something always did, he thought.

The ferry was in the open water when a sudden front moved in. Thick clouds rolled across the sun and a powerful, cold wind roiled the water. Caught unawares, the passengers shivered into sweatshirts and jackets or crowded into the lounge to escape the chill. Cubiak stayed on deck. He would rather be cold than sit inside.

How quickly things changed, he thought, and snapped his fingers. One minute, Jane Doe was breathing, and the next she was dead. In the same flash, a bow crossed a set of strings and a performance tent went from silence to sound. Like that, the wind came up and destroyed the calm.

As Washington Island receded in the distance, he tried to imagine Lake Superior, the source of the harsh wind that blasted across the Upper Peninsula and slammed down into Door County. Cubiak had never seen Superior, largest by far of the five Great Lakes, but he had heard many of the stories—fish as big as cars and, in some years, ice even in July. Probably all fanciful tales. But true or not, tales became the stuff of myths. And myths, well . . . they could bring grace to a stumbling world or give rise to a curse that damned the righteous.

THE GAR GROUP

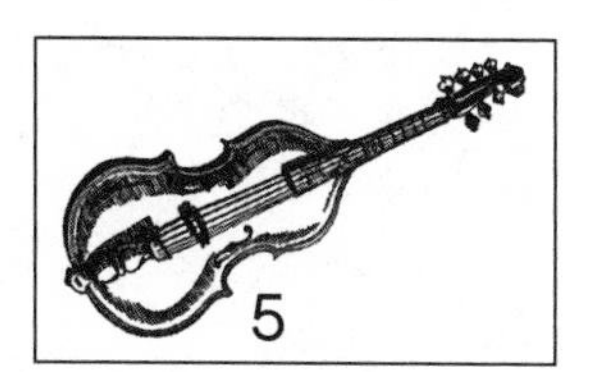

Cubiak emailed the names of the musicians and festival staffs to Rowe for him to run through the police databases. Then he headed toward Sister Bay. Near the south end of town, he noticed a crowd outside Sweet Eats. The stylish new bakery-café served only breakfast and lunch and was closing for the day. "Fresh Everyday" was the shop's motto, and those gathered in the narrow side yard were waiting for the daily giveaway of unsold bread, rolls, and pastries. They were mostly young, and many carried backpacks. They were probably campers or hikers—wanderers like Jane Doe.

The sheriff hesitated. Should he bother stopping? He had struck out all day. Then again, what was one more disappointment? He pulled to the curb and crossed between traffic to the other side of the road. The front door to the bakery was shut but an empty tray sat on the picnic table in the yard. As suddenly as it had come up, the cold front had retreated back north, and those who milled around were eating and enjoying the late afternoon warmth. He went around the crowd with the photo of Jane Doe and was met with a few shrugs, several blank stares, and mostly mumbles of "sorry, never saw her before."

Cubiak was starting to leave when the back door opened and a short, middle-aged woman emerged. She held a platter of doughnuts at shoulder height. "Don't be greedy. Please, let's share," the woman said as she moved through the cloud of outstretched hands. At the end of her pass, the dish was empty and she was standing in front of him.

"Sheriff?" she said, in a voice thick with curiosity. The woman smelled like vanilla and wore a name tag engraved with the unlikely moniker of Cookie.

Cubiak explained why he was there.

"May I?" Cookie said, brushing a flour-dusted hand on her cobbler's apron.

She scrutinized the image. "Yes, I've seen her several times. In fact, she was pretty much a regular the past week or so. I kind of got to feeling sorry for her. She was different. Older, more desperate. Hungrier, for sure," she said finally.

"When's the last time you saw her?"

Cookie furrowed her brow. "A couple days ago. I can't really be sure."

"Did she ever say where she was from or why she was here?"

"No." The baker frowned again. "But the last time I saw her, she had a flyer for the music festival on Washington Island. She showed it to a couple people and pointed to the name of one musician, asking if they knew where he lived."

"Do you remember who it was?"

"Sure. George Peter Payette. He's one of our regulars. George is a wonderful musician and Sister Bay's biggest celebrity. She said she had important news for him. Can you imagine?"

"Did you tell her where to find him?"

Cookie gave the photo back. "I was going to, but then I thought better of it. I figured if it was important enough she'd find him on her own. Besides, she seemed a bit touched, you know," she said, tapping a finger to her temple. "And I didn't want to be responsible if something bad came of it."

Payette lived north of town along the Green Bay shore. Retracing his route, Cubiak passed three luxury homes, each grander than the next, before he reached the musician's address. The other houses were visible from the road but not Payette's. The sheriff turned into a lane flanked by trees and followed it up a slope and over a berm until a modern, streamlined house came into view. L-shaped and flat roofed, it easily outsized those of the neighbors. A red sports car sat alongside the four-car garage. The one-story wing stood perpendicular to the shore, leaving the rest of the building to stretch along the water's edge. As if designed to both intimidate and impress visitors, the first-floor exterior that faced the yard was a solid stucco wall, interrupted only by a single wooden door, while the level above was wrapped in glass.

The large yard was cool and quiet. Wind whispered through the trees, and from somewhere on the other side of the house came the sound of waves lapping against the shore. At the richly oiled door, the sheriff pressed a button. Muffled chimes echoed through the interior and then faded. Back in Chicago, Cubiak had known a half-dozen artists, and all of them had lived in tight and often dismal quarters. How successful does a musician have to be to afford a place like this? he wondered. After a few moments, the walnut door opened. He was ready to announce himself to a maid or to introduce himself to George Payette. Instead, he found himself confronting Richard Mayes. The festival manager seemed as surprised to find Cubiak on the threshold as the sheriff was to see him in the role of butler.

"Sheriff, I'm sorry. I didn't realize you still needed to talk to me. I thought we were finished," Mayes said, stammering slightly.

"I'm here to see George Payette. I didn't expect to find you here."

"Ah, of course, you wouldn't. Besides my role at the festival, I am Mr. Payette's personal assistant."

"Are you?" Cubiak glanced at the red sports car parked alongside the garage. "You weren't on the ferry I took and there hasn't been another since we spoke last, so how'd you get here?"

"I came over on Mr. Payette's boat. We need to have transit available at all times and can't depend on the ferry schedule."

"He's in then, I take it."

"Actually he's on the island, meeting with the festival board. Not ten minutes after I arrived, he got called there. You know how it is with these events—always a fire to put out." Mayes waved his hands to convey a sense of activity.

"Well, as long as we're both here, let's continue our chat," Cubiak said. Before Mayes could object, he stepped across the threshold. From the foyer he had a view into a sunken living room that boasted a massive fieldstone fireplace and was filled with high-end, white leather chairs and sofas arranged in conversation-friendly clusters. Giant oak beams spanned the ceiling, and a glass wall overlooked a sloping lawn, a private dock, and a vast expanse of water that shimmered in the afternoon sun. He could only imagine the sunsets. "Why didn't you tell me earlier that you worked for Payette?"

"It didn't seem relevant."

"Really? I just learned that the woman who was found dead on the ferry had a keen interest in meeting with your boss."

Mayes smiled. "Proof that rock stars aren't the only musicians with groupies."

The sheriff let the comment slide and pulled out the photo of Jane Doe. "I'll ask you once again: Do you know this woman?"

"As I already told you, I'd never seen her before yesterday."

"That's not what I asked." He waited. The man was playing dodgeball with words.

Mayes was quiet. His shoulders twitched and then settled. "I'm telling you the truth when I say I never saw that woman before. But when she confronted me she claimed that she was Lydia Larson, the daughter of Annabelle Mary Larson. And Annabelle was a woman I once knew."

Suddenly the dead woman had a name. Jane Doe was Lydia Larson. And more than that, she was connected to Richard Mayes and possibly to George Payette, both of whom were involved in Dixan V. From the start Cubiak had suspected that the victim's visit to the island was related to the music fest. Mayes had just acknowledged that he knew Lydia Larson's mother; could it be that she had participated in the first festival four decades earlier?

"By any chance is Annabelle a musician also?" he said.

"She was at one point. I don't know if she's still playing."

"And you knew her when, forty years ago?"

Mayes tensed. "Yes. How'd you know?"

Cubiak ignored the question. "I'll need the whole story," he said.

Mayes let his gaze fall to the tiled floor. When he looked up again, resignation had replaced indignation. He reached over and closed the door. "Come with me, and I'll explain everything," he said.

From the foyer, Mayes led the way past the living room to a floating stairway. "The bedrooms and guest quarters are on the second level," he said mechanically, as if he were conducting a tour. Beyond the stairs, they followed a wide hall that ran the length of the house. The stucco wall remained on the right as they passed the kitchen, dining room, library, and media center. Finally, they reached a series of closed doors and Mayes spoke again. "These are the offices—Mr. Payette's and mine. Also, several practice rooms and the recording studio. George releases at least two new CDs every year. He even has his own label."

"Which is unusual or not?"

"Today's software makes it pretty easy to create your own label, but it's another matter to sell your music. George does both."

There was another large room at the end of the house. It was similar in size and shape to the living room, but instead of upscale furniture it held rows of padded pews arranged around a low stage. Beyond the stage, a wall of glass opened to the backdrop of Green Bay.

"A private recital hall," Cubiak said.

Mayes gave a smug smile. "Mr. Payette performs here several times a year, but mostly he reserves the room for the use of his students. George is a renowned instructor, and it's very prestigious to be invited to perform here."

"What does any of this have to do with Annabelle Larson?"

"She was part of this world. To understand her, you have to know something of it."

Mayes unlocked a door in the back wall and a light went on, revealing a steep flight of stairs. "You might want to use the rail," he said as he started down.

The stairwell was lined with cedar planks and felt cooler and dryer than the upstairs. At the bottom, Mayes opened another door and ushered Cubiak into a high-ceilinged underground chamber. The room was oval and dazzlingly lit and colder still.

"Mr. Payette's private collection," Mayes said, indicating the room's contents. The chamber held an array of antique instruments housed in glass display cases. There were few flutes and horns; most were strings, and all of them looked delicate and valuable.

"Mr. Payette started his collection when he was still a student. He had little money then and became a devotee of estate sales. You'd be surprised by the things people own that they don't even know the value of. Not that he ever stumbled across anything like a lost Strad, but he did find many exquisite instruments that he was able to procure at very reasonable prices. As his reputation grew, he was able to become more discriminating. This section"—Mayes pointed to the right quadrant of the room—"is devoted to the viola da gamba."

"There's what, a hundred instruments here? The collection must be worth a small fortune," Cubiak said.

Mayes laughed. "Wealthy collectors might not be interested in them, but to early music enthusiasts who'd appreciate the provenance of the pieces, it is a treasure."

"We still haven't gotten to Annabelle Larson."

Mayes flipped a switch and a soft spotlight shone on a slim glass case that stood slightly apart from the others. The case was lined with rich blue velvet, and the single wooden instrument inside shimmered under the light. "That's Annabelle's viol," he said.

A half-dozen framed posters hung on the wall behind the viol. The brightly colored posters promoted a series of concerts, and each featured the same abstract drawing of a needle-nosed fish. The word GAR appeared in prominent font, and below that odd word were three names.

"The GAR group was a trio of gambists," Mayes said, drawing the sheriff close enough to read the smaller print: George Peter Payette, Richard Paul Mayes, and Annabelle Mary Larson.

"All three of you," Cubiak said.

Mayes attempted a laugh. "Yes, all three of us. We were known as the Peter, Paul, and Mary of the viola da gamba world. Rather lofty praise perhaps, but a very small world, I assure you."

"So you're a musician, too."

"I was then."

"What happened to the group?"

"We went the way of all flesh. Here one day, gone the next."

"How long were you together?"

"Ten years or so. Looking back, maybe it was all too good to be true. We'd all just graduated and seemed blessed from the start. It was as if the world opened its arms and gave us a taste of what it would so quickly snatch away. The venues for gambists are relatively modest, but we played the biggest of them. The critics called us the *Wunderkind.* We were on our way, but then we had the good luck and the misfortune of appearing at the first Dixan festival. Like everyone there, we were tainted by the scandal."

Mayes looked up. "You know what happened?"

"I've heard the story about the missing yellow viol."

"Missing? It was snatched in the middle of the night in what was the biggest scandal in the world of the gamba. We were all shaken by it. You have to understand, the incident set musician against musician. Everyone watching each other, wondering if that person was the thief. Even after the authorities were convinced that none of us walked off with the viol, there was the suspicion that one of us might have helped whoever did."

"Making the disappearance an inside job?"

"Something like that, I guess." Mayes hesitated. "Everyone was suspect, but it seemed like the three of us—the GAR group—got more than our share of attention. It's all ancient history now, but back then there were other young and talented gambists who resented our success. And you know what human nature is like? The whispers, the innuendo, the snide looks. George and I recovered from the whole business, but Annabelle never got over it. She was always . . ."—he paused, searching for the right word—"fragile."

"What happened?"

"For nearly a year after the festival, it was a real struggle to get a gig, but we kept working together, waiting for the shadow to pass. George said we had to release a new album. He said this would reestablish our reputation and help absolve us of the past. Annabelle agreed to the plan but something had gone flat. Her playing was off, less than it should have been. She started arriving late for rehearsals and then started to not show up at all. George and I tried to coax her along, but Annabelle drifted away from us and further into her own world. She said we were doomed, that we'd been branded musicians non grata and that there was no going back to where we were before Dixan I. George and I did everything we could think of to convince her otherwise, but neither of us could reach her."

"Do you have any idea why she reacted so strongly?"

"Maybe because music came easily to her. She was a prodigy and the only child of two accomplished musicians. Annabelle was born with music in her blood and didn't have to work as hard at it as the rest of us. Before Dixan I, her gift was a blessing but afterward it became a curse. She didn't know how to fight for what she wanted because she'd never had to. She didn't know how to struggle."

"But you and George did?"

"That's how we got to where we were! The Dixan I fiasco knocked us down a few notches, but we'd climbed to the top before and we knew that to do it again we had to put our backs into our work. More than that, we had to want it and had to reembrace the drudge of routine practices, working ourselves as hard as we ever had. We couldn't afford to waste our energies brooding over what had happened, the way Annabelle did. Eventually the stress pushed her over the edge, and she had a bit of a breakdown. Once she fell apart, the group was no more."

"And she sold her viol to George?" Cubiak said, stepping back to the case that housed Annabelle's instrument.

"Sold? No, she gave it to him. It's a fine viol, and she knew he coveted it. George refused to take it, but she said if he didn't she'd pawn it. She didn't want to ever see it again, she said."

Mayes dimmed the light over the posters. "If you ask me, I think that losing Annabelle was as nearly as great a loss for the world of the gamba as the loss of the yellow viol."

"When was the last time you saw her?"

"Oh, I don't know exactly. Three decades at least."

"Then her daughter showed up and asked to be cast as an extra in the documentary of Dixan V."

Mayes colored. "Not exactly, Sheriff. I made that up. I don't know why. I apologize. Lydia wanted to see George. She said her mother had died and that she needed to tell him directly."

"You didn't know that Annabelle had died?"

"No, and I was so shocked by what she'd said, that I could hardly think. But that's not the only reason she'd come to the festival. She was quite blunt about her other motive. She told me she knew that there was money due the 'estate' and that as the rightful heir she was here to collect it."

"Money from . . ."

Mayes switched off half the lights. "From the recordings we'd made decades earlier. I told her that I handled the books, and that the last royalties had been paid out years before. She was very upset and wouldn't take no for an answer. 'There's money here, I know there is,' she insisted. I told her she had to wait until the festival was over before trying to see George and that if she was patient a little while longer, I'd talk to him and we'd see what we could do to help her out."

"You were stalling."

"Of course I was. I didn't know who she was. She claimed to be Lydia Larson, but as far as I was concerned she was a complete stranger. I didn't even know if Annabelle had a daughter. What if Annabelle was alive, and this woman was a scam artist?"

"Did you say anything to the festival organizers?"

"Are you kidding? They'd go berserk. Even the whiff of scandal sends them into paroxysms of hysteria."

"But you told George."

"Of course. As soon as I could. He was devastated by the news about Annabelle, but then he agreed that we should look into things further. Annabelle had dropped out of the music scene, but it seemed odd that we didn't hear as much as a whisper about her passing. George and I agreed that if this Lydia woman's story was true, we'd do everything we could for her. If not, we'd send her packing."

Mayes ushered the sheriff back into the small anteroom and then hit another switch. Behind them, the room went dark. "But now she's dead, too," he said. "And such a young woman. How did she die?"

"Suspicious circumstances."

"What does that mean?"

"It means I don't know yet for certain."

Mayes frowned. "But you have a theory."

"Several."

They were in the upstairs hall again when Cubiak asked Mayes about his career.

"My life as a musician ended twenty years ago," he said. Mayes was in front and as they walked, he held up his hands. His right index finger was crooked and both rows of knuckles were grotesquely swollen. "Rheumatoid arthritis. It wasn't easy giving it all up, but I had no choice. Since then I've kept plenty busy serving as George's booking agent, accountant, and publicist. In fact, I can honestly say that I take a great deal of satisfaction in supporting his career. He was always the more talented player anyway."

In the foyer Mayes gave a CD to the sheriff. "The GAR group at its finest," he said. Then he opened the door.

It was early evening and the yard blazed with the orange of the setting sun.

"What about Annabelle?" Cubiak said, squinting against the hot glow.

Mayes stepped out the door as if he were drawn by the light. When he turned back he was smiling. "Annabelle? Of the three of us, she was the best."

FATAL DELAY

Cubiak headed south again. After his talk with Mayes, he wanted to know more about Dixan I, and, as he so often did, he sought out Bathard. The retired coroner was not only a lifelong resident of the county but also a music aficionado, and there was a good chance he had attended the ill-fated festival. Forty years was a long time to cast back through the fog of memory, but the sheriff figured he had nothing to lose by asking.

When he reached the end of Bathard's cinder driveway, the old boat barn was lit up and strains of opera spilled into the yard. He rolled back the door and found his friend at his workbench. Bathard's hair was gray and longer than in his doctor days, and his shoulders had stooped slightly with age. He moved more slowly than when they had first met, but he had lost none of his mental edge.

"What do you think?" Bathard said, looking up from the replica of the Viking ship that was taking shape on the counter in front of him. The boat was three feet long and richly detailed.

"It looks great but will it float?"

The doctor chuckled. "It had better. I promised Sonja's grandsons they could try it out on Kangaroo Lake when it was finished, and I would sorely hate to see all this effort go to waste." He put down the crochet hook he was using to adjust the rigging and rose from his perch.

"And that?" Bathard said, pointing toward the vaulted ceiling where dust motes danced in the air.

Cubiak thought he meant the place where the *Parlando* had sat in its cradle while the two of them reworked the wooden sailboat, the most ambitious venture of Bathard's postretirement woodworking projects. Then the sheriff realized he was asking about the music flowing from the speakers that hung from the rafters.

"Verdi's *La Traviata.*"

The coroner frowned. "Too easy. You're getting good at this."

He walked over and, ever the gentleman, formally shook hands. "If you're not heading home for dinner, come join us. I believe we're having leftovers. Swedish meatballs and whatever else Sonja warmed up. There's always plenty."

When Cubiak first met Bathard, the doctor had been married to his high school sweetheart. Cornelia died soon after, and two years later, Bathard had remarried. Sonja was a notoriously good cook, and the sheriff knew it would be futile to refuse the invitation. Five minutes after he and Bathard left the boat barn, the three were sitting around the worn butcher-block table in the kitchen. Wine had been poured and platters of food were being passed.

"I've actually come to ask you about music," he said to Bathard.

"Ah." The physician smiled and raised his glass.

"Dixan I."

The smile faded.

"You were there?"

"Indeed. It was a proud moment in Door County history, until it turned into something quite different. I couldn't attend every performance, but I went to as many as possible. I wouldn't have dreamed of not going. Dixan I was the first viola da gamba festival held in the state. Musicians came from across the country, and, of course, the headliner was the famous Franz Acker, who, until that fateful weekend, was one of the world's premier gambists." Bathard glanced at his wife. "Sonja and I didn't know each other at the time, but she was there as well."

"You're a fan of early music?" the sheriff said.

"Not especially, but I lived on Washington Island then. I think all of us locals showed up at some point, out of curiosity if nothing else," she said.

Bathard shook his head. "All that preparation and promise and then, out of nowhere, disaster. First the death of Acker's wife and then the mysterious disappearance of the famous yellow viol. Afterward there were mad accusations and finger-pointing all around. For a while it seemed that everyone on the island was a suspect."

"Practically everybody on the peninsula really," Sonja said.

"True, all except for the unfortunate Franz Acker," Bathard said.

"Oskar Norling said something about a woman dying after leaving the island, but I didn't realize she was Acker's wife."

"Yes, it was all so terribly unfortunate."

"How much do you remember?" Cubiak said.

The coroner closed his eyes for a moment. "About the festival? The music, of course. Such exquisite harmony. It was a chance to hear rarely performed pieces by Abel, Boismortier, and Marais. And the wonderful musicians. They all seemed very young." He laughed. "I guess we were all very young then. They were so eager, so thrilled to be playing together, and the music was beautiful. It's a different sound from what we think of as classical music—simpler and purer. Everyone was so caught up in the euphoria I don't think they could have imagined the twin tragedies that lay ahead." Bathard sipped his wine. "What's most disturbing is that things didn't have to go so terribly wrong. To this day, I believe that the disaster could have been averted if Franz Acker had only listened to reason. Don't misunderstand, the man has my sympathies. He suffered greatly because of what transpired, but to an extent he was an architect of his own doom."

"I don't understand."

"Well, to begin with, the yellow viol didn't belong to him. The instrument was on loan from one of the old, aristocratic families in Germany, an offshoot of the Guttenbergs, I believe. Acker was entrusted with it on one very simple and basic condition: that he keep up the insurance premiums."

"And he didn't?"

"Unfortunately, no. Of course, there were various circumstances that he blamed for this misstep. He'd been recording and performing in New York for nearly a year and had the check ready to mail but he forgot, and then he brought it here to post from the island. With him also was his pregnant wife—Heike, I think her name was. She was seven months along but on the afternoon of the day he had to mail the check in order for the payment to arrive on time, she unexpectedly went into labor. Premature labor comes with its own potential complications, but her situation was even more problematic."

"Why?"

"Frau Acker had a condition called placenta previa." The doctor looked across the table at the sheriff. "It means the placenta is lying low in the womb. In her case, it was both blocking the birth canal and causing her to hemorrhage."

"You were there when she went into labor?"

"I wish I had been, but no, I was dealing with an emergency at the old clinic in Sister Bay. There wasn't a physician available on the island, so they called a midwife, which normally would be fine."

Sonja set out a tray with coffee, cookies, and sherry. She explained, "The midwife was my neighbor. Her car wouldn't start when she got the call, so I drove her. There was a huge gale bearing down. The reports said it was a hundred-year storm, the worst anyone could remember. I don't think I'd ever witnessed such wind and rain. There were moments I couldn't see the road and had to go by memory as much as instinct. Afterward, she told me that she did everything she could to stem the poor woman's bleeding. She even stayed with Heike on the ferry."

"The ferry was running?" Cubiak looked up from pouring the sherry.

"The schedule was put on hold because of the weather, but Acker went down to the landing and persuaded Norling to take his wife across," Bathard said.

"Oskar Norling's father?"

"No, his uncle Sven. The old captain had a reputation as something of a daredevil and was the only pilot willing to try. I don't know how he talked the owners into letting him take the boat but he did, and somehow he managed to get Acker and his wife over to the mainland. This was long before the ferry landing at Northport was built. So he had to dock at Gills Rock, and in those conditions it had to have been a real challenge. The ambulance was waiting, and as soon as they got Frau Acker on board, the EMTs radioed me. When they reached Sister Bay, I traded places with the midwife. I assumed we were headed to the hospital in Sturgeon Bay, but Acker wouldn't hear of it. He seemed to think we were a bunch of country rubes and insisted that his wife be flown to the university hospital in Madison."

Bathard grimaced. "What a horrible mistake. I tried to talk him out of it, but he said he had a colleague there, someone he knew and trusted from his student days. The man's arrogance was galling and worse. Heike had lost a lot of blood already, and I knew we were running out of time. I told him this. 'We can care for her here. You don't have to go to Madison,' I said. But Acker was adamant. He'd already called ahead and arranged for a private plane to transport her. I had no option but to stay with Heike. The ambulance tried to outrace the storm and get to the airport before the squall hit. It was the only chance we had. Ten minutes more and we would have made it. But just as we turned off the highway, the wind roared in off Green Bay and the airport was forced to shut down."

"Why didn't you turn around and go back to Sturgeon Bay?"

"If only we could have, but the rain was a deluge and the roads flooded almost instantly, making it impossible to get through. We were stranded at the airport for more than an hour. I did what I could but . . ." The elderly doctor shook his head. "It was all so sad and avoidable. Eventually the plane was able to take off for Madison. They landed in time to save the infant, but by then Heike had lost too much blood."

"The delay cost that poor woman her life," Sonja said.

"And that's the night the yellow viol disappeared."

"Sadly, yes. Acker returned to the island the next afternoon and discovered it missing. He sounded the alarm immediately," Bathard said. He turned to Sonja. "You were there; you know what went on."

"It was instant chaos. Nothing like that had ever happened on the island, and suddenly we were all under suspicion as possible thieves.

The next day, when Acker announced he'd give a reward for any information about the viol, everyone became a detective."

"How many people were on the island at the time?" Cubiak said as he refilled his glass.

"Easily six or seven hundred. There were the musicians and the tourists, and the summer people who hadn't left yet," Sonja said.

"Dutch Schumacher was the sheriff back then, and he put the island on what we've come to know as lockdown. The search went on for a couple of days but there was no trace of the instrument. There's never been a trace since. Because of the theft, Acker was left in financial ruin, and Washington Island was blackballed from playing host to the event for years. Of course, all that has changed now."

"Because of George Payette."

Bathard looked up. "You've done your homework." He added a touch of sherry to his glass and took a leisurely sip. "Now perhaps you'll tell me what this is all about."

"Does the name Annabelle Mary Larson mean anything to you?"

The coroner leaned back and studied the shadows on the ceiling. "Annabelle Mary Larson. Now there's a name I haven't heard in a long time. I always thought of her as one of those human beings blessed with an ability the rest of us can only dream of. She was an accomplished gambist, one of the few women in her day, and a delicate beauty as well. And if I remember correctly, she was part of a trio that performed at Dixan I. They had an odd name . . ."

"The GAR group."

"Yes, that's it."

"You heard them perform?"

"Oh, yes, and they were quite good. Superb, in fact, especially Annabelle Larson. There was something about the way she played, the intimacy of her connection with the viol, that set her apart from all the other musicians. I wonder whatever became of her."

"According to a woman who claimed to be her daughter, Annabelle Larson is dead. But the daughter, a Lydia Larson, is also deceased."

"This is the unfortunate woman whose body was found on the ferry from Washington Island yesterday?"

"Yes, that's her." Cubiak described the circumstances and repeated Emma Pardy's initial assessment.

Bathard set down his glass. "And you think Lydia Larson was murdered?"

"I consider it a possibility."

"Why was she on the island?" Sonja said.

"I don't know. I have the feeling she was there because of the festival but I've got nothing to back that up. No one affiliated with the event recognized her photo. And Richard Mayes, who was part of the GAR group, said that as far as he knows Annabelle isn't dead. So he thinks Lydia might be lying both about Annabelle's demise and about being the daughter. I haven't talked to George Payette yet—he was the third member of the trio—to see where he stands on any of this. Mayes said that Lydia was trying to see him and that she was after money."

Bathard sighed. "Another Dixan tragedy? History repeating itself? I surely hope not."

The three were at the door when Bathard asked Cubiak about Cate.

"She's fine. Working hard, as usual. In fact, she's been up on the island shooting the festival."

"We need to have the two of you over. We're due for dinner soon. I'll give her a call," Sonja said.

"Sounds good. I'll tell her," Cubiak said.

As he crossed the yard, the sheriff thought of the brief exchange he had just had with Bathard and Sonja. The mention of a dinner invitation was both incredibly commonplace and extraordinary, like the ring he wore on his left hand. In the two years since he and Cate had been married he had never removed the silver band, yet there were times when its presence seemed surreal. Times when even while looking at the ring he could not fully imagine that the two of them were together as a couple. For years he thought he would never marry again, never know happiness again. Bathard said he had felt the same way after Cornelia died, and yet here he was with Sonja, who had been widowed as well.

The currents of life were as unfathomable as the stars that studded the sky, he thought. When he lost Lauren and Alexis, he had lost everything, and yet somehow the universe had led him to renewed purpose, and given him, if not joy, then moments of fulfillment and a reason to embrace life again.

Without his even being aware, the current of life had swept him up and carried him to this new time and place, to an existence that was both familiar and strange, to a reality where a simple dinner invitation—unimaginable in the harrowing grief that followed the deaths of his wife and daughter—had become just that again.

A SOD HOUSE VISITOR

Later, if Cubiak was asked why he had used the back door when he arrived at work that Friday morning instead of walking through the front lobby as he usually did, he wouldn't have an answer. Perhaps he took the short cut because he was tired or because it was raining. But by doing so he missed the audience waiting for him in the front lobby.

"You're awfully popular today. Any more and I'd have to give out numbers," Lisa said.

"Meaning?"

"When I got in, there were already four people in line to see you. Three locals and a rather odd woman who appears to be from another century."

"Who was here first?"

"The visitor from elsewhere, but she says she can wait. The locals all own gift shops and are anxious to get going."

"Let's start with them then."

Cubiak had a feeling he knew the problem, and he was right. Each owner reported the recent theft of high-end merchandise from their shops in Ephraim and Fish Creek.

The three hadn't seen anyone suspicious, and their security cameras hadn't picked up anything unusual either.

"There are several festivals going on. Tourists love them, but they can make life hell for us," the Fish Creek merchant said.

"Aren't events good for business?" Cubiak asked.

"You'd think so, but they tend to attract crowds, which sometimes means that there are a lot of people in the shop at the same time, and that makes it hard to keep an eye on things. You can't stop every tourist who's carrying a canvas tote bag and ask to see what they've got in there. And for professional thieves, crowds provide good cover. Most people are honest, Sheriff, but if I trust everyone who comes in, I have a good chance of being fleeced. If I'm overly suspicious, I end up insulting innocent people," he said.

"There was an incident on Washington Island the other day. I wonder if they could be connected."

"Did you make an arrest?"

"The owner wouldn't press charges."

The merchants exchanged looks. "Figures," said one.

As they left, the spokesman turned to Cubiak. "Next time you catch someone stealing from any of us, throw the book at them."

The sheriff was mulling over the comment when Lisa reappeared, carrying two departmental mugs. "Black coffee for you and tea for the mystery visitor," she said as she set the cups on his desk.

"Any luck finding out her name?"

"Afraid not. I told her you'd be tied up for a while and tried to get her to talk to a deputy but she refused. She said she had to see to you." Lisa leaned in. "Like I said, she's a bit odd."

Cubiak expected to see a woman in outlandish futuristic dress, but the visitor who trailed Lisa into his office was from the other end of the time-warp spectrum. She looked like she had walked out of a sod house on the old plains. Her drab brown skirt hung to her ankles. Her muslin blouse was buttoned up tight around her neck, and the sleeves fell past her wrists. Her dark hair was pulled back, and when she finally looked up, he saw that her face was deeply tanned and scrubbed clean. The bulky cheap watch on her left wrist was her only modern adornment.

"Please, sit down," the sheriff said, indicating the chair opposite his desk.

The woman perched on the edge of the seat. She kept her back rigid and clasped her hands in her lap.

"You asked to see me?"

"Yes."

"And you are?"

The visitor pinned her amber-gold eyes on him. "Helen Kulas."

"You're Lithuanian."

"My grandparents."

Cubiak reached for his coffee and waited for her to elaborate. Instead she dropped her gaze and went silent. "The tea is for you," he said finally. She moistened her lips but kept her hands buried in the folds of her skirt.

"Are you from around here?'

She moved her head to say no. "Illinois."

"It's a big state."

Helen Kulas almost smiled. "Chicago."

"That's a long way to come to talk to me."

"It's important. It's about the woman they said was found on the ferry."

"Lydia Larson."

The visitor stiffened. "On the radio, the announcer said she was unidentified . . ."

"That was accurate when the announcement was made. But that was two days ago and since then, we've learned more," he said.

Helen crumpled into the chair as if suddenly deflated. "I see." The words came out like a whisper.

"How do you know Lydia Larson?"

"I used to babysit for her, when she was little."

"You hardly seem much older than her."

Helen dipped her head. "Lydia lived hard," she said.

"Then you knew Annabelle Mary Larson as well."

"Yes." Helen seemed surprised to hear the name. "We were friends. But that was a long time ago."

"How did you hear about the business on the ferry? News from up here generally doesn't travel all the way to Chicago."

"It was on the radio. The local classical station was doing a special segment on early music and as part of the report, they talked about the festival on Washington Island. They interviewed a musician who'd been at the original festival, Dixan I, and he started reminiscing about what happened there. You know the story about the yellow viol and the woman who died in childbirth the night it went missing? I'm not interested in viola da gamba, but I kept listening because I knew that Annabelle Larson—Lydia's mother—was at Dixan I, and it made me think of her. Then the announcer said that a young woman had just died during Dixan V, and the musician who was being interviewed said it seemed like history was repeating itself."

"And on the basis of what you heard on the radio, you assumed that the dead woman was Lydia?"

Helen took a sip of tea. "I was afraid it might be her, that's all. Lydia was aware of the festival. We'd talked about it, and after everything that had happened—everything I'd told her—I knew that she had good reason to come here."

Cubiak waited for the rest of the story.

"It all began with Annabelle." Helen paused and shifted her weight forward again. "I was teaching piano at the Crawford Avenue music school on the north side of Chicago when Annabelle started giving violin lessons there. Lydia was maybe eight at the time. They'd been through rough times, living in a car for a while, homeless for an entire summer, if you could believe the stories Annabelle told. She had lots of stories. About how she grew up with nannies and servants and how she'd been a star in the music world. I never paid much attention to what she said. Annabelle seemed like the kind of person who needed to feel important, so I thought she was making up all that stuff to impress me. The thing is, she didn't need to do that. Annabelle was good at her job. Once when she thought she was alone in the school, I heard her playing. She was good at that, too. Amazing, really."

Helen hummed a few bars and drummed her fingers on the edge of the desk. Then she caught herself and tucked her hands back into her lap. "I still didn't believe what she'd told me. If she was that famous, then what was she doing giving cut-rate lessons to a bunch of dopey kids and living in that moldy studio apartment?"

After a moment, Helen answered her own question.

"I finally figured out that she was sick. Mentally unstable, I mean. About five years after I met her, she disappeared with Lydia. God only knows where they went; she never said. Then a few years later, she showed up hoping to get her old job back. There was an opening and the owner of the school hired her immediately. Lydia wasn't with her and Annabelle said she was living with her sister. Annabelle had never mentioned a sister, but who knew. Everything was fine again for a while until she got sick. This time it was the other type of disease, the kind you can see. Skin cancer, the bad one."

Helen curled her fingers and tucked her hands back into her long sleeves.

"She was getting free, experimental treatment at Cook County, and when I went to see her, she said she needed me to do her a favor. She told me that she'd hidden a box in the back of her bedroom closet. And that it was full of stuff that she wanted me to destroy. When I asked her why, she said she didn't want Lydia to find it and learn what a mess she'd made of her life. She made me promise."

"Did you?"

"Promise? Of course I did. She was my friend. I found the box right where she said it would be. It was bigger and heavier than I expected, and it was hard for me to carry but I took it home like I said I would." She inhaled sharply.

"And then what?"

Helen colored. "I had every intention of keeping my word. I mean it, I really did."

"But you didn't."

"After all I'd been through with her, I felt that I had a right to know what she'd squirreled away. Maybe I needed to know. What if the box was full of money? Or expensive jewelry? I told you that she was mentally unstable. Maybe she didn't even remember what was in it. What if there were things in there that she could use? I figured I had an obligation to look, for her sake." She hesitated. "I admit that after listening to all those stories she told, I was curious, too."

"Did you find anything valuable?"

"No. It was crammed with junk—tattered notebooks and journals, an old diary, and memorabilia, the kind of sentimental stuff people put in scrapbooks. Pictures. Concert programs. Old newspaper articles. Even a magazine story. It turns out that Annabelle hadn't lied. Everything she'd told me about her life was true. The rich parents and big house in Winnetka. Private schools. Juilliard, even. I'd never believed her. I always thought we had so much in common, and suddenly I was faced with the proof that it wasn't even close to being true. Annabelle had lived in a different universe. I couldn't imagine growing up the way she had and then having all that talent and opportunity on top of it. I sat on the floor in my living room with all this stuff scattered around me and felt like a fool. What must the poor little rich girl have thought of me, I wondered?"

Helen turned a tearful face toward the sheriff. "Annabelle had everything I'd ever dreamed of, and I hated her for it. I never wanted to see her again. After a while, though, I started to feel sorry for her."

"Why was that?"

"Because something must have gone terribly wrong for her to end up like she did, living where she did and working at this sorry excuse for a music school. That's not a life you choose if you have the other."

"I assume you checked out the diary and looked through the other stuff."

Helen bowed her head. Her cheeks were pink. "A little, yes, and that's when I started to think that maybe it was wrong to get rid of everything, that maybe Lydia deserved to know the truth about her mother. They'd had such a struggle together, and I wanted her to be proud of her mom. I thought she deserved to have this legacy to hold on to and that maybe it would help her see her own life in a better light.

"The funny thing is, Annabelle got well again and lived another couple of years. She died five months ago, but in all that time she never asked me what I'd done with the box. She must have assumed I'd kept my word and thrown it away. And I didn't say anything because I was embarrassed about breaking my promise. I didn't see Lydia again until the funeral and by then I'd had plenty of time to read the diary all the way through."

Helen Kulas looked at him. "That's how I discovered the secret Annabelle had kept all those years." The visitor grew wide eyed. "The identity of the father. Annabelle never told Lydia who he was, but it was in her diary."

"And you told Lydia?"

Helen lowered her gaze. "I felt she deserved to know the truth. Lydia Larson was the daughter of two highly talented musicians: her mother and the famous gambist George Peter Payette. She had a right to know that, didn't she?"

When Cubiak failed to respond, Helen went on. "That had to be the reason Lydia came to Door County. She knew that Payette helped organize the festival and that she'd finally have the chance to meet her father."

"What did Annabelle say about Payette?"

"Oh, she went on for pages about what a talented musician he was, but the rest was the gibberish of a love-sick girl. Can't live without him, would do anything for him, love at first sight. All that kind of nonsense." Helen snorted. "And look where it got her."

"How about Richard Mayes? Did she mention him?"

"Yeah, he was in there, too. She went on and on about him and the trio they were in together. It had an odd name."

"The GAR group."

"That's it, and Mayes was part of it. Other than that, she seemed amused by the amount of attention he paid to her. Annabelle claimed he was crazy about her and kept telling her they were destined to be together forever."

"Mayes wanted to marry her?"

"That's what Annabelle said. According to her, he proposed three times, but she refused. She was stuck on George."

Helen smiled and reached for the cup of tea. It had to be cold by then but she didn't seem to mind. How much of what this strange woman had confided was true? Cubiak was sure the newspaper clippings she mentioned were authentic. But what proof was there that the Annabelle

Larson featured in the articles was the same woman Helen knew? Perhaps the story of the real Annabelle had been appropriated by this other woman or had been inflated by Helen's fantasies of a glamorous existence. Someone as pitiful as her could be seeking fame by association.

"Did you give Annabelle's diary and journals to Lydia?" he asked.

"Not right away. I started just by telling her things—a hint here and there about her mother's life, to see how she'd react. She seemed so thankful and so eager to know more that eventually, I turned them all over to her. I even told her it was her mother's wish. Oh, God, I didn't mean any harm. But look what's happened! She came here because of what I did and now I'm answerable for what's befallen her. It's all my fault. Maybe if I'd kept my promise to Annabelle all those years ago, her daughter would still be alive."

Helen began to weep quietly.

Cubiak slid a box of tissues across the desk. "Whatever happened, you are not responsible."

Helen sniffled and then, still looking down, she said, "How did Lydia die?"

He was intentionally vague. "We're still waiting for test results. And we still need to corroborate the identification of the woman on the boat."

Helen sat up, alarmed. "But you said it was Lydia!"

"I said we had a tentative identification. We need to be certain." He paused. "Do you think you're up to doing that?"

Helen Kulas glanced around in panic. "I've never . . ." She took a quick breath. "I owe her that much. I owe both of them that much. Yes, I'll do it."

Neither of them spoke on the way to the morgue.

"You're sure you're OK?" Cubiak said as they stood in the hospital basement outside the double doors of the morgue.

Helen nodded.

Once inside, she closed her eyes, and she didn't open them until the body was presented. "It's Lydia," she said almost instantly.

"You're sure?"

"Yes," she said and started to cry again.

When they were out in the hall, Helen crumpled. The sheriff caught her arm and kept her from sliding to the floor. She was ashen and barely able to stand on her own. He had hoped to question her further, but seeing her distress he knew that would have to wait.

"You're here alone?" he said.

Her head bobbled.

"Where are you staying? I'll take you there."

"No place. I have no place. I came straight to your office. I have to find something now." Helen Kulas looked around, confused, as if she didn't know where she was.

But there wouldn't be anything available. It was the weekend of the Tall Ships visit to Sturgeon Bay and the annual lighthouse tours, two highly popular Door County events. The hotels and guest houses around the city and up the peninsula probably had been booked for months.

The sheriff helped the visitor to a chair in the lobby. "Wait here," he said.

Lisa had two friends who rented their spare bedrooms to guests during the busy summer months. Cubiak asked her to check with them, but both said the rooms were booked. Bathard and Sonja had three spare bedrooms, but there was no answer when he called. The only other place he could think of was Cate's condo. The last renters had been called home on an emergency, so it was vacant.

He called her and explained the situation.

"Of course. It's no problem and I'm happy to help. The next guests aren't coming in for another week. She's welcome to stay until then."

"It's just for a few days."

"Whatever. That's fine. I'm home on a break, so I'll meet you there."

"You don't have to bother. I have the key."

A half hour later, when Cubiak reached the condo with Helen, he knew Cate had bothered. How like her, he thought. The AC hummed on low and the drapes were open, letting in the soft afternoon light.

Helen took in the pastel watercolors on the walls and bouquet of yellow daisies on the coffee table. "Nice place," she said, as she moved to the window and took in the view of the water. There was something off-putting in her tone but he ignored it. The woman had just identified a corpse. Not an easy task for anyone.

"Please, just relax and make yourself at home. The guest room is upstairs. You'll find everything you need there and here."

Cubiak showed her the landline and basket of herbal teas next to the toaster. Then he opened the fridge to juice, bread, eggs, and other basics.

Helen seemed startled by the food. "Am I under house arrest?" she said, trying for a joke.

"You're here as my wife's guest," he said.

"Free to come and go as I please?"

"Absolutely. And please stay through the weekend if you can. I'll probably have more questions."

"Thank you," she said. Then she turned and picked up a letter from the counter. "I think your wife forgot this," she said as she handed the envelope to Cubiak.

UNSETTLING NEWS

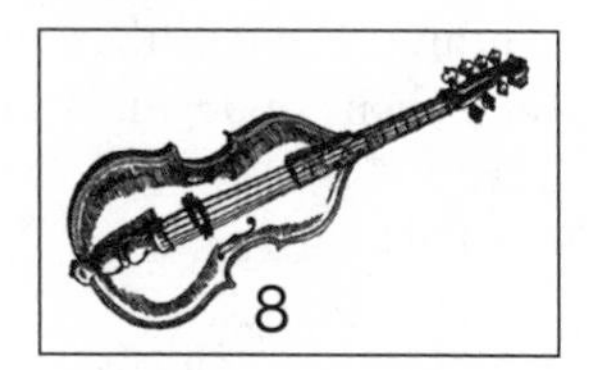

The sheriff headed north toward Jacksonport and home. He had barely seen Cate the last couple of days, and it would take only a minute to drop off the letter she had left at the condo and to pick up the photos she had printed for him. He needed the pictures for his investigation into Lydia Larson.

They had a beach house south of town. It was an eco-friendly, one-story structure designed by a Danish architect, a friend of Cate's. The two women had spent months putting together a list of basic musts: geothermal heating; solar panels for power; LEED certification; dual-pane, low-emittance windows; and a low-flow showerhead.

Cubiak thought the plans embodied a lot of costly razzle-dazzle that they couldn't afford, but Cate assured him that the house would eventually pay for itself. "We'll lead by example," she said. The thought of glass walls hadn't appealed to him either, but when the architect framed three sides of the house with old barn wood, leaving the fourth open to the lake, he couldn't say no. After the old-shoe feel of his rental on the rocks, he thought he would feel out of place in the modern setting. But after just a few weeks, he discovered that he liked the great wash of light and the openness that the design provided. Every time he crested the dune, he looked forward to seeing the house neatly rising up from the sand.

Cate waved to him from the shaded deck. She had poured iced herbal tea and put out a plate of ginger cookies. Two large envelopes lay at the end of the table.

"Everything OK with Ms. Kulas?"

"Yes. Thanks for setting her up." He grabbed a cookie and reached for the envelopes. He was eager to get back to his office. "I can only stay a minute. I'll take these and . . ."

"Come sit down. We need to talk," Cate said, patting the spot beside her.

He hesitated.

"David, please."

She never called him by his full name, and an uneasy feeling settled over him. He looked at her, and then he sat down.

Cate slid the envelopes off the table and leaned them against the bench. "We'll talk about these later, after you've had a chance to go through them."

"What is it? Is something wrong?" Cubiak said.

"Nothing's wrong." Cate locked her eyes on his and took his hand. "I'm pregnant."

He felt himself slip off a high ledge.

"I know it's a shock. It was a surprise for me, too."

"You can't be . . . ," he said.

She smiled. "Of course I can, and I am."

"But . . ." He remembered the first time they had really talked. It was years back, and they had just recently met. Earlier that day they had attended the funeral of a young girl who had been killed in a brutal attack at the state park, and later they found themselves sitting in Pechta's bar in Fish Creek, both depressed and drinking. Uncharacteristically, Cubiak had shared the story about his wife and daughter, and Cate had told him about her unhappy marriage, her ex-husband, the two devastating miscarriages that left her despondent and close to suicidal, and the doctor who advised her not to try again. Prior to the conversation, he had not liked Cate, or, more correctly, he had assumed that because they came from such different worlds he wouldn't like her. That afternoon, he discovered a common bond and began to view her in a new light.

When they eventually fell in love and discussed marriage, he never imagined they would talk about children. He had always assumed that the conversation that sad summer day insolated them from the talk they were having now. You can't be pregnant, he thought. You can't take that chance. You can't because the doctor told you not to. You can't because if the baby dies, it will destroy you.

Cubiak wanted to say all those things, but he couldn't find the words because Cate appeared so very happy, the happiest he had ever seen her.

"You're sure?"

She squeezed his hand. "I went to see the doctor this morning. She confirms it."

He stared at her.

"Please, don't worry. All that was before. Medicine has progressed. I'm well into my second month, and I have a new doctor, a better doctor, and she says I'm fine."

"But . . ." He tried again and faltered.

Cate put a finger to his lips. "I know this is hard for you. It has to be. It's not anything I expected either."

She kissed him. "Trust me, David. This will be good for us."

The conversation with Cate left Cubiak unsettled. Halfway to Sturgeon Bay, he spun off the highway and retreated deep into the countryside. Since that morning, nothing in the surrounding world had changed, yet everything seemed altered. Life was different now. He lowered the window hoping that the breeze would tamp down the roar in his head, but the rush of wind had no effect. "I'm pregnant," Cate had said, and her simple, powerful announcement played in an endless loop that he could not quiet.

Cate had been calm, almost serene, when she told him the news. Her message had been as straightforward and clear as the narrow road that stretched out before him, but the implications were daunting. A child affected the scope and rhythm of life. They had never talked about having children. And for good reason, he thought. He was nearly forty-nine. Given his age and Cate's medical history, he had never considered the possibility or thought to ask how she felt about being pregnant again. He had assumed that she would not want to take that chance. They had taken the appropriate precautions. But nothing was foolproof.

The reality she had eagerly shared with him that day was a reality he couldn't accept.

If only there was a way to step back in time and undo what's already been done, Cubiak thought. But second chances belonged to the future, not the past. He had learned that bitter lesson when Lauren and Alexis died.

What to do?

Nearing the ship canal, Cubiak hung a U-turn and detoured east toward the lake. He needed to sort through his confusion, and for that he needed to be by the water. Houses and cottages lined most of the shore, but there remained patches of wooded, undeveloped areas. He drove to his favorite spot and got out of the jeep. The wind had died and the air was warm. As he headed toward the lake, he rolled up his sleeves. He hadn't walked the trail since spring, when the way was open and easy to follow. During the summer, blackberry bushes had overgrown the narrow passage. He thrashed through the thick foliage, shoving past the thorny branches that raked his face and hands, drawing blood, and snagged his shirt. Sweat made the cuts burn, but he was thankful for the pain because it pierced the numbness he felt.

Cubiak often turned to the mighty lake for solace. That day he came hoping to find raging seas that would match his own turmoil, but with the wind gone, the water lay flat and quiet. The tranquility mocked his distress and left him feeling betrayed again. Distraught, he picked up a handful of rocks and hurled them at the water. How could Cate have been so careless to let this happen? He watched the ripples move across the surface and fade. Determined to stir the waters to meet his mood, he threw more rocks. But his efforts were futile. Lake Michigan swallowed his taunts and showed him only its peaceful side. Finally, exhausted, he stopped and rubbed his shoulder, letting his anger ebb until it matched the calm of the water. How could he blame Cate when he was as responsible as she?

"It will be good for us," Cate had promised.

Remembering what she had said, Cubiak shuddered.

He could not be a parent, again. As a young man, he was convinced that he could defy the legacy of his own miserable father, but when his chance came, he had failed in the worst way. "But . . . ," he had said to Cate and then silently recited the litany of logical reasons she couldn't—shouldn't—be pregnant. Her physical health. Her emotional well-being. He couldn't bear to lose her or bear to see her endure the agony of another miscarriage. All that was true.

But there was another layer of truth, and it was there that the real reason for his objections fermented. If he were to speak that truth, what he would say was: "We can't do this because I am afraid of failing again."

Somehow and soon, he would have to find the courage to tell her.

Cubiak didn't get back to the justice center until late afternoon. Again he slipped in through the rear door. In his office, he wiped the smears of dried blood off his face and hands and pulled on a clean shirt. He sat in his chair and slowly began to feel more settled. He had work to do. There were emails to read and calls to return. But more important, there was the mysterious death of Lydia Larson to investigate. He was still no closer to discovering who had killed her and why. Nor did he know when or how she had arrived on Washington Island.

He ignored the messages demanding his attention and moved to the conference table with Cate's photos. The first batch of pictures showed the musicians rehearsing and performing. The second group focused on the extras and the audiences at the different performances. He discarded nearly a dozen before he came across the first shot of Lydia Larson. She sat under a tree with her back against the trunk, her eyes closed and her face lifted up to the sunlight that leached through the branches. The photo was in black and white, and Cate had used a filter that gave it a gauzelike quality. The missing bag was on Lydia's lap, and her hands rested on it. She looked content, Cubiak thought.

In the next shot, Lydia was in a crowd that had gathered on the bleachers for a small outdoor performance. Except for her shabby attire, she was nearly indistinguishable from the rest of the audience. There were three more photos of Lydia, and in each of them she was with Richard Mayes.

It was clear the two were arguing. Lydia's eyes were wide and her mouth contorted as if she were shouting. In the first picture with Mayes, she leaned in toward him. He held both arms out and stood with one foot behind the other, as if he were trying to fend her off or flee from her.

Mayes initially said that Lydia had wanted a job and had become angry and unreasonable when he said he couldn't hire her. Later he admitted that he had fabricated the story, so that wouldn't explain her distress. Most likely she was upset because he had told her there was no money in her mother's estate.

There were two more photos taken in the same setting. In the first, Lydia was shoving a book toward Mayes. In the other, she held it open and pointed to something on the page, as if demanding that he look. In each of the photos, Lydia seemed to grow increasingly enraged and Mayes more bewildered and desperate to escape. Was she showing him the diary entry where her mother named George Payette as her father? Was that even true? He had only Helen Kulas's word on the matter, and he wasn't sure he believed everything she said, perhaps not even much of it. He needed to find the missing bag and the journals—if they existed.

Cubiak set the five photos aside and kept looking. But there was nothing more. He was about to give up when he came upon a group shot of seniors seated in folding chairs in the shade of the performance center. Behind them were the blurred figures of a man and a woman caught in earnest conversation. Something about the woman's outfit seemed familiar. He looked at the photo through a magnifying glass. The woman was Lydia Larson, and the man with her was Eric Fielder, the catering employee.

"Well, well, how about that," the sheriff said.

According to the date in the lower right-hand corner, the photo had been taken the day before Cubiak saw Lydia eating the free lunch Fielder had given her.

Fielder claimed that he didn't know Lydia and that he hadn't met her until Wednesday when he gave her the leftover food. Either he had confused the dates or he had lied.

Cubiak added the group shot to the pile with the other photos of Lydia Larson and continued sorting through Cate's work. She was good, he thought as he scanned the photos. He hoped to find more of Lydia but that was it: six pictures. Not much, and yet plenty for him to work with.

He called the catering company, hoping to learn more about Eric Fielder. It was a small, family business headquartered in Egg Harbor, run by the owner and his daughter and son-in-law. They hired cooks and servers as needed for the summer, their busiest season.

When Cubiak asked to speak to the HR person, the owner laughed. "My daughter does the hiring, but she's out."

"Did she hire extra help for this week?"

"She had to. Landing the contract for the music festival was a real coup. We were up against stiff competition and didn't think we had much of a chance. So it was also a surprise and she had had to bring on more staff on short notice." The man paused. "We've had no problems with our licensing or our food. So what's this about?"

"Just routine," he said and explained that he was looking for information on Eric Fielder.

"Eric's one of the good ones—and he's fully documented."

"Of course. But have your daughter call me anyway."

Shortly after he hung up, Cubiak's cell phone rang. An unfamiliar number flashed across caller ID, and he figured it was the daughter from the catering company getting back to him.

Instead, the gruff voice of Oskar Norling boomed out.

"That you, Dave?"

Cubiak hoped the ferryboat captain was reaching out because he had remembered important details about Lydia Larson's death, but his worried tone hinted at something quite different.

"What is it?"

"We got another one, Sheriff," Norling said.

ACROSS DEATH'S DOOR

Oskar Norling was a man of few words, but there was no escaping his meaning: the captain had discovered another body on his ferry.

"Male or female?"

"Male."

"Do you know who it is?"

"I've seen him around but I don't know his name."

"Where are you?"

"On the island. My grandson will be waiting at Northport. He'll bring you over."

Cubiak reached the ferry landing in time to see the lopsided oval of a moon lift above the horizon. In Chicago, the luster from a quarter-million streetlamps made the celestial body seem an afterthought in the night sky. But up north, the moon was queen. Her magical light cascaded over the ferry landing, transforming all it touched. The forest looked ready to reach out and reclaim the nub of land that had been stolen from it to build the harbor. But the inanimate buildings, the restaurant, and the ticket booth seemed shrunken and defenseless. Even the three ferries, massive enough to carry semis and tour buses along with convoys of cars and SUVs, bobbed like toys alongside the dock.

Only the great water refused to bow before the power of the moon. Undulating quietly, the inland sea spread out to the horizon, where its distant reaches spilled beyond the scope of the light and lolled in total darkness, as if taunting the lunar orb to try harder, to reach farther.

Against this backdrop, the familiar blue motorboat idled by the dock. Waiting onboard was the same young man who had transported Cubiak from the island the day Lydia Larson's body was found. What was his name? The sheriff remembered just as he stepped over the gunwale.

"Kevin, good to see you. Sorry to have to bother you again," he said.

"It's no trouble."

As soon as Cubiak sat, the boy started the motor and spun the prow around toward the harbor entrance. Once past the breakwater, he opened the throttle.

"Hang on," he said as they sped into the strait.

Instantly, the heat of the land disappeared and the two plunged into the ghostly chill that rose up from the deep water. Kevin tugged the hood of his sweatshirt over his head. The sheriff pulled his jacket closed and wished he had brought a hat.

Despite the cold wind in his face, Cubiak looked out over the bouncing prow. In the silvery moonlight, the ride across the Porte des Morts was both beautiful and terrifying. Kevin knew many of the old stories and legends and, perhaps sobered by the repeat purpose of his mission, he shared them as they sliced through the heaving rollers.

"You know how the strait got its name?"

"I thought it was because of the ships that went down."

"Naw, that came later. The name originated with the Indians. There was a war between two tribes, the Winnebago on the mainland and the Potawatomi on the islands north of the peninsula. The Potawatomi were paddling down and the Winnebago were heading north when a storm capsized their canoes. Something like six hundred warriors drowned. After that the Indians called the channel the doorway to death. When the French trappers showed up, they picked up on the idea, and everyone's called it Death's Door ever since."

Kevin was quiet for a moment. Then he went on. "The strait has been killing people forever. My great granddad used to talk about island men who tried to walk across in winter when the ice seemed solid enough. Just when they were too far from shore to get back, it would crack under their weight and they'd be stranded on floes that would carry them out into the lake or break up in the waves before anyone could reach them. Not that there was anything that could be done to help them. Once they were out here, they were on their own.

"And now this," he said, shouting over the roar of the boat motor. "In two days, the strait has claimed two more people."

"They didn't drown," Cubiak said. Well, at least Lydia hadn't. In truth he wasn't sure what he was going to find this time.

"Does it matter?" Kevin said. As they approached the entrance to Detroit Harbor, he eased up on the throttle and his voice jarred in the sudden silence. "Dead is dead. And whatever happened, happened here."

"The stories don't seem to keep you from going back and forth."

Kevin shrugged and responded with adolescent bravado. "It's my job."

Captain Norling waited at the pier, his silhouette vivid in the light. In movements that were second nature, he caught the mooring line and tied up the small boat. Norling nodded to Cubiak and gave his grandson a pat on the back that stopped short of becoming a hug. "Go wait in the truck, son," he said.

The captain's shoulders were stooped, and his eyes stared out from sunken sockets: signs of a worried man. He offered the sheriff a frown and a crushing handshake, and then he turned and headed toward the dock where the ferries were docked for the night. Norling stopped alongside the *Fiardakolla*. It was the largest of the boats and sat directly behind the *Ledstjarna*, the ill-fated vessel on which Lydia Larson had died.

"At least it's not the same boat," Cubiak said, thinking this small grace might mute any gossip about bad luck and keep it from morphing into a rumor of a jinx, but Norling's scowl let him know that this fact brought little consolation to the ferry captain.

Even in the moonlight, much of the cavernous vessel remained in shadow. They were onboard and halfway across the bottom deck before the sheriff spotted the black Lexus parked at the rear of the ferry. Tinted windows made the car seem even more foreboding.

Norling stopped several feet from the sedan. "It was one of the last cars on and would have been one of the last off, so we didn't notice anything wrong until the rest were offloaded. Even then, we weren't overly concerned at first. It happens occasionally that a driver takes his sweet time coming down or stays in the car and falls asleep and then has to be rattled awake."

"Who found him?"

"Tim Vultan. Poor sot. He could see the driver sitting there behind the wheel, so he yelled and pounded on the window. When he couldn't get a response, he called me down. He said he figured maybe the man had had a heart attack. It happened once years back. One of the locals. Anyways, I knocked and yelled but still with no result. We had to break the window to open the door."

"He was dead when you got to him?"

"Aye."

"Did anyone move him or touch anything else?"

"No. I put my hand to his neck to check for a pulse, that's all. Otherwise, nobody came near the body. This is just how we found him."

"Why'd you call me and not the coast guard?"

Norling scrubbed his brow and turned his deep, sad eyes on the sheriff. "Because of the garlic smell. Same damn stink as with that woman."

The dead man was Richard Mayes.

What the hell? First the young woman and now the festival manager—Payette's assistant. What's going on here? Cubiak thought.

There was nothing unusual about Mayes's appearance. His hair was neatly combed. His twisted, manicured hands lay quietly in his lap. He wore a light-blue button-down shirt and khaki pants. A navy-blue blazer lay neatly folded on the passenger seat. Mayes's eyes were closed, as if he were napping. Cubiak verified what the captain had told him about the tell-tale aroma. Then he searched the body and the car.

Mayes wasn't carrying a wallet, but his driver's license and insurance cards were in the glove box. The two credit cards and eighty dollars in cash the sheriff found in the inside breast pocket of his blazer and the expensive cell phone perched on the dash ruled out robbery as a motive. Unless the killer or thief was after something else, he thought. The key fob was in the ignition but there were no house keys to be found. Had they been taken or did Mayes not have any on him?

But more curious: Why was Richard Mayes on the ferry when he had access to a private boat that would transport him back and forth anytime he wanted? Whose car was it? Was he driving because he had planned to meet someone on the mainland when he returned the next day? Or because he needed it for a rendezvous on the island? The sheriff slipped the phone into an evidence bag. He didn't dare try to open it. He would give it to Rowe tomorrow. The deputy was good with technology. Maybe he could get into it and check the calendar and voice messages.

That done, Cubiak called the medical examiner and told her the latest. Pardy's husband was out of town and both kids were sick. It was already past ten, and she sounded exhausted.

"Do you need me now?"

"There's nothing you can do here tonight. I'll take pictures and then we'll lay the body out for you."

"OK, thanks. The sitter's coming at eight. I'll be there as soon as I can."

"Call Rowe."

Pardy managed a small laugh. "Deputy Speedy," she said.

Norling waited stoically for Cubiak to finish. "I heard what you said about the body. I can get a tarp, if that would help."

While the captain was gone, the sheriff photographed the scene. Then the two men eased the body from the car. "There's no place down here to keep it overnight. We'll have to put it in the lounge," Norling said.

Mayes weighed in at probably less than 150, but it was still tough going up the stairs. "I don't want to ask Kevin to help," Norling said.

"Of course not. We're fine," Cubiak said, ignoring the sweat trickling down his back.

When they were finished, the captain locked the door and took him up to the pilothouse.

"This was the last run for the night?"

"Yes."

"How many passengers onboard?"

"Twenty-five. More than usual but I figure that was because of the festival."

"But no names?"

Norling sighed, the fatigue etched deep in the lines that crisscrossed his forehead. "I told you, we don't track passengers. Although I recognized three of them. They're musicians here for the festival. They were all pretty loaded."

"How do you know they're with the festival?"

"I heard them play at a concert on the first night."

"You're a fan of early music?" Cubiak tried to keep the surprise from his voice.

Norling made a face. "Until now I didn't even know what that meant. My wife talked me into it. She said that since the festival was going on in our backyard we might as well take advantage. Besides, the preview was free to island residents."

"Do you know the musicians' names?"

"No, but they played the eight o'clock concert on the first day."

"Did you like it?"

The ferry captain considered the question. "It was a little subdued for my taste. I prefer horns, but still, it was OK. Nice to get out, too. We don't have much time for fun in the summer with all the work to be done."

Norling opened a thermos. He poured something hot into a cup and passed it to the sheriff. "Herbal tea," he said, embarrassment lacing his voice. "Can't handle the caffeine anymore after the middle of the day." He filled a second cup for himself and blew on it. "If you want to go back tonight, I can have Kevin run you over."

Through the window, Cubiak saw the boy waiting in the truck.

"It doesn't worry you to have your grandson out there in the dark?"

Norling shook his head. "It's practically like day out there now, and the boy knows how to handle himself in a boat. I made sure of that." He hesitated. "But truth be told, I'd rather not have him out on the water this late."

"If I stay, he'll spend the night with you?"

"Yep."

That was reason enough for Cubiak to book a room on the island. In fact, he was relieved to have an excuse not to go back and face Cate.

He waited until he was at the hotel to call her and explain the situation. "I'm sorry but I'm stranded here for the night," he said.

"Of course. I understand."

"You're OK?"

"I'm fine." The disappointment in her voice made him feel guilty, but the fact that she believed him made him feel even worse.

Cubiak couldn't sleep, and after thirty minutes he got up and checked his email. There were no updates from the deputies, but a note from the film producer said neither the cameraman nor sound guy remembered seeing Lydia Larson at the reenactment. "Hope you find something here," she wrote and gave him the password to the raw footage the crew had shot. He spent several hours scanning the material. He was convinced that Lydia was on the island because of the festival, and he was disappointed that she wasn't in any of the footage.

Instead, someone he didn't expect to see—the woman who had been caught shoplifting at the harbor store—popped up in the audience at three different concerts. Two of the performances were prior to the incident at the gift shop, but the third took place several hours after her near arrest for stealing. The sheriff had watched her drive onto the ferry. Damn it anyway, he thought. She must have ridden over to the mainland and then turned around and taken another boat back. So where was she now and what was she up to? Cubiak wondered.

OFF THE RADAR

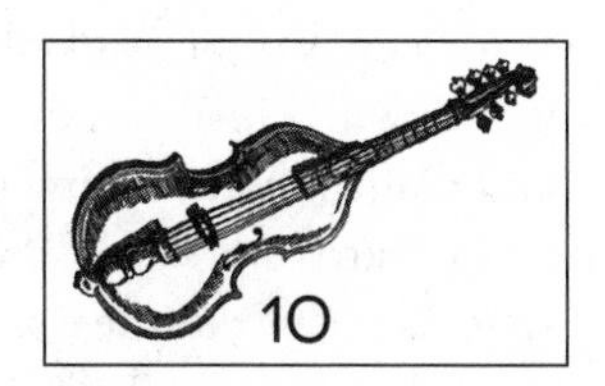

On Saturday morning, Cubiak was first in line at the harbor restaurant getting coffee and doughnuts for the crew of the *Fiardakolla*. Along with the senior deckhand, Tim Vultan, it was same team that had been on duty when Lydia Larson's body was discovered. A run of bad luck, especially for the teens, he thought.

The boys were clad in thin T-shirts and shorts, and they shivered in the brisk air. Vultan and the mustachioed assistant were similarly dressed but used plaid shirts as jackets. All four seemed grateful for the hot coffee. The sheriff didn't expect to learn much and wasn't surprised. Just as with Lydia, none of them had noticed anything unusual on the short trip from the mainland to Washington Island.

"Still got this?" Cubiak held up one of his cards. The first time he had questioned them he had passed them out with instructions to call him if they remembered anything.

Embarrassed, the crew members shook their heads. So he gave out the cards again. "Even the smallest thing could be important," he said, but he didn't hold out hope for much. The fateful crossing had been the last passage of the day, a sorry end to a twelve-hour shift.

As he left, Vultan pulled him aside. "The boys are getting a bit spooked," he said, indicating the two teens. "I'm gonna ask Norling to put them to work on the dock for a while."

"Good idea," Cubiak said, touched by the man's concern. "How are you doing?"

The deckhand shrugged. "I seen plenty in my life. I'm OK. But thanks."

When Vultan walked away, his shoulders were erect but his head was down. This business was getting to people. They expected results and Cubiak had nothing to offer. Not yet.

A text from Pardy popped up. The medical examiner was on her way. As she put it, she was "flying north" with Rowe. *Hang on*, the sheriff replied. Whatever she could give him would be another important piece to the puzzle.

As he passed the bike rental shop, the owner gave a nod of recognition, and the sheriff returned the gesture. He was starting to feel like a regular on the island. The previous night he had called the three musicians Norling had seen on the last crossing and asked them to meet him at the café. He found them in a rear booth looking pale and subdued.

"Hard night?" he said as he pulled up a chair to the end of the table.

They grunted in unison. Cubiak waved to the waitress. "Four cups and a pot of coffee, please."

The men gave their names. They were all from the greater Midwest: Milwaukee, Fargo, and Saint Louis.

"You guys just meet each other up here at Dixan V?"

"Not at all. We've known each other for eight, ten years now. We're 'festival friends.' We play a lot of the same gigs so our paths probably cross two or three times a season. When we're all together in the same place, we take advantage of it," the man from Milwaukee said.

"You party a lot."

The musician smirked. "Not really. We spend most of our time in rehearsals. Plus Bob's wife keeps pretty close tabs on him, so we usually get away only when she's shopping."

The Saint Louis player laughed. "But lucky for us, she likes to shop a lot."

Bob looked down sheepishly. His last name was Sandusky, which at first confused Cubiak because he was from North Dakota and not from Ohio, where there was a city by that name. He was also older and more reserved than the other two. "Does your wife usually travel with you when you're on the circuit?"

"Most of the time, yes. Why not? A lot of spouses do. Their wives are here, too." He pointed at his colleagues. "It's a free vacation."

The sheriff showed the trio a photo of Richard Mayes. "Do you recognize him?"

"Yeah, sure. He's with the festival. We see him around all the time," Bob said.

"Anyone have problems with him that you know of?"

"No, nada," they said, one after the other.

"Did you see him on the ferry last night?"

The two from Saint Louis and Milwaukee shook their heads. "As soon as we got on, we went to the top deck to get some air. He wasn't up there."

"You're sure?"

"Sheriff, in that moonlight, I could have read the paper. If this guy was sitting anywhere around us, we'd have seen him," the Milwaukee player said.

"What about you?" Cubiak asked Bob.

"I stayed in the car."

"You were on the vehicle deck the entire time?"

"Yeah."

"Did you see anyone there?"

"Someone on the crew might have walked by, but I wasn't paying attention."

"Where were you parked?"

"We were among the first on, so we were right up front," Bob said.

Which was as far from Mayes's car as it was possible to be.

"What's this all about anyway?" Bob asked.

"Richard Mayes died during the passage last night."

The three gawked at him and spoke nearly in unison. "What happened?"

"We don't know yet." Not completely.

By the time Cubiak finished with the musicians, Pardy and Rowe had reached the harbor. The sheriff found the medical examiner bent over the body and the deputy standing nearby.

"Nice car, this Mayes had," he said.

"Second one this week," Cubiak said. He told Rowe about the shoplifter he had escorted to the ferry on Wednesday.

"Two Lexuses? Or is it Lexi?"

"Who knows?" Cubiak laughed. "Every spring when I was a kid our landlady watched for the first sprouts so she could announce the arrival of the 'croci.' Drove my mother crazy. 'It's crocuses,' she'd insist, and they'd have a running argument until the flowers finally died. Neither of these women spoke English as a first language, so it was pretty funny listening to them debate this obscure point of grammar."

"Who was right?

"Both of them, actually."

"That doesn't answer my question."

"I think you were correct the first time," Cubiak said.

He gave Mayes's cell phone to the deputy. "You know what I need from it."

"Gotcha."

"Are you taking Emma back?"

"If she'll ride with me again." Rowe spoke loud enough for Pardy to hear.

The medical examiner looked up and mouthed an exaggerated *Ha* at the two men.

Cubiak waited another couple of minutes. "Anything?" he asked her.

"I'll know more this afternoon."

"Similarities between this one and . . ."

Pardy cut him off. "This afternoon, Dave," she said.

It was midmorning when Cubiak got back to the peninsula. He should have driven straight to work but guilt pulled him home first. He still wasn't sure how he would explain his feelings to Cate. No matter how he lined up the words, they came out sounding harsh and selfish.

From the dune, the house looked very still, and he was relieved to find that she had left already. There was a note on the kitchen table: "Thinking of you. Much love."

He made coffee and walked the dog. Kipper's droopy ears and shaggy coat reminded the sheriff of Butch, the mongrel that had limped out of the dark and into his life not long after he was first elected sheriff. Technically, Kipper was Cate's pet. She had chosen the pup from Butch's first litter, but his resemblance to his mother endeared him to the sheriff as well, especially now that Butch was gone. Playing fetch with Kipper, Cubiak tried not to think about Cate's message and the reason for it. He was being a coward and he knew it.

Anxious to hear what Pardy had learned from the autopsy on Richard Mayes, the sheriff made another detour to the west side and the medical examiner's office. For the second time that week he settled into the worn wooden chair that faced her desk. Pardy was on the phone and had her back toward the view of the old steel bridge. On his first visit she had been discussing kid issues—music lessons and playdates. This time, the talk was technical and sprinkled with medical jargon, not unlike the words in the titles of the books that lined her narrow bookcase and stood piled on the floor.

Pardy's voice shot up an octave, and when Cubiak realized she was talking about Mayes he paid close attention. She doesn't give up easily, he thought as he listened to her pressure the state medical lab to run the tests she had requested. "It's an emergency. I need the results so the department can proceed investigating the man's death. In fact, Sheriff Cubiak is sitting with me right now," she added, as if his presence underscored the urgency of the situation.

When the medical examiner reverted to scientific jargon, Cubiak let his attention wander to the primitive rainbow painting that hung on the wall over her left shoulder. Alexis had drawn the same lopsided images in preschool, and for a moment, he drifted into the memory of the sweet times he had shared with his daughter. "No."

Pardy looked at him quizzically and he realized he had spoken out loud. He motioned that he was fine but he felt his pulse race. What had he meant by the word? That he wasn't going to deny the memory of his own child or that he didn't want to imagine a new child in his life? No one will ever take your place, he silently promised Alexis as he turned away from the drawing and tried to concentrate on the stack of books near his feet.

"Right, then. Thank you," Pardy said. She dropped the receiver into place and looked across at him.

"We better be careful, or people are going to start talking," she said.

Cubiak tried to laugh. "Any news?"

"Yes, and none of it good, I'm afraid. Although from my perspective, it's certainly interesting." She raised both eyebrows, a sign that an explanation was coming.

"Preliminary results indicate that Richard Mayes may have died from selenium acid poisoning, just like Ms. Larson. Someone in my position doesn't come across this type of situation often, maybe never, and for me to have it drop into my lap twice in three days can hardly be considered a coincidence."

"Were there any signs of trauma on the body?"

She shook her head. "Mayes had a faint bruise on his left forearm, but it was old and unrelated to his demise. The only obvious symptom was the garlicky odor, which the captain mentioned to you. But the autopsy revealed the telltale swelling of the brain and dilated blood vessels, along with the other symptoms. And just as with the first victim, stomach contents indicated that he had eaten several hours before."

"And you think the poison was introduced in the food?"

"It's possible. In fact, I'd say it's very likely that's the way it was administered."

"Is there any way to determine if the poison used in both cases came from the same source?"

"If the same person killed both Lydia Larson and Richard Mayes, it's a pretty good assumption that it did, but not knowing the one, I can't speculate about the other," Pardy said. "We're scientists, Dave, not wizards. But nice try."

Rowe was waiting at the office.

"I got those reports," the deputy said as he laid several folders on the desk. "I checked all the names on the three lists. The musicians move around a lot, but they're clean. A few traffic tickets, but that's about it. One guy had issues with child support a couple of years ago but that's been cleared up. The film crew's a bit dicier." He opened the top folder. "The soundman's got two drunk and disorderlies."

It's the quiet ones that are always the most surprising, the sheriff thought.

"What about the caterers?"

"Nothing on the owner or his daughter. The student workers are clean. Two others have been here since May, typical summer employees. But there's one who's been in the country for a couple of years."

Cubiak skimmed the copies of the passports. The photos were not flattering but he remembered seeing two of the workers and recognized another immediately. It was the photo of Eric Fielder. Fielder held an Austrian passport.

"He said he was German."

"A lot of Germans live in Austria. Maybe he associated more with the one than the other." Rowe flipped through his notes. "According to immigration, Fielder came in through JFK. He stayed in New York for a couple of months and then headed to Madison and Chicago. Eighteen months ago, he renewed his visa, and after that he fell off the radar, until he showed up here working for the catering company."

"What did he do back home in Europe?"

Rowe arched his shoulders. "That's the funny part of this. There's no record of an Eric Fielder in Austria or in Germany either—I checked with authorities there as well."

"The passport could be fake."

"That's what I thought, too. But why?"

"Good question. And why did he lie about his first encounter with Lydia Larson?" The sheriff showed Rowe the incriminating photo. "In fact, why's he working here now, during the Dixan festival? He could have gotten a similar job anywhere on the peninsula. Keep digging and see if you can come up with anything else."

"On it, sir."

"Mike."

"Yes?"

"Don't call me *sir*."

Rowe saluted. "Yes, Boss."

Cubiak waved him out the door and called the catering service. Eric Fielder had not shown up for work that day. All attempts to reach him had failed.

"Did you talk to his landlady?"

"Yeah, and she said she hadn't seen him since late last evening."

"You tried his cell?"

"It's been disconnected."

A member of the sheriff's traffic detail was near the boardinghouse where Fielder had been staying. Cubiak sent her to check the premises. Twenty minutes later, she reported back that his room had been cleaned out.

Pardy had been evasive when Cubiak pressed her about the source of the toxin that had killed Lydia Larson and Richard Mayes. "If the same person killed both victims," she had said. The sheriff didn't share her reservations. Given the similarities in the two deaths, he was sure he was after a single culprit.

Both victims had died while riding the ferry. Lydia Larson perished as she went from Washington Island to the mainland, and Richard Mayes died while traveling in the opposite direction. The medical examiner's theory that Lydia and Richard both died from a slow-acting poison meant that the killer had struck well before the victims got onboard. But what if Emma was wrong? If the poison had been administered while they were crossing Death's Door, the murderer had been riding the ferry with them.

More than just location and cause of death linked the two victims. Both were connected directly to Annabelle Larson. Lydia was the self-proclaimed daughter of the supposedly deceased woman, and Mayes was a former colleague and friend. But was Annabelle dead, and, if so, how had she died?

Lisa was working until noon that day. He buzzed her and asked her to contact the coroner's office in Cook County. "We need a copy of the death certificate for Annabelle Larson. Ask them to scan and email it ASAP. The actual document can come later," he said.

The Dixan V festival also tied the two victims together. Mayes was directly involved with the event, so his presence could be explained. But Lydia had been on the grounds as well. What was she doing there?

What about Eric Fielder? What role, if any, did he play? He had been seen talking with Lydia before she died. And then, by the time Mayes's body was discovered, he was gone.

Finally, there was the mysterious George Payette, the bright light to which both Richard and Lydia were drawn. Payette was credited with bringing the early music festival back to Washington Island. He was also part of the GAR group, and with Mayes and Annabelle dead, he remained the sole survivor of the once-famous trio. That left Annabelle's daughter, Lydia, as the only other person who had a claim on the group. But Lydia was dead, and she had been killed in the same week and in the same way as Mayes.

Richard claimed that Lydia came to Door County searching for a legacy from her mother's days with the GAR trio, but the timing struck Cubiak as odd. Lydia could have shown up anytime after Annabelle's death. Was there a reason she chose the weekend of the Dixan festival?

Until yesterday, the sheriff had pegged Mayes as a possible suspect in Lydia's death. Mayes had opportunity and two possible motives for wanting the young woman out of the way. One was to protect Payette from her claims that he was her father, and another was to profit from marketing the trio's old recordings. Mayes had been dependent on Payette for his livelihood for years. Maybe he feared the well would run dry if there was another mouth to feed. But now Mayes was dead, as well, and Cubiak doubted that the poison that killed him had been self-administered.

There had to be a connection among the deaths, the GAR group, and the festival. Perhaps George Peter Payette held the answer.

Cubiak grabbed his keys. It was time to visit the famed gambist of Door County.

MAESTRO

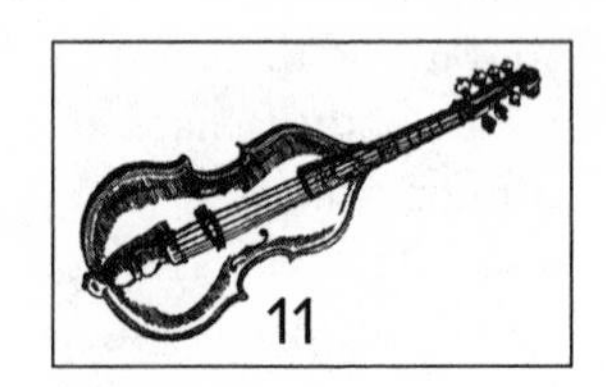

By noon Sturgeon Bay was hot and sunny, but at George Payette's estate, heavy tree cover and a breeze off the bay cooled the temperature by several degrees. When Cubiak pulled up, two vehicles were already in the yard, the familiar red sports car by the garage and a bright yellow van with a locksmith's logo painted on the side. Two young, leather-tanned workmen in shorts and T-shirts were busy outside the front door. One was removing the old lock while the other unpacked a new, more complicated mechanism. Cubiak said hi and rang the doorbell. Then he stepped past them into the cool interior of the house.

He waited in heavy silence. After a couple of minutes, a plump, stern woman appeared at the far end of the hall. She approached in choppy, nervous steps, with her hands bundled in her housekeeper's apron and a frown imprinted on her face. "Mr. Payette is in conference and not to be disturbed," she said, not bothering to ask the visitor's name.

He held up his badge. "I'll wait."

The furrow in the woman's forehead deepened, and for a moment he wondered if she wasn't going to insist that he leave. But the housekeeper finally decided that his credentials carried more weight than Payette's orders. She turned with a grunt and led him back down the hall.

"I'll tell Mr. Payette you're here," she said, showing him into the library.

The room was warm with wood and splashed with color from the bounty of books, CDs, and records on display. With an eye on the open door, Cubiak wandered around and admired the collections. He recognized most of the authors and a few of the major composers, but the names of most of the musicians were unfamiliar. Fifteen minutes passed. From somewhere inside the house, a door opened and soon the hunched and harried figures of the three festival organizers scurried past the library. Either they didn't see him or they pretended not to as they hurried toward the front entrance. The three had been decidedly more upbeat when he had talked with them the previous day.

Moments later, the inner door snapped shut, and a series of slow, steady footfalls brought a tall, well-dressed man to the library entrance. He was slender and had thick salt-and-pepper hair that reached his collar. "I am George Peter Payette," he said, in a regal tone. Payette paused for a beat, and then he entered the room like a man accustomed to stepping onto a stage. For a fleeting moment, Cubiak had the notion that he was expected to applaud. Instead, he extended his hand and offered his condolences.

Payette inclined his head. "Thank you, Sheriff. Richard's loss will be deeply felt. He was more than an able assistant; he was a friend. A very dear friend," he said, and his manner suddenly but only momentarily turned humble. "I'm sorry we have to meet under these circumstances, and while I appreciate your follow-up to this sad occasion I don't quite understand . . ."

"This isn't a social call," Cubiak said. He waited for the impact of the statement to penetrate Payette's cool façade.

"I don't understand."

"I'm here on official business."

The gambist's elegant face clouded. "Surely you don't think there was anything untoward about Richard's death? There was no mention of an accident. He had a bad heart, among a number of serious ailments, and I assumed . . ." The musician ran his fingers along his chin.

"Richard wasn't in an accident. But unfortunately, there are indications that he didn't die of natural causes."

"Oh, God." Payette sank into a chair. He looked puzzled, and moments passed before he spoke. "What do you mean? What are you getting at?" He hesitated again. "You aren't telling me that someone killed Richard?" The question was a whisper.

"It's a strong possibility, yes,"

Payette was ashen. "Richard didn't have an enemy in the world. Are you sure?"

"We're still sorting out the details, but there seems to be little question that he was murdered. Unless he took his own life, but I doubt that."

"Richard would never have killed himself. Not now, not after all he did to help revive the festival. But what makes you think he didn't die by his own hand?"

"For the simple reason that there appear to be several similarities between Richard's death and that of Lydia Larson."

Payette nearly sprang from the chair. "That horrid young woman. But the radio said nothing about murder, only that she was found dead on the ferry." His face darkened with fury. "The rumors have already started. First about her. And now Richard! Are you absolutely sure?" he asked again.

"I am investigating both deaths as possible homicides."

"Oh please, God, no. This is a disaster! You have no idea what this could mean. A lead player has already pulled out, claiming a personal emergency. If word about Richard gets around, the festival will hemorrhage musicians before we wrap up tonight. Everything will be ruined."

"Like Dixan I."

Payette seemed not to have heard. He stumbled across the white carpet to the drinks table and picked up a clear decanter of what looked like whiskey. He poured a generous amount into a glass and tossed it down. Arching an eyebrow, he raised the carafe but the sheriff shook his head at the offer of a drink.

"Have it your way," Payette said and sloshed another two fingers of amber liquid into the tumbler. "What do you know about music, Sheriff? And by that I mean classical music."

Cubiak didn't think his rudimentary grasp of opera would stand up to scrutiny. "Not much," he said as his host took a hearty sip.

Payette snorted. "Most people don't, thanks to our philistine educational system. In Russia, even the peasants know music, but here if you ask someone to name a famous composer the best you get is Beethoven if you're lucky, and most times you're not lucky."

The contents of the glass disappeared. "Music is important in more ways than I can explain. It does so much. It lifts us up from the mundane. It feeds our joy. It sustains us in time of sorrow. People can appreciate a good painting or a beautiful statue but they can't re-create it. Not like they can music. They might not be able to play an instrument well or at all, but everyone can hum a tune. Music is the only art form you can take with you wherever you go, no matter who you are."

Brandishing the empty glass, Payette dropped back into the chair. "Music touches what's inside our hearts, the very elements that make us human. Without it, we would all wither into dust." He looked at the sheriff and laughed. "Not literally, of course. I'm not being stupid. But if we didn't have good music, we'd spend our lives grunting at each other like apes and posting pictures of tuna sandwiches on Facebook or shopping for toilet tissue on Amazon."

"That's a pretty harsh judgment."

"Perhaps, but I believe it's true. Sadly, not enough people believe it. Not even enough musicians."

"Did Richard?"

"Yes, yes, he did." Payette set the tumbler on the floor. "Richard was a true lover of music as well as a true musician. Not just dedicated, but excellent at his art, as well, until he became unable to play. A good many musicians are technical geniuses, but it's the rare players who go beyond the score and the pages littered with notes and reach a deeper level of understanding. Richard was one of those, and it's horribly unfair that fate treated him as it did."

"The arthritis."

"Inherited from his mother. When it became obvious that he couldn't continue playing at the level he aspired to and demanded of himself, he put aside his instruments. It was painful to witness the impact. It was like watching his soul wither. He went away for more than a year, just disappeared. I never learned where he went or what he did. Then one day, he was at the door. He was leaner and sadder than before, but he said he wanted to reconnect with music again, as much as was possible. He told me he couldn't exist otherwise and that he decided he would devote himself to the profession in any way he could."

"You took him on as your assistant."

"It was his suggestion. I urged him to look elsewhere. A man with his talent could teach or work anywhere. But he insisted on staying here and helping me, and finally after a lot of back and forth, I agreed. We were friends, of course, with similar interests and philosophies of life, but as colleagues we shared an even stronger bond, a common purpose of furthering the reach of classical music in general and the gamba in particular."

Cubiak took a seat facing Payette. "He lived here, with you?"

"Of course. There's plenty of room, and it made things easier all around. Richard had one of the guest suites. That allowed him all the privacy he might need or want, but also, well, it was just less complicated and better all around. He had no commute, and unless there was a pressing deadline, he could work whatever hours he chose."

"Does he have any relations? Anyone I should contact?"

"Richard was an only child and his parents are both dead. There's an uncle somewhere. Montana, I think. I was going to call him after the festival, as soon as the arrangements were made."

"You'll have to wait on those."

Payette looked puzzled. Then he nodded. "Of course. You'll let me know," he said.

"I will. In the meantime, I'll need the uncle's name and number. No one else?"

"There may be cousins, too. I'm not sure."

"Was Richard ever married?"

"No."

"Did he have any offspring?"

"You mean children? No, of course not. At least none that I ever knew about and I think I knew him pretty well."

"And you met . . ."

"At Appleton. We were both at the Lawrence Conservatory." The answer came before the question was completed.

"What about Annabelle Larson?"

Payette was halfway to his feet. He grunted and dropped back down again. "Ah, Annabelle. I wondered how long it would take before you got around to her," he said, as a sad, sweet smile flitted across his face.

"Didn't she go to Juilliard?"

"Yes, she did." The musician looked past Cubiak, as if lost in the past. "Richard and I met her at a conference in Milwaukee and then we started playing together as a trio. But I'm sure you heard all about that already from Richard. He told me you'd talked."

"You were the GAR group."

"We were, and we were good."

"So I understand. Richard gave me one of your CDs but I haven't had a chance to listen to it yet. Would you say Annabelle was the linchpin of the trio?"

"I think we all contributed differently but equally. But a trio requires three people and once Annabelle pulled out, we were no more."

Payette stood. "It was tragic, really. Annabelle had the gift and the calling but she lacked the strength to sustain her talent. Music demands more than love and natural ability. It requires discipline and stamina. What do you think it took to keep Beethoven composing after he went deaf? Or Mozart when he was penniless? How does a man who cannot afford to buy a crust of bread ignore the pangs of hunger to create the most complex and beautiful music? The rest of us, those of us who make music, have to practice for hours every day to attain the basest competence. The drudgery is enough to discourage most people. It's a daily struggle. Even if you are born gifted, as Annabelle was, you have to work to nurture your skill. And beyond all that you must find a way to believe in yourself when the world turns its back. That is what we all must do.

But Annabelle? She could not sustain her faith, in her ability or in herself. Annabelle fell apart because someone stole a viol."

"She was a suspect?"

"We all were."

At the drinks table, Payette stirred up a fiery red drink. "Campari and soda. Very bitter, just like the memories." He hoisted the glass and gave Cubiak a knowing look. "But you're not here to rehash history or to critique Annabelle's musical talent. You're here because of that poor woman who claimed to be her daughter."

"It appears that Lydia Larson is her daughter. We have a positive ID on the body from a source who claims to have known them both."

"Ah," Payette said again. He drained the glass in a long, slow sip.

"Lydia also alleged that you were her father."

Payette still had the glass in hand, and Cubiak waited for him to pour another drink, but instead, he set the tumbler down. Then he closed his eyes and pressed his coupled hands to his mouth as if he were praying or remembering.

"Yes," Payette said finally. "Richard already told me about that, but isn't it obvious what she was up to?"

When Cubiak didn't respond, the musician went on.

"It's no secret that Annabelle ended up badly. From what little I know, she'd had a rough go of things and struggled financially for years. I, on the other hand, had made a success of my career. And this woman, Lydia, wanted money. That's all. I don't mean to sound harsh or disrespectful, but facts are facts. And if you think that I had anything to do with her death, you are very wrong. Indeed, to be honest, I resent the implication."

Most people do, Cubiak thought. Even the guilty ones.

Payette continued. "The real question is why would anyone want to kill both Richard and this Lydia woman? There's no possible connection between the two." He hesitated. "You're assuming the same person is responsible for both deaths, aren't you?"

"I'm not assuming anything at this point, but I am looking for information. For example, how many people here might have known both of them?"

Payette shrugged. "No one that I can think of. As I understand, this Lydia was a young woman. Richard was from a different generation."

"The only link between them was Annabelle."

"It would appear so."

"When was the last time you saw Annabelle Larson?"

"Our professional relationship ended nearly forty years ago when GAR dissolved. That was some eighteen months after the Dixan I debacle."

"That doesn't answer the question." Cubiak wanted a beer but resisted the urge to ask for one. "Did you ever see her after that?"

There was a long pause before Payette replied. "Once, a few years later. I was at a music conference in Aspen, and she was waiting tables at a local restaurant. I went to dinner with a group and she came over in her waitress outfit to take our order. You can imagine how awkward it was. I recognized her immediately. But she pretended not to know who I was, so out of respect for her, I said nothing. It pained me to see her like that. To look at those beautiful hands that I knew were capable of producing such beautiful, delicate music instead balancing platters of pasta and salad."

"When was this?"

"I don't remember exactly, maybe twenty-five, thirty years ago. I attend four or five festivals a year. After a while they all blend together."

"Did you try to help her?"

Payette frowned. "What do you mean?"

"Did you offer her any financial support?"

"No. I would have liked to but she was a proud woman. It would have been an insult."

Cubiak wasn't sure he agreed.

"You met with her, though?"

"Yes, before I left the restaurant that evening I arranged to see her again. The following morning, we had breakfast at a little café and talked for more than an hour. For a while it was like old times, except that she never mentioned music—and neither did I. Maybe I should have. I wanted to, but there was something in her manner that put me off."

"And you never saw her after that?"

Payette looked away. "No."

He's lying, Cubiak thought.

The musician checked his watch. "I'm sorry, Sheriff, but we have performances the rest of the afternoon and then the final concert tonight, and I'm already well behind schedule." He hesitated. "You think we should have canceled, don't you, out of respect for Richard?"

"It's a tough decision to make."

"I considered it, of course, and discussed it with the board. Ultimately we decided that the finest tribute to him was for the festival to go on as planned. This was Richard's event as much as ours and he would have wanted us to see it through."

Payette stood. "Do come, if you can. It will be a special performance, dedicated to Richard. I'll leave two front-row tickets for you at the box office."

As if summoned by secret signal, the housekeeper appeared in the hall outside the library. Wordlessly, she led Cubiak down the corridor and held the door for him. When he reached the walkway, she slammed it shut.

He looked back at the fortress wall. What secrets lie buried here? he wondered.

Payette had neither confirmed nor denied that he had fathered Annabelle's child. And then talking about Lydia, he had referred to her as "this Lydia woman." Why? Was he trying to divert attention from himself or had Mayes said something to confirm Payette's suspicion that the dead woman was an imposter? Perhaps Mayes had information that would either substantiate or disprove her claim. It was possible that Payette knew he was Lydia's father and didn't care.

In the jeep, Cubiak checked his phone. There was a text from Cate. *Call me. Important.*

A rush of panic hit him. Something had gone wrong already. He knew it. Hadn't he wanted to warn her? He tamped down his fear and called.

"Are you all right?"

"What? Yes, I'm fine, but Helen Kulas is gone."

"What do you mean?"

"She's not at the condo."

"Maybe she went for a walk."

"No, she's vanished. I went over to see if she needed anything and the condo was deserted. There was no sign of her anywhere."

"Did she leave a message saying how to contact her?"

"There was nothing. It was like she was never there."

"Did anyone see her?"

"I talked to a couple of people on the beach but they said they didn't see anything. And the caretaker was busy fixing a faucet at the other end of the building, so he didn't notice anybody coming or going. There's no one else around."

"Is anything missing?"

"Not as far as I can tell. And she did leave the key."

"So she's not coming back."

"Apparently not."

Cubiak heard the hesitation in her voice. "What else?"

"I'm probably being silly, but I found two mugs in the dish drainer. When I drink coffee or tea, I use the same cup over and over. It seems odd that she wouldn't do the same."

Unless someone else was at the condo with her, Cubiak thought, but he kept his concerns to himself. He didn't want Cate connecting dots that maybe shouldn't be connected. "I'm sorry I got you into this."

She gave a small laugh. "You were just trying to help. I wouldn't worry about it. Helen was pretty strange, so perhaps we shouldn't be too surprised by her odd behavior. At any rate, no harm, no foul," Cate said.

Payette said that music soothed the soul. But that didn't seem to hold true for the Dixan festivals. During the first event, an innocent woman died needlessly and a priceless viol was stolen. During the second, which was still ongoing, two people had been murdered and two more were missing.

Although the two festivals were separated by four decades, Cubiak was starting to wonder if the incidents weren't related. He was sure Payette hadn't revealed everything he knew. As for the two who had disappeared, it could be coincidence that both Eric Fielder and Helen Kulas had dropped out of sight, but the sheriff didn't believe in coincidence. If they knew each other, Fielder could have been at the condo with Helen. And what about the strange Ms. Kulas? What was the real reason she had shown up at his office the previous day?

MISSING, PRESUMED DEAD

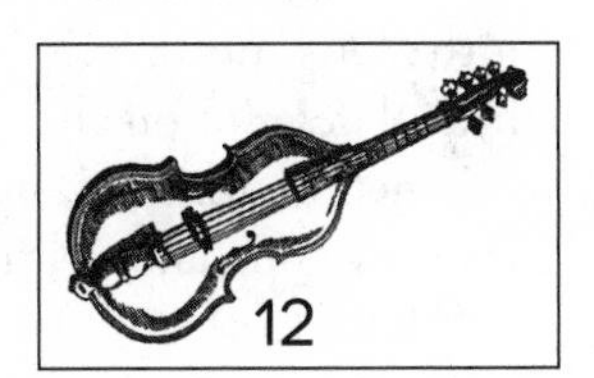
12

Onboard the ferry to Washington Island, Cubiak searched the internet for information about Helen Kulas. No matter what key words he entered, he came up blank. Which really wasn't that unusual, he thought. Most people didn't leave a trail in cyberspace.

But someone as well known as Annabelle Larson would have. He entered her name and found a flood of information, including a profile on Wikipedia and a half-dozen feature articles in several music magazines. A small notice mentioned her death earlier that year, but there was no reference to any children. Most of the material dated back to Annabelle's early career and performances throughout the region, including at the Birch Creek Music Festival when she was sixteen. The stories focused on her lofty status as a member of GAR and a rising star in the small universe of viola da gamba. Back then, she was a delicate beauty, with a petite face framed by tumbling long dark hair, her gray eyes intense with intelligence and spirit and a sweet smile. Nothing at all like her ostensible daughter. A more recent article listed Annabelle as the head violin instructor at Chicago's Crawford Avenue music school, the same school where Helen Kulas said she taught.

Cubiak viewed the school's website. Annabelle was no longer on the list of current staff, but Helen Kulas was. Her posted credentials pretty much matched what she had told him earlier, but the profile photo was that of a kindly woman on the far side of middle age. The Helen Kulas on the website was a little plump, a little sad, a little frumpy, and decidedly not the woman who had sat in his office earlier that week and said she was Helen Kulas.

At Detroit Harbor, he issued a BOLO notice for the imposter: Be on the lookout for missing woman. Last seen near Valmy. He gave a physical description and then added: may have altered appearance.

When he finished, he called the Crawford School of Music. The director was on another line.

"I'll wait."

After several minutes, a man's voice boomed out at him. "Harry Toramic here. Why is a Wisconsin sheriff calling me? What's going on?"

"I'm looking for information on one of your employees, a Helen Kulas."

"Former employee, you mean. Helen no longer works at the music school."

"She's on your website."

"That thing's always out-of-date. What's Helen done? Is she in trouble?"

"Nothing like that, but what happened? Did she quit or get fired?"

"Neither. With no warning, she stopped showing up for work. No call, no message. Nothing."

"When was this?"

Toramic thought a moment. "About five months ago. We were in rehearsals for the spring recital. She couldn't have picked a worse time to walk off the job."

"Did you try to get hold of her?"

"Of course. We called and sent urgent emails, but there was no answer, no response. I even went over to her apartment—she lived just a couple blocks from the school. The landlord said she'd left a check for six months' rent and said she was going on vacation."

"He didn't think that was odd?"

"How the hell would I know? He got his money; that's all he seemed to care about."

"How long had she worked for you?"

"Nearly twenty years! We were planning a party for her."

"And she'd never done anything like that before?"

"Never. Until this, Helen was an exemplary employee, the kind of person who got along well with everyone. I have no idea what came over her. But with these spinster ladies, well, you never know." He coughed. "Though I've got to admit, she was a bit quirky. Maybe she came into an inheritance and, poof, off she goes to Tahiti. But Wisconsin? What's she doing there?"

Cubiak ignored the question. "What do you mean by quirky?"

"Fussy, I guess. We rotate the rooms depending on who's got students that day, but Helen insisted on using the same room for every lesson, even if it meant rescheduling a student. And pretentious too. If someone famous was in the city, she'd talk like she knew them personally. It was kind of pathetic really."

"Did Miss Kulas live alone?" the sheriff said.

"I . . . I'm not sure. I think so. There was never any mention of . . ."

Cubiak cut him off. "When we're finished, you're going to contact the police and request a wellness check on your Miss Kulas." He used the possessive advisedly, hoping to instill a sense of guilt into the man.

"Helen is a very private person. We wouldn't want to . . ."

"Helen may be in serious trouble." He paused to let the notion sink in. "Call the district office and tell the desk sergeant exactly what you told me. Explain that you have reason to believe your former employee is in danger, that you've done everything you can to reach her, and that you need help from the authorities. Explain that you're following up on a lead from the sheriff's department in Door County, Wisconsin. That the sheriff has new information about Helen Kulas's unexplained disappearance."

"You do?" Toramic sounded alarmed.

Cubiak grunted and hung up.

A lot of things—good or bad—could happen to a person in six months, the sheriff thought as he wandered around the marina. From a distance he looked like any other tourist as he checked out the two-masted schooner that was tied up at the dock and read the historic plaque about the island's history. He even wandered through the small museum and ate an ice cream cone. But the sheriff wasn't in a vacation frame of mind. Instead, he was thinking about the dead and the missing. About Lydia Larson and Richard Mayes, who had been fatally poisoned; the deceased Annabelle Larson, who was Lydia's mother and Richard's former musical colleague; the man with the assumed name of Eric Fielder, who had gone missing; Helen Kulas, who had disappeared from her Chicago apartment several months ago; and the pretend Helen Kulas, who had vanished twenty-four hours after she arrived in Door County and identified Lydia's body. Had she told the truth when she said she knew Lydia or had she lied? What if the fake Helen Kulas was the real Lydia Larson?

Cubiak was on his second circuit around the harbor when he spied Oskar Norling at a picnic table outside the restaurant. He was working his way through a cheeseburger and a mound of french fries.

"Mind if I join you?" the sheriff said as he slipped in across from the ferry captain.

Norling shooed a hungry sparrow away from his plate. "Be my guest, only don't tell the wife. She's always after me to eat more salad. 'Lettuce will keep you healthy.'" He grimaced. "Whatever. You want something? I'll get Agnes."

Cubiak shook his head but Norling had his hand up and the waitress was heading their way. She had a smile on her face and came toward them with a mug and coffeepot. "Sheriff?" she said.

He knew it would be rude to refuse but even before he had a chance to respond, Agnes set the cup down. "Cream and sugar?"

"Black's fine," he said and waved away the menu. "Nothing else. Thanks."

"The ladies work hard here," Norling said as the waitress retreated.

"Everyone does. You sure had your hands full this week."

The ferry captain harrumphed. "Comes with the territory. Whenever there's a special festival, we do whatever's needed to accommodate folks. Used to be people here could make a living off the water or the land. Some still do but more and more the locals depend on the tourists." He shrugged. "Well, what are you gonna do?"

The query needed no answer, so Cubiak gave none.

"You've been doing this a long time," he said finally.

"Pretty much all my life. But I got no complaints. There are worse ways to make a living. And it's a helluva nice place to live."

"You were here for Dixan I?"

"I sure was."

"Was it this busy?"

"Not so much. I was a punk kid back then but I remember it as being what I'd say on a scale of one to ten was about a four or five in terms of how hectic things were. It was a much smaller event, but there were still plenty of people coming and going. And, of course, we had fewer boats then too. After that fancy violin went missing, it was slow and tedious as hell getting people off the island."

"Viol. The instrument was a viol, not a violin."

Norling shrugged and scooped up a handful of fries. "Whatever. It was worth a small fortune. Whole place went into a panic. Every vehicle was searched top to bottom. All the instrument cases opened and checked at the dock. Same with every large suitcase and duffle. Took forever to load the ferries. Folks were not happy."

"I imagine not."

"It wasn't just the time they had to spend waiting in line; it was the weather too. It's usually pretty cool up here on the island, but that year it was hot as blazes, and those stuck on the road in the sun were downright miserable. But Dutch wasn't to be hurried. It didn't matter how important you were or where you said you had to be, he made them wait. Every single person leaving the island went through the process."

Norling pulled at his chin. "He searched the ferries, too, every square inch. He made us open every door and cubby. He maybe figured that someone had squirreled it away, though there aren't many hiding places on any of the boats. All of us crew were scrutinized as well. He was real polite about it and said he didn't mean to insult us, but he couldn't ignore the possibility that one of the locals was in on the heist.

We practically had to turn our pockets inside out to convince him we had nothing to do with it. No, sir. Nobody got a pass from Dutch Schumacher."

"What about before the festival, when the musicians were arriving?"

The boat captain ran a fry through a pool of ketchup. "Before the festival? Nothing unusual that I can remember. The musicians straggled in at their own pace. Some showed up at the last minute, in time for the first rehearsal, and some came early with their families, so they'd have a little vacation time up front. That German fellow, the man who owned the stolen . . ." Norling hesitated. "What did you say it was called?"

"Viol."

"Yeah, that. He was here with the early birds. Came over with his wife. I remember that she was very young and very quiet, kind of scared-like or maybe just shy. I took them both up to the bridge to meet my uncle Sven—he was the captain—and remember her saying that it was her first time in America outside of New York City. She spoke good English and said she hadn't realized what a lovely country it was. Too bad, what happened to her."

"Nobody inspected instrument cases?"

"You mean, coming in? Not that I recall. Why would they?"

"No reason, just wondering." Cubiak swallowed a mouthful of coffee. "What about the storm?"

Norling pushed his plate away and folded his arms on the table. They were muscled and leathery brown. "Now that's a day I'll never forget. I've seen plenty of weather in these waters since, and I can tell you that was one of the worst storms ever. We knew it was coming and urged anyone who needed to leave the island to get down to the harbor as fast as they could because at some point all the runs would be canceled. Things were all shut down already when that German musician showed up and begged us to take him and his wife across. We didn't dare. We couldn't."

"She'd gone into labor, hadn't she?"

"I don't know exactly. She was having some kind of pains, and a couple of the local ladies said it was probably those false ones, whatever they're called. My uncle said he couldn't chance the run but the foreigner kept pleading and finally old Sven relented. 'If we go down it's on your head,' he told him. We got word out in case there were folks who wanted to cross. Told them they had ten minutes to get to the dock. But nobody else showed up. And so we took off."

"You went, too?"

Norling nodded. "I was part of the crew. My uncle didn't want to take me but he was shorthanded and had no choice. Scariest damn ride of my life. And then to land at the old dock at Gills Rock? I don't think there was another ferry captain who could have managed it. We got the lady there, like her husband wanted, but in the end it didn't matter. The poor woman died anyway."

In the nearby park, a child squealed and then a man shouted. "Saaammee!" he called out again and again. The captain laughed. "Look at that," he said.

Cubiak turned to see a young boy barrel headlong toward a young man who sat on the edge of a wooden bench. The two had the same olive complexion and dark curly hair and wore matching Door County T-shirts. Both were laughing.

"Daddy!" the boy shouted as he ran toward his father's outstretched arms. When the boy was nearly in his father's grasp, he spun on his heel and started to dart away.

But the man was too fast for him.

"Saaammee!" he cried as he pulled the boy into his arms and swung him in the air. All the while Sammy shrieked with delight. For a moment they were nearly nose to nose, the young man on the park bench and the boy with his arms and legs outstretched as if he were flying.

Then the man set Sammy back on the ground, and the boy started running in circles and pretending to dodge his father's reach, but invariably giving in and letting his father catch him. Over and over the game went on. People walking past stopped and watched but the father and son were oblivious.

Norling swiped at his eye. "You got any kids?" he said.

The question stopped Cubiak, as it always did. He took his time answering. "I have a daughter, but she died," he said.

Norling cleared his throat. "Sorry. That's gotta be really tough."

They fell into an uneasy silence as the Sammy game continued behind them. Finally, Norling spoke. He was subdued, almost wistful.

"You know, when I was a kid, I was always a little scared of my dad. I never knew how he felt about me because he never said. Hell, I can't remember him ever so much as giving me a hug, but I figured he loved me. He had to. I guess I never really gave it much thought. Things were what they were. But that boy"—the ferry captain watched Sammy and his father stroll hand in hand along the dock—"that boy is never going to have any doubts. He is going to grow up knowing he is loved."

Cubiak left Norling with a slice of cherry pie and headed to the ferry. He was on the top deck when his cell buzzed. The call was from the 312 area code, not the same number as the music school but from Chicago. He answered and found himself talking to a homicide detective from his former district. It was an odd sensation: the county sheriff talking to a version of the city cop he had once been. Their conversation was sprinkled with the raised *a*, a linguistic feature of the old rust-belt cities that made a word like *cat* sound like *cayet.*

The detective was no-nonsense and direct. Whether he was oblivious to Cubiak's history with the force or didn't care about it, the sheriff couldn't parse.

"I got your number from the owner of the music school. He came into the station nearly hysterical, going on about us needing to check on a missing woman named Helen Kulas. Based on what he had to say, it sounded urgent, so I figured I'd better contact you myself. Call it professional courtesy or whatever," he said.

"You checked her apartment?"

"Just got back a few minutes ago. The apartment was locked up nice and tidy. No sign of forcible entry to the apartment, but we discovered the remains of a woman in the bedroom. We'll need dental records to ID the body but it bears a resemblance to the missing woman."

"Any obvious cause of death?"

"No trauma that we could see. The coroner's ordered an autopsy. I'll get those results to you ASAP. I'll tell you one thing; someone went through a lot of trouble either to preserve the body or to prevent anyone from finding it after the victim was dead."

"What do you mean?"

"The bedroom was sealed and the body was sprinkled with salt and herbs and wrapped in layers of linen. The pathologist said it looked like an amateur attempt at mummification. Never seen anything like it before and I've been doing this a long time."

"Was the apartment ransacked?"

"Nope. Everything in its place."

"What about the neighbors?"

"We found two at home. They said Helen Kulas had lived there for as long as they could remember but neither had seen her for several months. She generally kept to herself so they weren't alarmed. The upstairs tenant said she remembered her saying she was going on vacation," the detective said, and a touch of sadness tinged his coarse laugh.

Cubiak called Cate again. Until she answered, he didn't realize he had been holding his breath. "You're OK?" he said.

"Of course, I'm OK. Why wouldn't I be?"

He told her about the body in Helen Kulas's apartment.

"But who . . . ?" she said.

"I don't know."

Cate went quiet. "Do you think all this has something to do with the yellow viol?" she said finally.

"It's possible. The viol is either at the bottom of the strait or someone has it."

"And that someone could be in Door County?"

"Or anywhere else in the world." He hesitated. "You still have your uncle Dutch's notebooks, right?"

"They're at the farm, along with everything else."

Cubiak sensed the tension in Cate's voice. *At the farm* was how she referred to the small homestead where her aunt Ruby and uncle Dutch had lived. It was where Cate had spent her childhood summers and where she had last seen Ruby. As far as he knew, Cate had never been back, even though she had inherited the house and property after Ruby's death.

"Why?" she said.

"Dutch was the sheriff during Dixan I. That first evening I was invited for dinner, Ruby showed me a few of the notebooks, and I remember being struck by his attention to detail. It might help me now to find out what he knew then."

"You have the key." It was both statement and question. They each had a key, in case of emergency. Cubiak didn't know where Cate kept hers but his was in the glove box of the jeep.

DECIPHERING DUTCH

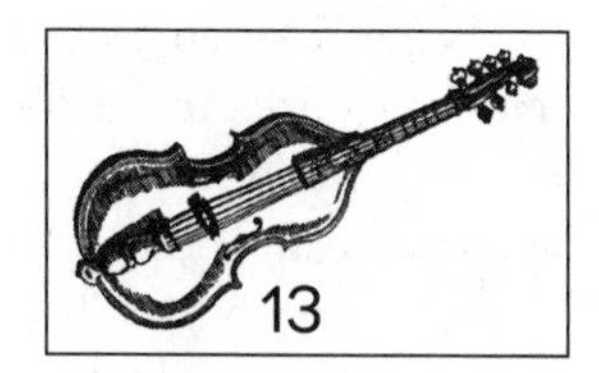

The sun was level with the treetops when Cubiak left Northport on the two-lane blacktop that cut across the top of the peninsula. He drove slowly through the lacy patchwork of light and shadow that covered the road. It was still early, but he knew that the deer would start their nocturnal roaming soon. As he rounded a curve, a doe emerged from the thick woods that flanked the road. The animal's cinnamon silhouette melted into the backdrop, and he barely noticed her in time. But the deer had seen him. Standing knee-high in a patch of milkweed on the narrow shoulder, she froze, head up and alert.

Cubiak flashed his lights and slowed even further. Would the deer cross the road in front of him or run back into woods? He watched. The deer waited. He was about fifty feet away when the animal pivoted on its front hooves and leapt back into the forest. He crept forward another few yards. Then, just as he started to pick up speed, the doe sprang from the trees and vaulted into the middle of the road. He hit the brake as it flew past, with head and white tail high. A fawn trailed behind, inches from the jeep.

Door County was home to some twenty thousand deer. They showed up in open fields and fenced-in backyards. But a good many of the animals favored the rich forests at the northern tip of the peninsula.

The sheriff didn't mind the slow pace. In fact, he was relieved to delay reaching the house where Ruby and Dutch had lived. He had been there twice, and each time Ruby had talked about her late husband, Dutch Schumacher, the legendary sheriff of Door County and the love of her life. Listening to the memories, Cubiak felt her suffering almost as much as his own.

When Lauren and Alexis died, pain became the air he breathed. There was grief in the food he ate and guilt in the vodka he drank. He escaped drowning in that dismal well, but he never fully escaped the agony of losing them. "You don't ever leave the pain behind. It's a truth that those who have lost know, and that those who have not cannot fathom," Bathard had said once.

Cubiak's pain shrank into a tight capsule that burrowed into a corner of his heart, invisible but viable. A single word was enough to release the tsunami. A memory would do the same. For that reason, he would rather not enter Ruby's house again. But he had no choice. There would be no dallying. He would grab the notebooks and leave.

From the driveway, he was struck by how little the yard had changed. Although the large vegetable garden was overrun with weeds, the firewood remained piled in neat rows and the old barn that had been Ruby's weaving studio was barely more weathered than it had been the first time he saw it seven years prior. The familiar scent of cedar still perfumed the air, and the eternal waves still battered the rocks at the base of the cliff.

A ghostly silence greeted him at the back door. Eyes downcast, and with the weight of memory dogging his footsteps, he walked into the kitchen and then through the dining room to the front hall, where Dutch's notebooks were piled in a narrow pine cupboard. Cubiak grabbed the knob, but instead of opening it, he looked into the vaulted living room. The room was empty and the heavy woven drapes were pulled across the wall of windows at the far end, but no matter. He could still imagine the tall pines and the waters of Death's Door that lay on the other side of the glass, and he could hear Ruby's rich voice as she talked of her deceased husband. He had liked Ruby, and although he had never met Dutch, he would have liked him too, and he understood how she had suffered when he died.

The stillness inside the house was paralyzing. Cubiak wasn't sure how long he stood before the cupboard before he finally opened the door. There were more notebooks than he had remembered. Five shelves were piled with rubber-banded stacks of pocket-sized spiral pads. The notebooks had rainbow-colored covers and were arranged chronologically by years, the most recent on the upper shelves. Kneeling, he searched for the early records. When the yellow viol was stolen, Dutch had been head of the department for a little more than four years. On the second shelf from the bottom, Cubiak found what he had come for: four notebooks filled with information about the event. With those in hand, he retraced his steps through the house, careful not to disturb the thick fog of reminiscence that hung in the air.

Back in the jeep, Cubiak tried to reach Cate again. When she didn't answer, he left a message. *Call me. It's important.*

Then he phoned Bathard.

"I picked up Dutch Schumacher's notebooks from the Dixan I investigation to see if there's anything in them that I could use. I thought maybe we could go through them together and see what we learn. Maybe something will jog your memory. I'm heading back from Gills Rock now," he said.

"Good. I just left Baileys Harbor. I'll meet you at your house."

Bathard was on the deck watching a flock of seagulls circle above the shore when Cubiak pulled up.

The coroner held up a white paper bag. "Specials from that new restaurant. I figure the two of you are too busy to cook these days."

"Thanks." The sheriff reached for the door, and Kipper trotted out to greet them. "Cate's up on the island getting ready for tonight. We can save some for her."

"How is your lovely wife? I haven't seen her in a while," the physician said. He petted the dog as he glanced at the hand-painted ceramic tiles that lined the walls, work that Cate had done.

"Cate's fine." Cubiak put out food and fresh water for Kipper and set two bottles of beer on the table. "She's pregnant."

Bathard grinned and clapped his friend on the shoulder. "Well,

well, I must say this is a surprise, but congratulations. That's wonderful news. What a good thing for you, for both of you."

"That's what Cate said." There was a hard edge to Cubiak's voice.

"And you don't think so."

The sheriff sat down heavily. "No, I don't." He looked at his old friend as if wanting him to agree. "There's her health to consider. She said the doctor assured her that medicine has improved and that things will be better, but I don't know."

"She's probably right. Doctors generally don't mislead their patients." When Cubiak didn't react, Bathard sighed. "Sorry, that was my pathetic attempt at a joke. Sonja told me not to try to be funny; she said that I can't carry it off." The doctor took a chair across the table. "What about you?"

Cubiak grunted. "Me? I can't do this again," he said. He reached down and scrubbed Kipper's head. "It's complicated."

"Actually, Dave, I don't think it's that complicated. I think it's pretty obvious what's bothering you." Bathard softened his tone. "You're afraid of having another child because you think something horrendous will happen, like it did to Alexis."

Cubiak hung his head.

"You also think that having a second child makes you disloyal to your daughter's memory."

The sheriff did not respond.

"It's only natural that you feel that way."

He looked up. "So you agree?"

"No, I don't. I said it's natural to feel that way, but that doesn't mean you shouldn't forge ahead. I know you feel guilty about your daughter's death. What parent wouldn't? But Alexis was killed by a drunk driver. The man behind the wheel is the guilty party. You're never going to forget your daughter. And no other child will ever replace her, either. Just as Cate didn't replace Lauren.

"We hold on to the past like a drowning man clings to a life raft, but sometimes the only way to reach shore is to let go and swim for it."

Bathard hesitated. "If I may quote the good and wise Buddha: 'No one saves us but ourselves. No one can and no one may. We ourselves must walk the path.'" The coroner rested a gnarled hand on Cubiak's arm. "Perhaps this is your path, Dave."

They ate in silence, each man caught up in his own thoughts. Afterward, while Bathard cleared, the sheriff made coffee. When they were ready, he laid Dutch Schumacher's notebooks on the table.

"What do you want me to do?" Bathard said.

"Sit back and listen, and stop me if anything jars a memory or doesn't sound right."

Cubiak opened the first notebook and began to read.

"'August 10, 3:43 p.m. Call from Washington Island. Dixan I organizer reports rare instrument missing. Yellow viol.' And then a question mark." The sheriff looked at Bathard. "Dutch didn't know what it was."

"No one did except the gambists and people who followed early music," the coroner said.

"Right. Then he wrote: 'Viol equals 250K. Verify.' He underlined the figure in red. 'No insurance? Why?' also underlined. 'On loan to Franz Acker: German musician. Owner?'" Cubiak scanned the next two pages. "He answers his questions and then the rest is about the musicians: forty-six players, fifty-eight instruments. Twelve more instruments than players.' Several question marks after that. His list of the players includes date of arrival, island address, and number of instruments. And again he writes: 'Verify? Check records—police, financial—musicians and organizers.' There are markings after each name, probably Dutch's own code. But here"—he pointed to the bottom of the page—"again in red: 'Nothing.'"

A festival program was folded and stuck between two of the notebooks. Cubiak pressed it flat on the table. "Dutch compared the program to the musician list from the organizers. All the players' names are checked off," he said.

The sheriff opened the second notebook. "There's a lot here on Franz Acker. 'Photo, verified. Passport number, checked. Vita—verify.' That's checked too. Much the same for his wife, Heike. Then: 'Check backgrounds. Acker's financial situation. Details of theft forwarded to Interpol and FBI.'"

"What about the yellow viol?"

"That comes next. 'Produced: 1594 by Augusto Fiorrelli. Verify history, value, description. Need pics from three sources.' With an exclamation point he notes that the viol is brown, not yellow. 'Strings dyed.' Finally, Dutch poses a series of questions: 'First: Premeditated or crime of moment?'"

The coroner listened with his eyes closed.

"What do you think," Cubiak asked.

"Premeditated and carefully planned."

"Dutch thought so, too. 'Second: Motive?' He came up with three."

"Three?" The coroner opened his eyes and sat up. "I can think of two: money and revenge. If Acker had crossed someone, they might have stolen the viol to get even."

"Dutch's thinking exactly, but he added a third: 'Covetousness. Collector-slash-musician equals sickness,' he wrote."

"And?"

"Nothing came of the first two motives. Leaving the third. Which makes a lot of sense. People lust for power. They lust for sex. They lust to own things that are rare and beautiful."

"That leaves a wide-open field of suspects," Bathard said.

"The thief could have been a musician or even someone in the audience. Another gambist or a collector. Or the person hired to do the dirty work. The musicians were still on the island when the theft was discovered, but there was no way to track the movements of the audience members or tourists who were also there at the time."

"Hence, everyone was a suspect."

"Right. Third question: 'Hide viol on WI?' Dutch says they searched every structure, including vacant garden sheds and abandoned barns. 'Long-term?' he wrote. I wondered about that myself. If someone had planned this, could they have left the viol in a hidden location with the intention of coming back months later to retrieve it? Dutch conferred with experts in Madison and New York. 'Not likely. Need controlled climate. Impossible on island without special chamber.'"

"And constructing a climate-controlled chamber would have been a big tip-off that something was in the offing," Bathard said.

"Exactly."

"Fourth question: 'How remove viol from WI?'"

"What did Dutch say about that?"

"Pretty much what we've gone over before: that it was carried away inside an instrument case, hidden inside another instrument, or secreted in a large suitcase or duffel. But after the theft was reported, every vehicle, boat, case, and piece of luggage was searched, so these were all dead ends."

"Leaving only the theory that the yellow viol was whisked away by boat before anyone knew it was missing," Bathard said.

"Dutch didn't like that theory, but in the end it was all he was left with."

Cubiak skimmed the third notebook.

"What's in there?"

"A rundown of the musicians' accommodations during the festival. More than half were put up in cottages and houses that were provided by local residents and sponsors. 'Nothing,' Dutch noted. But there's an asterisk by the address for the Knotty Pine cottage: 'Owner returns two weeks later. Finds ashes in the fireplace. Nights on island usually cool, but record heat fest week: Why fire?'"

"Good question."

Cubiak stretched and poured another beer. "If you don't need a fire for warmth, there are two other possible explanations for making one: First, to create a romantic or sentimental mood. Second, to destroy evidence. Dutch checked with the musician who'd been assigned to the house, but he said he never used the fireplace."

"Maybe the ashes were from an earlier fire."

"Not likely. The owner told Dutch the house was spotless when she left. No ashes, she said."

Cubiak went back through the notes. "Hold on, there's more. The musician admitted that he only stayed there the first night. Seems he hooked up with one of the single female players and moved into her cottage for the rest of the festival."

"Leaving the house empty for several days?"

"Correct, but there was no sign of a break-in."

"That doesn't mean anything. Even today, a lot of island people don't lock their doors. Back then, I'm sure hardly anyone did."

"Someone made a fire in that cottage. Why, we don't know. Who, we don't know. Dutch called all the musicians, and every one denied knowing anything about a fire. But it didn't have to be one of the players. Anyone could have done it, even a couple of kids."

CURTAIN CALL

That evening Cubiak reached Washington Island in time for the final performance of Dixan V. True to his word, Payette had left two front-row tickets at the box office for the sheriff. Absent Cate, who was shooting the event, he took in the first half of the concert alone. But even from that vantage point, he found it hard to focus on the music. Instead, he imagined Franz Acker center stage, and a thief skulking in the background, plotting to get hold of the yellow viol.

At intermission, he met up with Cate. While others in the sell-out audience discussed the performance, she brought up the fake Helen Kulas.

"If the woman who stayed in my condo isn't Helen Kulas, who is she?"

"I don't know."

"And what's she doing here?"

"I don't know that either. There's an alert out about her, but whoever she is, she's probably altered her appearance by now."

"She must have had some reason for the charade."

"Besides identifying the body of the dead woman as Lydia Larson, I don't know, but I have my suspicions. Everything keeps coming back to the music festival."

Cate took a sip of water. "I'd much rather have a flute of champagne, but there'll be plenty of time for that later," she said and smiled.

Cubiak smiled back, but it was a false gesture of support and made him feel like a louse.

How long before things turned bad again for her? he wondered. Cate had been on the island since noon photographing the final phases of the festival. Musicians who had avoided the camera earlier suddenly wanted souvenir photos, and she was flushed from exertion.

He tucked a stray strand of her hair behind her ear. "You shouldn't overdo things," he said.

"I won't." Cate's tone was light but then it flipped to somber. "If the woman claiming to be Helen Kulas isn't her, does that mean the dead woman on the ferry isn't Lydia Larson?"

"Not necessarily, but I don't know that either. If fact, I don't know for certain that Lydia Larson even exists. The fake Helen Kulas talked about her, but there's no credibility in anything she said. Richard Mayes ID'd Lydia from the photo I showed him, but that's because when he met her earlier she told him that was her name. If someone was masquerading as this Kulas woman, maybe someone else was pretending to be Lydia. Both Mayes and Payette said they had never heard anything about Annabelle Larson having a baby, which brings us back to the ersatz Helen, who claimed she babysat for Lydia when she was a child." Cubiak frowned. "There's too much about this situation that's puzzling."

"You'll figure it out. You always do." Cate raised on her toes and kissed his cheek. "Sorry I couldn't join you in there. The music is really lovely. I see why people are so enthralled with it."

She set her glass down. "I hope I run into this phony Helen character again. I'd like to find out what her story is."

"What? No." The prospect made Cubiak uneasy. "I'd stay clear of her if I were you. She's wasted valuable police time and may have interfered with a murder investigation. Also, she knew the real Helen Kulas, who is presumably dead."

"And that makes her a suspect?"

"It could. If you see her, call me."

A chime sounded and white perimeter lights flickered, indicating the end of intermission.

"Are you going in?" Cate said.

"Yeah, but I want to keep an eye on things. How about you?"

Cate hefted the camera and smiled. "I wish I could. Music is good for babies, but I'm not done 'til the applause ends."

"We'll go straight home afterward. You need to get some rest," he said and gave her a hug.

Cubiak handed the ticket stubs for the front-row seats to a surprised young couple, and then he watched the crowd filter in. Was the fake Helen here in yet another disguise? he wondered. What about Fielder?

The audience members seemed almost reverential as they settled into their seats. All eyes looked to the front; all ears strained to catch the first pure notes that would signal the start of the second half of the concert. And once the music flowed, they barely moved, so captivated were they by the sounds that rose up from the simple, traditional instruments. Payette had worried that the defection of his premier player would spark an exodus, but the ensemble seemed unaffected by the deserter's absence. Perhaps he really did have a family emergency, Cubiak thought. Maybe despite his actions, Dixan V would emerge a grand triumph.

The sheriff kept to the back of the house and paced from one side of the auditorium to the other as the various ensembles moved on and off the stage. Besides Cate, he wasn't the only person working. The craggy cameraman was shooting from the wings. At the rear of the hall, the sound technician hovered over an electronic board dotted with lights and switches. Mitchell Stone watched from the wings, with his aristocratic hands clasped and long pale face aglow.

Payette had talked about the hold that music had over people. It was certainly true that evening. In the hushed auditorium, the audience paid no mind to anyone but the players on the stage and to anything but the music.

In the first half of the evening, the music had exuded a light, almost whimsical touch, but after the intermission the pieces started bittersweet and melancholy and grew increasingly somber, as if the composers and the musicians had conspired to turn their listeners' thoughts to the serious aspects of life. This was music to move and inspire, not merely to entertain.

The concert had opened with a solo performance by Payette. For the final piece, he joined three other gambists in playing Purcell's *Music for the Funeral of Queen Mary*. The selection had been transcribed for strings and was presented in memory of Richard Mayes. As the ensemble played, the audience sank into a heavy silence. When the final strains of the mournful melody faded, a beat passed. Then the crowd rose as one. Shouts of *Bravi* and *More* rang out with the applause. Flowers were tossed to the stage, and the quartet basked in long minutes of adulation before Payette called out the rest of the musicians. Onstage the players joined in an encore, and then another. By the time the last pristine notes faded between the rafters, everyone in the room—the audience, players, and organizers—thrilled with the grand success of Dixan V.

The audience members carried their elation back to the ferry landing and to the island hotels and cottages they had booked for the event. The organizers took their delight to the box office, where the receipts were being tallied. George Payette nourished his personal triumph through a series of interviews with local media and music critics from Chicago, New York, and Los Angeles. The musicians responsible for the joyous celebration bore their cheers off the stage and down to the lower level warmup room, where their enthusiasm instantly halted. The players' tote bags, briefcases, and purses had been ransacked and the contents strewn across the floor and tables. Cameras, phones, and wallets filled with credit cards and cash were gone.

Cubiak was out front waiting for Cate when his phone buzzed with word of the theft.

"How'd the thieves get in?" he said, then incredulously added, "The room was left unlocked?"

He found his wife downstairs with her camera. "Looks like I'll be stuck here overnight again. There's probably not much I can do, but I have to stay and sort this out."

At least there was no chance of another scandal equal to the loss of the yellow viol, he thought. The gambas were the most valuable items in the hall that night, and they had been on stage with the musicians when the thieves struck.

The sheriff walked in on the players just as Veronica Winslow was assuring them that the festival would reimburse the losses to the extent possible. "We are properly insured," she told the anxious crowd, but the wobble in her voice conveyed her concerns more than her downcast appearance.

Stone was up next. He was as stiff and polished as the Roman numerals behind his name, and he made it clear that his primary concern was protecting the festival's reputation. "What happened tonight is an act of cowardly vandalism. This kind of unfortunate incident could have happened anywhere. For all our sakes, the less said about it, the better. Certainly, it is not to be laid at the feet of a Dixan curse," he said.

The musicians responded with skeptical silence. No doubt the news had already been released on social media, where the line between truth and rumor was growing increasingly thin, Cubiak thought.

Even he was starting to wonder. Although he didn't believe in curses and such, he knew that charms and spells had a long and lively history. People wanted life to make sense, and they looked for ways to connect seemingly unrelated events. It wouldn't take much imagination to link the Dixan V robbery to the infamous thievery that had marred the first Dixan festival. Or to connect the deaths of Lydia Larson and Richard Mayes to the unfortunate death of Heike Acker forty years ago.

Cubiak hadn't exaggerated when he told Cate earlier that he was puzzled by the odd parallels in the two events. Were the similarities real or was someone using the notoriety of Dixan I as a cover for current misdeeds? In four days, three very public crimes had been committed: the two murders on the ferries and the daring theft during the final performance. He still didn't know who was responsible for the deaths, and he was right when he told Cate there was little he could do about the situation that night. There were no security cameras or witnesses. He, along with everyone else, had been upstairs at the concert. The thieves had been free to take what they wanted and then to melt into the departing crowd.

The sheriff doubted that any of the disheartened musicians could provide useful information. Nonetheless, he felt they were entitled to air their grievances, and so he met with them individually and took down their statements.

It was nearly midnight when he finished at the festival and checked in with Cate.

"You got home all right?"

"Traffic was a little heavier than usual, but it was fine."

"Remember to lock the doors," he said. He had never urged such caution before and wasn't sure why he had that night.

"I will. I'm fine. Besides, I've got Kipper to protect me."

At the sound of her name, the dog barked.

"I love you," Cubiak said. But he didn't mention the baby.

AMERICAN BORN

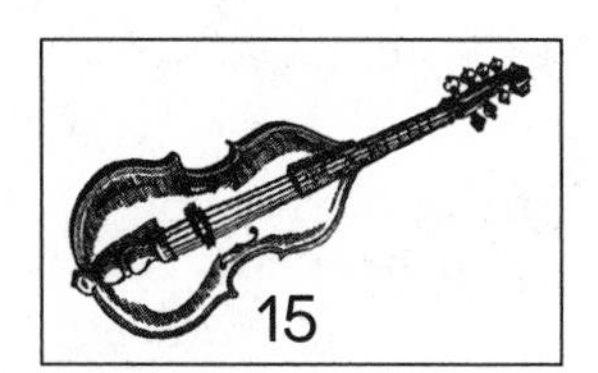

The sheriff spent a restless night. Phantom figures from the past zigzagged through his dreams. Relatives he barely knew in life loomed up and jeered at him. Soldiers he had loved like brothers cried out for help. Strangers grabbed at his arms and legs. In the midst of the muddled chaos he found himself on the muddy bank of a wide, raging river. Laura and Alexis were on the other side. They were walking away from the water, toward a field of yellow daisies. He called to them but they didn't hear. He shouted repeatedly, but they kept on. As they approached the flowery meadow, Lydia Larson and her mother appeared alongside the river and began to follow them. Then suddenly Cate was on the same path, running to catch up.

"No!" Cubiak yelled and jolted awake.

The room was dark and cold. The blanket lay on the floor, and he shivered in the icy blast from the air conditioner that had been churning at full bore. He closed his eyes and tried to dislodge the image of Cate rushing after the others. Even when the dream had dissolved, the message remained vividly clear: yet another mother and child were doomed to die and he was powerless to help.

The red digits on the bedside clock read 5:22. He rolled out of bed and switched off the AC. Still cold, he retrieved the blanket, wrapped it around his shoulders, and poured water into the hotel coffeemaker. The familiar routine grounded him. Freud be damned, he thought as he tossed the bedspread over the mattress. A dream is the mind playing tricks, nothing more.

When the coffee was ready, Cubiak pulled on his rumpled clothes and carried the first cup outside. To the east, a spear of neon orange light slit the horizon. In the crisp morning air, the coffee steamed and warmed his face. He waited for the night sky to shrink under the sun's assault, and then he went back in and showered. When he was dressed again, he poured a second cup. By the time he was back outside, the sun was fully up and the new day abloom. Cate once told him that photographers called this blip of time the golden hour, for the softness of the light.

Cubiak started toward the dock. A ribbon of mist blurred the shoreline. Farther out, four black dots emerged from the fading, gossamer fog. Like a loose string of ebony opals, they danced across the waves toward Detroit Harbor. He finished his coffee just as the four smudges transformed into a convoy of ferryboats.

The vessels were running well ahead of the usual schedule, a gesture made to mollify the musicians and audience members who had been forced to spend an extra night on the island because of the theft. From the chatter he had overheard, the sheriff knew that many of the musicians were heading out to other gigs and were worried about being late for their commitments. The others, the music lovers and hangers-on, were either returning home or rushing off to fill their remaining vacation days with fish boils, golf, shopping. Everyone was in a hurry to leave.

A dozen vehicles waited to board the first ferry. Bob Sandusky, the North Dakota gambist, was driving the lead car, a silver Lexus. Curious, Cubiak walked over. Sandusky was unshaven, and his hair was wet. A woman sat in the passenger seat. She was slumped low and had wrapped a checkered scarf around her head, but the sheriff recognized her as Meryl Gregory, the tourist who had been accused of stealing from the harbor gift store earlier that week. So this was the wife who liked to shop?

"Bob. Ms. Gregory. We meet again," he said.

The musician looked confused. "You know my wife?"

"We've met." Before Sandusky could say anything, the sheriff went on. "I know you're anxious to get going but I have to ask you to pull off to the side so I can search your vehicle."

"Why? What's this all about? What do you mean you need to search the vehicle? Don't you need a warrant?" Sandusky said.

"It's a random check. No warrant needed."

"You haven't pulled anyone else over."

"That's because I'm just getting started, and you're first in line. Don't worry, I'll get to the others," Cubiak said, knowing he probably wouldn't be searching many other cars, if any, that morning.

The gambist started to object further but his wife interrupted. "It's fine, honey. The man is just doing his job. We can catch the next ferry."

Meryl smiled. Her smug demeanor told him that he would find nothing incriminating in the car, and he didn't. Sandusky's viol and two suitcases with their clothes were in the trunk. There were three bags on the back seat filled with two new dresses, several T-shirts, sandals, and a straw hat. She showed him the receipts.

"You like to shop," Cubiak said.

"I do."

The sheriff had no choice but to let them depart on the next ferry. Again he watched the car drive on, but this time he noted the license number, just in case. For the next half hour, he made his way down the line of vehicles, questioning the drivers. Most of them were musicians from the festival. The others were tourists. Except for the early hour, it looked like a typical day at the ferry landing. There wasn't anything suspicious about anyone or anything he encountered. Still Cubiak kept checking.

As the fourth ferry loaded, a silver Toyota pulled up to the landing. The driver was a blonde woman, about the same age as Bob Sandusky's shopaholic wife. She put the car in Park and smiled. It was a friendly gesture, unlike the smug look the shoplifting woman had given him earlier. He swore softly.

"What's wrong?" a dockhand asked.

"I've been duped."

Earlier that week when Cubiak escorted Sandusky's wife from the store in Detroit harbor, she was carrying the turquoise jewelry and silk scarves that she had paid for to avoid being arrested. But he hadn't found any of those items when he searched the car that morning. She must have stashed them off island. The new dresses and other purchases in the vehicle were things she bought for herself; that's why she had the receipts. The rest isn't for her, he realized. While her husband played the festival she was out stealing merchandise, which she then hid on the mainland. She would pick it up on her way out and sell it on eBay after she got home. What was it the musician's friend had said? *Lucky for us she likes to shop.*

Did Sandusky know about his wife's scheme? Cubiak wondered.

It was too late to nab the couple at Northport but they had to cross one of the bridges at Sturgeon Bay to get off the peninsula. He called the city police chief with the make, model, and license number of their car and asked him to post his deputies at the bridges. "We need to stop the car before it goes any farther," he said.

Out on the water, another black spot appeared. It was too small to be a ferry.

"I think it's your guy," the dock worker said as the *Speedy Sister II* swung around the harbor buoy.

Rowe's energetic leap onto the pier made Cubiak realize how tired he was.

"What are you doing here? I thought you had the day off," said Cubiak.

"I do but I'll take it another time. This is too important. Remember you asked me to keep checking on Eric Fielder? Well, something about the name kept bugging me. I took a couple years of German in high school, and it dawned on me that in German the name Fielder is Acker. So I went back and checked under that name and bingo. It looks like our Eric Fielder is really a man named Ubell Acker. The DOB is the same as on his fake ID, but place of birth is Madison."

"You're telling me that Fielder was born here?"

"Yes, sir. And he holds dual citizenship. US and German."

"The viol that was stolen at Dixan I belonged to a German musician named Franz Acker. Acker's wife was pregnant, and she died in Madison after giving birth to a premature infant."

"Boy or girl?"

"I don't know. No one ever said, and I didn't think to ask."

"Give me a minute."

The deputy retrieved his laptop from the boat. "Nothing," he said after he had worked the keyboard for several minutes. "Nothing," he said again.

Cubiak stayed quiet. He knew that Rowe was churning through sites he wasn't even aware existed. If there was any information to be found, his deputy would ferret it out.

Finally, Rowe looked up. "The baby was a boy."

"A child born under the worst circumstances on a night from hell," Cubiak said.

Rowe bent over the computer again. "I'll be damned. You know what Ubell means?"

The sheriff shook his head.

"It's German for *evil.*"

Cubiak started toward the boat. "I need to talk to George Payette again. You got enough gas to get us there?"

They were midway across the strait when Rowe's phone dinged.

"It's a response from Interpol, sir. Acker has a record. One charge of domestic violence, which was dropped, and a conviction for assault and battery. Seems he put two men in the hospital during a fight. Also, an email from the merchant marine. They have no record of either an Ubell Acker or an Eric Fielder."

The sheriff remembered the steely cold in Acker's eyes the first time they talked. "The son of Franz Acker turns out to be a liar with a violent temper who spends time in Chicago, where Annabelle Larson lived with her daughter and the mummified remains of a woman are found in the apartment of the missing, real Helen Kulas. Then, pretending to be just another pleasant foreign worker, he gets a job serving food at Dixan V, where two more people are murdered. Why?" Cubiak tilted his head and squinted at the horizon. "The bastard is here for the yellow viol."

"You mean it's in Door County?"

"He thinks it's here." Cubiak remembered what Cate had said about seeing two mugs in the dish drainer at the condo. "And if I'm right, the woman who claimed to be Helen Kulas is in on this with him."

They're all connected, he thought. He pictured the principals—Ubell Acker, the fake Helen, Lydia Larson, Richard Mayes, Annabelle Larson, and George Payette—lined up like dominoes in a parade that stretched from Dixan I through the years to Dixan V. If he discovered the truth about the man at either end, the pieces would all topple.

Cubiak had a bad feeling about where this was heading. He wished he could go back and not involve Cate. How could he live with himself if he had put her in danger?

He needed to warn her, but he wasn't sure about whom or what.

She didn't answer his call, so he sent a text: *New developments. Take extra care today.*

The sheriff and deputy talked little on the rest of the ride. At Payette's Sister Bay estate, they tied up behind his white yacht and followed the cinder path to the house. Both levels on the water side were glass, but the first-floor drapes and blinds were pulled, preventing them from seeing in.

Cubiak knocked on the patio door. There was no answer. Rowe pounded on the window but still there was no response. He tried the door, but it was locked. They moved to the yard and rang the bell by the stately wooden door, but still there was no answer, and the door was locked as well.

The red car hadn't moved from its spot. Rowe peeked inside the garage. "There's a bike against the wall. Maybe Payette walked into town," he said.

"Does he strike you as the kind of man who walks anywhere?"

Rowe shrugged. "Not really. Maybe he's in the recording studio. He wouldn't hear us from in there."

They continued to circle the house and found another door behind a row of hedges.

Cubiak pointed to the small pane nearest the knob. "Try that," he said and braced for the shriek of the alarm. But when Rowe smashed the window, there was only the sound of glass hitting the floor.

"Let's go," the sheriff said.

They passed through a narrow porch to a short hall that opened onto the kitchen. The room was in shambles. Broken pieces of plates and glasses were scattered over the counters. Cupboard drawers had been wrenched from their glides and turned upside down, the contents spilled out. The refrigerator doors were open and the shelves emptied. Milk pooled on the floor mixed with broken egg yolks and shells. The walls were splashed with vinegar.

"Jesus, that stinks," Rowe said.

Cubiak held his hand up. "Listen." He thought he had heard a noise.

A second passed, and they both heard a sound, like that of a can rolling across bare wood. It came from behind the closed pantry door.

The housekeeper lay inside on the wooden floor. She had been beaten and gagged and left curled in a fetal position with her arms and legs bound together behind her back. There was a can of soup near her blood-smeared face. Somehow she had managed to push it with her chin.

Cubiak knelt by the woman. "Call for an ambulance and then search the rest of the house. Hurry," he told Rowe as he loosened the cloth from around her mouth.

When she was free, he helped her sit up against the wall. "Anything broken?" he asked. She stared at him. She's in shock, he realized.

He filled a cup with water and brought it to her. "How many were there?"

She murmured something that sounded like *un*.

"One?" The answer surprised him.

She blinked.

"A man?"

Another blink, a second sign he interpreted as yes. Ubell Acker, he thought. It had to be. But where was the pretend Helen Kulas while this was going on? He had paired up the two because of the two mugs at Cate's place and because they both disappeared around the same time, but what if she wasn't Fielder's accomplice?

"Did he have a gun?"

The housekeeper's eyes opened wide with fear, and she tried to move her head.

"Did you ever see him before?"

"No." The word was a whisper.

"Sir!" Rowe called out from somewhere in the house.

Cubiak brushed the hair from the housekeeper's forehead. "Help is on the way. It'll be here soon. You're going to be OK," he said.

The deputy shouted again. "Up here. The second floor."

As he moved toward the staircase, the sheriff took in the mayhem along the way. In the living room, furniture stood upended and cushions were slashed. The drinks table had been smashed and the bottles tossed to the floor. In the dining room, the china and crystal were shattered.

Rowe watched from the landing. "Watch your step, sir. They poured something on the stairs."

An empty olive oil bottle lay near the bottom riser, and oil dripped down the newel post and center of the treads.

Cubiak climbed up along the edges.

"Payette?" he said when he reached Rowe.

"He's breathing but unconscious. In there," the deputy said and pointed to the master bedroom.

The room was a confluence of velvet, marble, and mirrors. Payette was naked and lay on the floor of the walk-in closet. He had been bound and gagged with brightly colored ties from his designer collection. The halo of blood around his head looked almost black in the dim light. The flesh around his eyes was pulpy, and his lips ballooned to caricaturist proportions. Several of his fingers were mangled, and there was a nasty slash on his shoulder.

"I called for another ambulance," Rowe said.

"Good."

Cubiak felt for a pulse, as a siren screamed from the yard.

"Go and warn them about the steps," he said.

While he waited for the medics, the sheriff photographed the scene. He was relieved that Payette was alive but puzzled by the fact as well. Why didn't Ubell kill the musician when he had the chance? he wondered.

He heard voices and the EMTs entered the room.

Cubiak left them with Rowe. "If Payette comes to, call me immediately. I have to go back downstairs. I promised the housekeeper I'd be back," he said.

The sheriff stayed with the traumatized woman until the second ambulance arrived. While the medics tended to her, he helped the first team of medics lower the gurney with Payette to the first floor.

"Do you have any police tape on the *Sister*?" Cubiak asked Rowe as the ambulance crew rolled the injured man through the door.

"Yes, sir."

"Get it and secure the premises."

Once the second ambulance left, silence again muffled Payette's imposing home. Cubiak walked through the unnatural quiet to the back rooms. He expected the damage to the business side of the dwelling to be worse than that in the living quarters, but he was still surprised by the extent of the violence. The gambist's office had been ripped apart. Everything that could be overturned was upended, every drawer emptied. Holes were punched in the walls and ceiling. Mayes's office got the same treatment. Next door, the equipment in the recording studio was smashed and damaged. Along the hallway, every closet had been turned out, every storage bin emptied and the contents strewn about like rubbish. The track lighting in the performance room had been torn from the ceiling and the sturdy oak stage hacked into pieces.

The desecration in the lower-level museum was even more extreme. The flutes and horns were untouched but the GAR posters hung in shreds, and the glass cases that held the string instruments had been toppled from their stands and smashed open. Payette's collection of antique cellos, violins, and viols had been ripped apart. Strings were torn loose, the delicate necks cracked and smashed into brittle shards of wood, the carved face pieces wrenched off and splintered, and the elegant bows cracked in half.

Cubiak regarded the wreckage with great sadness. The instruments had survived wars and plagues, only to be destroyed in an angry rampage. This was more than a search-and-find mission; this was a search-and-punish vendetta.

But did you get what you came for? he wondered.

The tourist brochures labeled Door County a peninsula but technically the description was a deceit. The Sturgeon Bay Ship Canal, which was dug in the late 1800s, severed the land-link between the mainland and the readily identifiable long finger of land that jutted out between the waters of Lake Michigan and Green Bay. The project left the northern portion of the county completely surrounded by water. It was, in fact, an island. And the only way off was to cross one of the three bridges at the city of Sturgeon Bay.

Cubiak called the bridge superintendent and ordered the bridges raised.

"Must be someone you don't want leaving," the tender said.

"That's right."

"It's going to be a mess down here."

"Can't be helped."

"How long you figure this is gonna take?"

"Don't know. My deputies are on the way now to help sort things out," Cubiak said, hoping it wasn't too late.

Finally, the sheriff issued an APB to the counties of Door, Kewaunee, and Brown for one Eric Fielder, aka Ubell Acker. White male. Approximately forty years old. Six feet. Blond. Blue eyes. Suspect in assault and robbery. Armed and considered dangerous. May be traveling with a woman posing as Helen Kulas. Approach with caution.

ONE MAN'S REVENGE

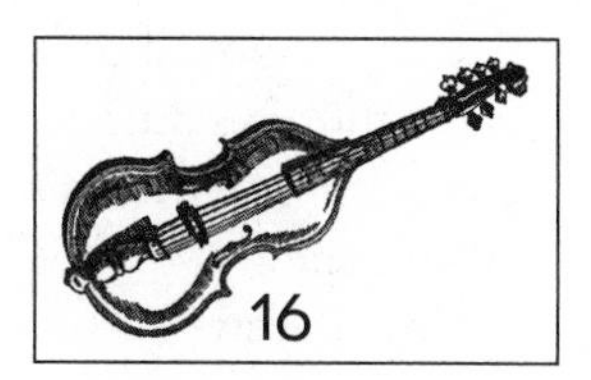

His years as a city cop had made Cubiak wary of hospitals. Working in Chicago, he had spent countless sad and angry hours in emergency rooms with perps and innocent victims—women, men, and even children—who had been shot, stabbed, or mercilessly battered. He knew the doctors and nurses who worked hard to save lives within those walls, but he couldn't help but associate the institutions with death and despair, and so he avoided them as much as he could, even in normally peaceful Door County.

When he was notified that George Payette might be able to talk that afternoon, the sheriff shoved aside his discomfort and settled into the third-floor visitors' lounge to wait. A number of crimes were unsolved, and the gambist was both the victim of an assault and a suspect in another, older crime. He had to be questioned as soon as possible. Cubiak stared at the bland art on the walls and thought about what he would say to the musician. He also wondered what he would say to Cate when he saw her at home later.

The sheriff was convinced that Payette was involved in the disappearance of the yellow viol and wished he would come clean about his role, but he didn't hold out much hope. He held out even less hope that he would be honest with Cate about his feelings toward the baby. In truth, he was no longer sure what his feelings were. He thought of Alexis and the joy she had brought to him. He thought of the boy Sammy and the delight he shared with his father. And he began to wonder if hope could ever outweigh his fear.

"Sheriff?"

Cubiak looked up at a man in a white coat. For a moment he expected the attending physician to announce that Payette had died, and he was relieved when the doctor told him that the victim had regained consciousness.

"Mr. Payette is fortunate that he came through the assault with no serious internal injuries, but he suffered a concussion and he may not have a clear memory of what happened. He also may have difficulty following your questions. Take it easy with him. You can have twenty minutes but no more," he said.

Cubiak checked his watch. He hoped to be done in half that time.

The blinds in Payette's room were closed and the lights dimmed. The bed was cranked to a partial sitting position, and a bounty of pillows was arranged behind the patient. Other than being bathed, clothed, and bandaged, the musician looked little better than he had when the sheriff saw him bound and bloody on his closet floor. His lips were puffed and his eyelids were swollen nearly shut. The bruised flesh on his face and arms was turning a sickly blue-green. His left arm was in a sling.

"Do you know who I am?" Cubiak asked.

"Yes."

"Good. Do you remember what happened?"

"I think so." Payette's normally strong voice was muffled, as if he were talking through cotton.

"There was only a lone attacker, a man," Cubiak said, hoping that the patient would verify what the housekeeper had told him.

"Yes."

"Was it this man?" He came alongside the bed and held up a photo of Eric Fielder.

The gambist flinched. "Yes."

"Does the name Eric Fielder mean anything to you?"

"No." Payette moistened his lips. "Should it?"

"That's the man whose photo you just identified. Fielder worked with the catering crew at the festival. But the name is an alias. Eric Fielder's real name is Ubell Acker." Cubiak watched for a reaction from Payette. It wasn't much, a slight tic in the left cheek, but it told him what he needed to know.

"You recognize that name?"

Payette slowly moved his head back and forth.

"No? Of course, you do. He is the son of Franz Acker, the famous gambist who headlined the Dixan I festival."

The musician closed his eyes.

"Acker was the musician who brought the yellow viol to Washington Island. He was the man whose wife died in childbirth the night of the big storm and whose life fell apart when the viol went missing. But, of course, you know the story, because you were there. You and Richard Mayes and Annabelle Larson, the up-and-coming GAR group."

Payette looked at the ceiling. "It was a long time ago."

"Forty years. That's half a lifetime for many people, but it's nothing in the life of a fabled treasure like the yellow viol. How old would the instrument be now? Nearly four hundred years?"

Payette lifted his free hand off the mattress. "Irrelevant. The viol is gone—phfft."

"Maybe it is. And then again, maybe it's not." Cubiak let the comment hang in the air. Then he spoke again. "I think the yellow viol is very much in existence."

The patient pushed to his elbow. "Impossible," he said. He struggled to sit up farther and then fell back against the pillows. "You don't know what you're saying. People spent years trying to find it, but nothing."

"You coveted the yellow viol, didn't you?"

"We all did. It was a magnificent instrument."

"But you not only coveted it, you figured out a way to get it."

The musician's sharp laugh disintegrated into a fit of coughing.

When the room was quiet, Cubiak continued. "I have to admit it was pretty clever how you managed to whisk the viol off the island in full view of the authorities."

"Really?" Payette's voice was still weak but his dry, arrogant manner asserted itself.

"I couldn't figure out how you managed it, but that's because I didn't really understand the simple mechanics of how a stringed instrument is put together. Seeing the carnage in your little museum—all the bits and pieces scattered around—got me wondering. I still need to check with a couple of experts but I have a few ideas. If I'm right, it wasn't all that hard."

Payette scoffed. "You're fishing, Sheriff. You know my thinking might be muddled and you're trying to take advantage of that and lure me into admitting to something I didn't do."

"Am I?"

Payette glared at Cubiak. "Why would you accuse an innocent man?" The musician smirked again. "Oh, I get it, you want the glory of solving the mystery of Dixan I, don't you? That's what you're after. If you ID the culprit, your name will be in headlines all over the world."

"What I want is to find out why Lydia Larson and Richard Mayes were killed and to figure out who did it. I'm convinced that the yellow viol figures into the puzzle. I know that it's important to Ubell Acker, and that he's pegged you as the thief. That's why he attacked you and ransacked your house. He was looking for the viol."

"You can't prove that. I already told you I didn't steal the yellow viol, and I've never heard of this Eric Fielder or Ubell Acker or whoever he is. You said those are the two names he uses. Maybe he has other aliases as well."

Something I'm looking into, Cubiak thought.

Payette went on. "The man broke into my house demanding money. That's what he was after. He must have seen me at the festival. Maybe he heard people talk about my instrument collection. It wouldn't take much to find out that some of the pieces are fairly valuable. And when he saw the house, he figured I was loaded. A lot of people make that mistake."

"What happened at your house doesn't come across as an ordinary robbery. If Ubell was interested in the instruments in your collection, he would have taken them instead of destroying them. If he wanted money, why waste time ransacking the house? I think he wanted revenge for what he believes you did to his father, and he wanted the viol because he's convinced that it's rightfully his."

Payette stiffened. His look was pitiless. "Franz Acker forfeited his claim to the yellow viol when he failed to pay the insurance premium on time. That was part of the contract with the Guttenbergs, and everyone knew it. No one in his family can lay claim to the instrument, certainly not now."

"Apparently his son doesn't see it that way. Ubell came to Door County to recover his birthright. Either he worked it out on his own that you stole it or his father passed on that knowledge as his legacy."

Payette's face contorted into a sneer that exaggerated the remnants of the beating he had endured. "That's absurd."

"Is it? Perhaps Lydia Larson had much the same idea. Maybe she came here searching for you because of what her mother had told her or confided in her diary. Even if Lydia didn't believe you still had the instrument in your possession, she'd assume that you sold it on the black market for what I've been told would have been a fortune. Lydia didn't want the viol. She lacked the wherewithal to dispose of it with the discretion such a transaction required. No. Lydia needed money, and if she could prove she was your daughter she figured you would help her out financially. Even if she isn't your daughter she may still have believed that she could blackmail you with whatever knowledge she'd gained from her mother."

"You think I killed Lydia?" The question was barely audible.

"It's possible, but I admit that you were my second choice. Initially I thought it was Mayes who murdered her."

"Why?"

"Because he felt threatened by her. If Lydia could prove that she was your daughter, he feared that he might be cut out of your will or that he'd get a smaller slice of the pie."

"And now that Richard is dead?"

"You're a logical suspect in his death as well."

Payette turned toward the wall. "No, never, not either of them," he said.

"Why not? If Lydia claimed she had proof that you'd stolen the yellow viol, you might silence her to keep her from talking."

Payette's face was still turned away. "And Richard? Why would I kill him?"

"Because he knew too much. Richard couldn't have worked that closely with you for all those years and not known or suspected what you'd done. Maybe he was in on the deal from the beginning. Maybe all three of you were the culprits. Richard told me that Annabelle fell apart because she couldn't handle the stress and stigma of being a suspect in the theft of the yellow viol. But maybe the truth is that she couldn't handle the guilt of being one of the thieves."

Payette struggled to sit up again. "Annabelle wasn't a thief."

Cubiak regarded the battered man. "That may be the only true thing you've said this afternoon. But what if she suspected that you, the man she loved, had stolen the yellow viol? Wouldn't that be enough to destroy her?"

Before Payette could respond, a nurse appeared in the doorway. She tapped her wrist. "Time's up, Sheriff," she said.

He raised a hand. "Almost done."

The nurse hesitated, but then she turned away.

When the two men were alone again, Cubiak leaned over the bed. "You think you're in the clear, don't you? Fielder forced you to give up the viol and now you figure he'll disappear with it, and with him goes all chance of tracing it back to you and nailing you as the thief of Dixan I. But I wouldn't be so sure if I were you. I'll find Fielder and get to the bottom of this. And then I'll be back for you."

Cate was out when Cubiak got home. Kipper was gone as well. He was relieved. Home on his own, he had time to think and work. He went through Dutch's notebooks again, looking for the information the former sheriff had garnered from the experts. Their comments focused on what needed to be done to safeguard the yellow viol: proper steps for storage and transportation. All well and good, but the information didn't go far enough. Dutch hadn't asked one critical question: could the instrument be taken apart?

Of course, he hadn't. The yellow viol was a masterpiece. Only a lunatic would consider committing such an atrocity.

Or maybe not. What if someone familiar with the old viols had tried it? Cubiak wondered. What then?

Luthiers don't keep Sunday hours, and the best the sheriff could do was leave messages with three of the experts, urging them to return his calls.

With nothing to do but wait, he grabbed his phone and went for a run. He normally did five miles but pushed for seven that afternoon. The phone call he was waiting for came when he was in the shower. He was dressed and back in the kitchen when he noticed the red light blinking. One of the experts had called back. As he was listening to the message he heard a noise from outside. It sounded like a branch rubbing against the house or something scratching at the wooden deck. He ignored it. The noise came again and was followed by a whimpering. Then silence.

From the door, the deck and beach looked deserted. Cubiak was turning to go back in when the soft whining started again. He was halfway around the house when he spotted Kipper crouched beneath a bush. As he approached, the dog struggled to get up. His head and left flank drooped and he seemed to have trouble standing. Déjà vu swept over Cubiak. Butch had been injured too the first time he had seen her.

He ran to the dog and scooped him up. Kipper yelped and hung limply in his arms. His white and brown fur was wet and sticky. His front paws were streaked with blood.

"My God, what happened?" Cubiak said. The possibilities were all bad—accident, fight, attack.

Inside, he laid the dog on the table and gently muzzled him with a dishcloth.

"Where's Cate?" he said.

Kipper whimpered and tried to raise his head.

Something was terribly wrong. Cate would never leave the injured dog. Where was she?

The sheriff punched his wife's number into his phone. There was a pause and then a click as the connection went through. Another moment passed and the familiar jingle of Cate's cell rang out from the living room.

Cubiak froze. Cate never left the house without her mobile. She took it if she was going to the garage or walking the dog. She carried it everywhere, a habit she had developed as a photographer for *National Geographic* because she never knew when she would get a call or when she might need to make a call. Given the nature of some of her assignments, the phone could be a lifesaver.

He had to do something.

The sheriff called Rowe. There was no answer.

He phoned Bathard. "Cate's gone and Kipper's hurt." He ran his hand over the dog's left flank. "I think he's been shot and I found Cate's cell in the house. She'd never leave without it. I think someone grabbed her. They took Kipper, too, and then shot him. They could have killed the dog, but they didn't. Why not?" he said.

"Slow down, Dave. I don't understand, what are you saying?"

The sheriff pressed on, thinking out loud. "Whoever took Cate injured Kipper and left him here as a message to me: look what we did to your dog; imagine what we will do to your wife." My pregnant wife, he thought.

"Do you have any idea who's behind this? Any idea where she might be?" Bathard said.

Cubiak didn't hesitate. "It must be that fucking Ubell and that woman, the fake Helen Kulas. I'm sure of it. They're probably holding her at the condo, waiting for me to show up. I'm guessing that they have the yellow viol and need my help to get away."

"What are you going to do?"

"I've got to go find her. I need you to take Kipper to the vet. Keep your phone with you. I'll try the condo first. If you don't hear from me within a half hour it means I'm right about them holding her there. If that happens, I want you to call me at the condo. Not my cell but the landline. You have it?"

"Yes."

"We won't answer but don't hang up. Let it ring. They can wonder who it is. When it goes to voice mail, pretend it's a social call and leave a message. Then contact Rowe and tell him this: The fake Helen must have copied the key to Cate's townhouse, and she and Ubell are hiding out there. They have the yellow viol and are holding Cate, and I'm there as well."

"What do you want him to do?"

"Tell Mike not to do anything until he hears from me."

"I don't like the sound of this. Be careful."

THE BLUE HOUR

Be careful. Bathard's parting words echoed in the stillness as the jeep rolled over the dune into the fading light. It was the blue hour, what Cate called *l'heure bleue*, the period at the end of day when the deep blue of twilight melted into the inky black of night, a time when the day's promises were recalled and the night's revealed.

"Be careful? No," Cubiak said. He had to be smart and fearless. Caution was an option, not a priority. Three lives were at stake: Cate's, the baby's—their baby's—and his. Without his realizing it, his misgivings about the child had vanished with the threat of impending danger. He couldn't afford to think of a time that existed before or beyond the next few hours. Only one thing mattered: that he protect his wife and unborn infant from harm. Even if it meant his life.

The first star sparkled low in the southeast. The light was vivid against the charcoal sky and glowed like a talisman from a different world. As he drove toward it, he felt a strange calm settle his nerves. What was it that Bathard had said? *No one saves us but ourselves.* Well, then, he thought, I have a job to do if I'm going to save anyone.

The sheriff had no chance of surprising Ubell. The German expected him to show. Cubiak had options: he could call his deputies in and also request assistance from the sheriffs' departments in neighboring counties, but either would take time. Even with backup surrounding the complex, what chance did he have of negotiating a peaceful surrender? Probably none, given Ubell's criminal record and the sheriff's suspicion that he had already killed three people and had nearly beaten George Payette to death.

Ubell didn't want to talk. He wanted to escape Door County, and for that he needed the sheriff's help. The most Cubiak could hope for was that he could convince him to release Cate and take him in her place. That was Plan A. There was no Plan B—not yet.

Without traffic, the sheriff could make it from the house to the condo in just under ten minutes. But this was summer, and a long string of cars and trucks filled the roadway, like a trackless train. Anywhere else, he could crisscross the backroads to get around, but in this part of the county the main drag was the shortest and only direct route. He had to stay with it. He left Jacksonport riding the bumper of a blue convertible from the Sunshine State. As soon as space opened up, he flew past and then hopscotched around three more cars. And after that, another two and a truck. On each attempt, he played chicken with the approaching traffic. Finally, he reached Valmy and turned onto a side road. From there, he sped east toward the lake.

They must have grabbed Cate at the house. That would explain why her phone was in the living room. But how did they know where to find her? Either they tailed her there or—"Fuck," he said—the fake Helen had seen their home address on the letter Cate had left on the kitchen counter. Ubell was on his own when he attacked Payette and tore the house apart looking for the yellow viol because he had sent the fake Helen to stake out their lakeside home.

"Bastard," the sheriff said.

If the fake Helen had hidden in the surrounding woods, she would have been far enough from the house not to alarm Kipper but close enough to see who came and went and to know when Cate was there on her own. Cubiak had wondered why Ubell hadn't killed Payette when he had the opportunity. Now he understood. When the German got the call from Helen, he had already found the viol, and rather than spend more time at the estate, he decided it was more important to snatch Cate than to finish off the musician.

Poor Cate. She must have been terrified.

Cubiak continued trying to piece together the scenario. Ubell nabbed Cate and then shot Kipper to frighten her even more.

Why take Cate?

There was only one explanation. It was to scare him and to force his hand. They wanted him to play their game by their rules, and so far, they were winning.

Cate's townhouse overlooked a pristine sand beach along the Lake Michigan shore. The condo was in an upscale development that was popular with tourists, retirees, and second-home buyers. In the off-season most of the units were empty except on weekends, but this was still prime time on the peninsula. When Cubiak reached the driveway, the parking lot was nearly full and lights were on in more than half the units. Through open curtains he saw flashes of cartoons and through another, Humphrey Bogart at the wheel of the *African Queen*. It was a warm evening and people were out. From the tennis courts across the road, he heard the thwack of the balls hitting the rackets over and again. There were voices coming from the water side of the building, which meant people were still on the beach. Snatches of conversation drifted down from the restaurant at the south end of the complex. Locals tended to eat early. These were tourists sipping cocktails on the patio.

With so many people around, it seemed odd that Ubell would chance being seen. But the German seemed to enjoy tempting fate, and maybe it made sense to hide in plain sight. No one would notice a little extra noise or a few raised voices in the middle of the summer season. Folks were out to enjoy themselves. Besides, the condos in the complex were well built and soundproofed. Each had a private entrance and was designed for maximum privacy. And thanks to him, these were all features the fake Helen had plenty of time to check out.

He coasted into the lot and parked at the north end, near the last unit. He pocketed his phone and had a foot on the ground when he stopped and slid his gun and holster under the seat. Unarmed, he felt unnerved, but he knew he couldn't chance a false step. He couldn't do anything that would endanger Cate.

The townhouses backed up to a forest of tall pines, and Cate's end unit stood in deep shadows, like the deer he had seen earlier that evening. Inside, Ubell would be on the alert, behind the drawn shades and curtains, looking, listening, and poised for action.

Cubiak followed the brick pathway lit by solar-powered lamps. Five feet from the door, he stopped and waited for the automatic light to switch on, but nothing happened. He tossed a pebble at the doormat. Still nothing. The motion detector had been disabled.

He ducked around the corner and crept alongside the white brick building. Second-floor windows that were usually open were shut. The front deck was unlit. On the beach, a couple and their three teenage kids folded up towels and packed a large cooler. A sudden gust tumbled an umbrella, and one of the boys ran after it across the sand. When they had their things gathered together, they traipsed toward the middle door. Mom and Dad argued about dinner: she wanted to go out and he wanted to stay in and order pizza. The kids were each glued to their phones. The door slammed after them and the beach went quiet. The dock near the restaurant was empty as well, but the people he had heard when he arrived were still on the patio. Either they were waiting to go in to eat or were lingering over dessert and coffee.

A sharp wind rustled the trees and pushed large puffs of clouds down from the north. As the restless lake rubbed against the shore, the waves shushed quietly over the sand. From the grass came the chirp of a lone cricket. He tried the patio entrance. The sliding door was locked. Careful not to make any noise, he set a chair in front of it. If Ubell and the fake Helen were inside and tried to run out that way, they would trip over the chair.

Back on the other side, the sheriff used his key to slip into the downstairs hallway. He had come in through that door dozens of times and took for granted the ordinariness of the surroundings. But tonight, he sensed something unfamiliar and menacing in the house. The usually welcoming silence seemed tense and heavy. There was something else different too: the faint odor of burning tobacco. Cate didn't smoke. But Ubell did. Cubiak had seen his nicotine-stained fingers.

He announced his presence. "I'm unarmed. And I'm coming in." He tried to keep his voice neutral, but in the stillness the words sounded loud and threatening.

There was no response, and he imagined the German poised and waiting, perhaps in the next room, as he waited in the hall. Why the cat-and-mouse games? he wondered.

"I know you're here," he said.

Still nothing.

He took three blind steps into the darkness and bumped into the wooden coat tree that had been left in the middle of the hall. The pine table that normally stood along the wall had been moved as well. He edged past it. Farther along, the surface underfoot changed from tile to hardwood, telling him that he was moving from the hall into the first-floor expanse of living room, dining area, and kitchen. The area had been designed to pull in the outside light, but at night with the drapes pulled tight, it was a dark cave. A little more than forty-eight hours had passed since he and Cate had left the fake Helen standing by the kitchen counter. Was she there now, waiting for him? Was Ubell with her? What had they done with Cate?

Cubiak continued to move cautiously. He kneed a low table that was out of place, bumped into the sofa that had been pulled from its usual spot, and then nearly tripped on an overturned cane chair. Glass crunched beneath his foot; he guessed it was from one of Cate's framed photos. He toed a hard object that rolled away and wondered if it was one of the trio of tall candles from the teak sideboard. Had there been a struggle or was this disarray evidence of spite and meanness?

Slowly, his vision adjusted to the darkness. When he reached the kitchen he could make out the gaping cabinet doors and the contents spilled out on the floor. Stepping around the mess, he came to the alcove where the washer and dryer stood and ran his hand over them. The dryer was warm. The bastards had done laundry!

There was more havoc in the first-floor guest room, which Cate used as a photo studio, but no sign of her or her captors.

Cubiak started up the rear stairs. As he climbed, the stench of cigarettes grew stronger. On the second floor, thin ribbons of light filtered through the blinds in the two guest rooms. Both were empty and undisturbed. Nothing had been touched in the utility closet or the guest bathroom either. He crept down the hall toward the front. Had Ubell and the fake Helen trashed the downstairs and then taken Cate and moved on? Was he too late?

If they weren't in the front bedroom, he had wasted precious time. Worse, he had no idea where else to look for them.

The master suite took up the front third of the second floor, on the far side of the main stairwell. The room faced the water, and even with the drapes open it would be dark on a cloudy night. The door was closed but as he got closer he saw a sliver of pale yellow light along the bottom.

The knob turned easily in his hand. He nudged the door open with his foot. Through a haze of cigarette smoke, he saw three shadowy figures silhouetted against the partially lit back wall. It took him a moment to realize that the fan-shaped illumination came from a flashlight propped upright against the baseboard. One figure reclined on the king-size bed, another was in the red barrel chair that Cate had bought at a charity auction, and the third sat upright at the cherry desk. It took Cubiak another moment to identify each of the trio. The reclining shape on the bed was the fake Helen. Cate sat at the desk. The upright shape in the barrel chair was Ubell Acker.

"Sheriff, welcome to our little party," he said, and then he snapped on a small table lamp. Enough light filtered through the dark glass shade for Cubiak to see their faces.

"*Willkommen*," the fake Helen echoed. She held a small silver hand gun that she kept trained on Cate. Unlike the wan creature who had visited his office, she was heavily made up with the black lips and kohled eyes of a gothic horror.

Ubell sneered. Smoke curled from the cigarette that hung from the corner of his mouth and swirled up into a veil that blurred his features. A pistol rested in the flat of his hand. It was a Glock, and the barrel pointed in the direction of Cate. Despite the two weapons aimed at her, she refused to look cowed.

"Are you OK?" Cubiak asked her.

"Yes . . ."

"You do not speak!" Ubell barked out the order.

The sheriff ignored him. "Have they hurt you?"

"No."

"Shut up!" Another order, louder and harsher.

Cate blinked as if slapped, but she continued to look at him with an intense fearlessness. He held her gaze. *I will get you out of this,* he tried to tell her. As if in reply, as if saying *Yes, I know,* Cate inclined her head. The movement was small but enough for him to see.

Cubiak edged over the threshold and scanned the room. A tan canvas bag and two bulky backpacks leaned against the wall behind the round chair. A black cello case stood propped up between the knapsacks. The case was shiny and made of black metal or carbon. It was the kind of protective container made for an expensive instrument. On the nightstand at the German's elbow was a phalanx of empty beer bottles. The door to the balcony, which had been closed earlier, was open a few inches, and through the breach came the susurrus of the water caressing the shore.

"I am unarmed," the sheriff said again.

Ubell sniggered and motioned to his colleague.

The fake Helen put down her pistol and approached him. She had traded her bulky Amish skirt and Pollyanna blouse for tight motorcycle pants that showed off her slim figure and a black leather jerkin with deep cleavage.

"You aren't Helen Kulas, so who are you?" Cubiak said as she ran her long fingers along the inside of his thighs.

"It doesn't matter," she said. A raw, guttural twang replaced the soft, feathery voice she had used in his office.

"It does to me. I'll call you Helen-Marlene, because you're such a good actress," he said.

She laughed.

"Shut up," Ubell said.

The fake Helen kept her hand on Cubiak's belt and whirled toward the barrel chair. "Why should I? It doesn't matter, so what difference does it make if he calls me Marlene? He could call me Queen Victoria and it wouldn't matter."

Ubell blew a plume of smoke at her. "There is only one captain on the boat. Remember that."

Helen-Marlene lowered her eyes in fake submission. "Aye, aye, sir." She shoved Cubiak away. "Sit," she said and pointed to the floor near the balcony door.

When he was seated, she picked up the flashlight and held the beam beneath Cate's chin, angling it so the light shone grotesquely upward into her face and onto the ceiling. Cate stared straight ahead.

"Blink, bitch," the woman said, but Cate didn't flinch.

"Your wife's a real stoic, isn't she?" Helen-Marlene said. "Something she learned at finishing school, no doubt." Bored with her little game, she tossed the flashlight to Ubell. "Bet she's cold as ice, too. But rich!" The fake Helen flung her arms open and rolled the *r*'s on the word, repeating it several times. "Married up, didn't you? Sheriff."

He said nothing.

She laughed. "Oh, I read all about you, Herr Cubiak. Poor little policeman. Wife and daughter die, and then he meets the rich princess. Such a sad story, tears all around, but what a happy ending." She snickered at him.

"Shut up," Ubell said again, more irritated this time.

Helen-Marlene made a face. "The internet is a wonderful invention, so full of information," she said, glaring at the sheriff.

"Sit down."

"Whatever," she said and flounced onto the bed next to the silver pistol. "This is fucking boring. Maybe I will take a little nap. You join me?" Her eyes widened as she leered at Cubiak.

He ignored her taunts.

"No? How about you? You want to lay down with me and make nice?" she said, this time to Cate.

Cate did not respond.

"No? Well, suit yourself, cunt," Helen-Marlene said.

Ubell hurled an empty beer bottle toward the bed.

"Enough," he said, and the room went quiet.

Cubiak studied the two. They were a pair of sociopaths, two sick people bent on shaping events to their own perverse view of the world. He didn't mind when they focused on him, but he did when they amused themselves at Cate's expense. He needed to draw attention away from her.

He looked across the room at the man with the gun. "Your name isn't Eric Fielder. It's Ubell Acker, and you shot my dog," he said.

The German lit another cigarette and let out a trail of smoke. "You are correct, it is and I did. I reasoned that it was a way to invite you here to join us without having to communicate directly. And look, it worked. You put two and two together and got four. You are a clever man. Just don't let yourself become too clever."

"You have what you came for, why not leave?"

Ubell puffed out his chest. "I do indeed have what I came for, as you say, but it is not so easy to leave, my friend. There is a little problem with the bridges."

"One word from me and they go down."

The German snickered. "Are you tempting me, like Eve with the apple? You think I will fall for your little plan? Don't play me for a fool, Sheriff. I am not a fool."

"I know that. I respect that. You figured out how Payette got off the island with your father's viol. Why not use the same method and outwit the authorities again?"

The captor smiled. "It takes a bit of time to do it right, and unfortunately I do not have the luxury of time."

"Or you're afraid of screwing up. One little mistake and the viol is ruined forever."

"I do not 'screw up,' as you say," Ubell retorted, but Cubiak suspected he had touched a nerve.

He pointed toward Cate. "Let her be, and I'll get you off the peninsula, even if I have to drive you over the bay myself."

Ubell's laugh was cruel, like his name. "Oh, you will get us away from here all right, only not in anything on wheels. I want a boat, a fast boat. With someone who can pilot it and with enough gas to go a long distance." He rose to his feet and gestured toward the unseen water. "No coast guard. No police boat. A plain brown wrapper—that's the American expression, isn't it?"

"My deputy has a boat."

"He is police." Ubell spoke with derision.

"He is my friend. He has a good boat and he likes to go fast."

"Does the boat have a big tank?"

Cubiak had no idea. "Yes."

"How big?"

The sheriff didn't dare push his luck. "I don't know."

Helen-Marlene sat up. "Don't believe him."

"Shut up. I need to think."

At the desk, Cate stirred. "I have to use the bathroom."

"Women." Ubell curled his mouth in disgust. "Can't you wait?"

"I have waited."

The German gestured to the fake Helen. "Go with her."

When Cate pushed the chair away and stood, she bobbled unsteadily on her feet. Then she took a few clumsy steps, and Cubiak saw that her wrists were bound and her ankles shackled.

He started to get up. "That's not necessary."

Helen-Marlene shot over and shoved him down hard.

"Good girl," Ubell said to her.

The fake Helen smiled as she retraced her steps and prodded Cate with her fist.

Then the German turned to the sheriff. "You do not tell me what is necessary."

When the women disappeared into the bathroom, Ubell got up and paced. "If your compatriot hadn't stolen the yellow viol, if he hadn't destroyed my father, if he hadn't ruined my life, then it would not be necessary for me to be here," he said.

He stopped in front of Cubiak. "Do you know what my name means?"

"Yes."

"I see." The demonic laugh again.

"It's a very unusual name," Cubiak said, determined to rile the man. "Was it chosen in honor of someone in the family, or did your father consider you evil because of the circumstances of your birth?"

Ubell kicked the sheriff in the shin. "We do not need to talk about my father."

"Why not? Parentage can be so interesting. If we had time I would tell you my own unhappy story, although it's probably not as interesting as yours. Franz Acker gave up on life, didn't he? He stopped playing his music. He turned his back on you. He was weak. Not like his son."

Ubell started toward Cubiak again but was interrupted by the fake Helen, who kicked the bathroom door open and pushed Cate back into the bedroom.

"She tried to buy me off. The rich bitch tried to buy me off," Helen-Marlene said.

Ubell spun away and took three quick steps toward Cate. "Cunt," he said, and slapped her.

Cubiak jumped to his feet. "Leave her alone."

The German turned and leveled the handgun at his chest. "I will do as I wish."

Cubiak ignored the weapon. "If you hurt her, I don't help you," he said. Then he looked at Cate. Her cheek was red where she had been struck, but she remained stoic. She caught his gaze and shook her head slightly, a signal that what the fake Helen said wasn't true. The woman had lied.

"Everybody, sit," Ubell said.

They retook their positions and settled into an uneasy truce. Ubell unfolded a map and bent over it, tracing his finger in one direction and then in another. Helen-Marlene leaned against the headboard and stared at the ceiling. Cate remained immobile. Somewhere in the dark, a voice called out a bright farewell, and Cubiak saw his wife's shoulders stiffen as if the sound conveyed hope. Then a car door slammed. After a couple of moments, another door thudded shut and the car drove away. Cate's resolve dissolved. There was no one to help them. Still, she offered him a weak smile that tore at his heart.

In the silent room, the black phone on the desk rang.

Ubell snapped to attention. His eyes narrowed and Cubiak imagined him counting the rings, calculating his next step. The sheriff wasn't sure how much time had elapsed since he had left home, and he didn't dare check his watch. The call could be from anyone. It might mean nothing, but he prayed it was Bathard phoning as planned. He pushed up and moved as if to answer.

The German reacted the way the sheriff expected him to. "Let it go," he said.

After six rings, the voice mail clicked on, and the retired coroner's cheerful, cultured voice spilled into the void. "Cate, it's Evelyn. I tried to reach your husband but he didn't answer. I'm calling to invite the two of you to dinner tomorrow. Sonja is making her special dessert. I hope you can join us around five thirty. Dinner will be served at six. You know we like to eat early. Let me know," he said.

Ubell snickered. "You Americans. Six o'clock is late lunch, not dinner. But see, I can be reasonable about this. If you do as you are told tonight, you will enjoy a lovely meal tomorrow with your friends."

"That would be nice," Cate said. She understood, Cubiak realized. They both knew that Bathard and his wife preferred dining late, and further that Sonja was visiting her sister in Wausau and wasn't due back for another week. Whatever Bathard had meant, it was a message, and Cate was telling him that she assumed he understood what it was about.

Ubell started pacing again. "Enough of this nonsense. Back to the boat. Where is it?"

"It's either docked in Sturgeon Bay or somewhere out on the water."

"How long to get here?"

"From Sturgeon Bay, an hour, maybe less. If Rowe is out fishing in Green Bay, it would be longer."

Helen-Marlene grabbed her partner's arm. "I don't like it. It's a trap," she said.

He shook her off and turned to Cubiak. "Give me your mobile," he said.

"I can make the call," the sheriff said.

"So you can give secret messages or codes or whatever? No. I will text your friend. What is the name of the boat?"

"The *Speedy Sister*."

"Ah, good, sounds fast."

He typed out the message: *Come alone. Bring SS to . . .*

"How will he know to come here?"

"Tell him Cate's condo. He's been here before."

Ubell finished texting. "How to sign off?"

Now was the time for the lie. "Kubi." Cubiak spelled out the word.

Ubell gave him a curious look. "Kubi?"

"Departmental nickname."

The German sniggered. "I told you, don't play me for a fool. You are not a nickname kind of man. The number is enough. Unless your friend is an idiot, he will know who it is from," he said as he hit Send.

The simple act of conveying the message seemed to energize Ubell. Holding the phone loosely in his hand, he stalked the perimeter of the room. He was just under six feet and from where the sheriff sat on the floor, he looked even more formidable. As he strode back and forth, he muttered an incomprehensible sequence of gibberish. Then he smiled and said, "*Ja*." A moment later, he frowned and muttered a word that Cubiak didn't understand. From the pattern of the monologue, Ubell seemed to be going over a plan.

Every few minutes the German glanced at the phone as if expecting a response to the text. Would Rowe reply? Probably not, Cubiak thought. Given an order, the deputy usually did as requested and then asked questions later. If anything he would send an *OK* or *Got it* to indicate that the message had come through. But not always and today, Cubiak hoped he wouldn't. He wanted to keep Ubell on edge as much as possible.

Five minutes passed.

The German waved the cell at the sheriff. "Why is he not answering?"

Cubiak shrugged.

Another ten minutes elapsed. Ubell stood at the balcony door, his back to the others. Helen-Marlene lounged on the bed and inspected her nails. Cate remained ramrod straight but Cubiak sensed the ache in her shoulders. He started to edge away from the window toward her but Ubell whirled on him.

"Stop. Halt. No fraternizing." He glared at Helen-Marlene, who pulled herself upright and tried to look alert. Then he hurled the cell at the barrel chair. "Your friend is not very dependable."

"He'll be here," Cubiak said.

Ubell made a harsh noise. "You better hope so." He frowned at his cohort. "I want food. See what there is to eat in this place."

"I'm not your servant."

Ubell barked something in German and pointed to the door. When she didn't move, he lifted the gun from his side. She scowled. "Fucking men," she said as she slid off the bed.

The fake Helen slammed the door and stomped down the uncarpeted stairs. They had no trouble following her progress through the downstairs to the kitchen. Cabinet doors were opened and then banged shut. The silverware drawer rattled. A pot slid across the tile floor. "Damn!" she said, loud enough for them to hear. A moment later two plates pinged against the granite counter.

After five more noisy minutes, Helen-Marlene reappeared. She had several bottles of beer tucked against her side and carried a tray piled with bread, cheese, and a garlicky salami or sausage. She gave a beer to Ubell, who had returned to the chair, and then divided the food on plates for each of them but nothing for Cate or Cubiak. He didn't care. He wanted a cigarette, not food. But he worried that maybe Cate was hungry, and he was surprised when Helen-Marlene half-heartedly held out a slice of bread to her.

"No, thank you," Cate said.

"No, thank you," the fake Helen repeated, mocking her.

"Shut up," Ubell said. He drained his bottle and set it at his feet. Then he tucked the gun between his leg and the arm of the chair and began eating. After several bites, he glanced from the sheriff to the Glock.

"Don't even think about it," Ubell said before he shoved more food into his mouth.

A DESPERATE GAMBLE

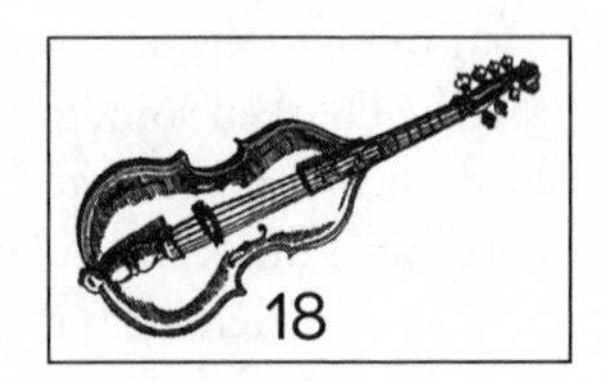

As Ubell ate, he peppered the sheriff with questions.

"This Rowe, you said he liked to go fast."

"Yes."

"How old is he?"

"Twenty-nine."

"Good. Is he a careful man or a man who likes to take chances?"

Cubiak pretended to cringe. "Not careful enough sometimes."

Ubell laughed. "Good, again. I like a reckless man. What about you?"

"Do I like a man who takes chances?"

"No, are you one?"

"You'll have to decide that for yourself."

The German smirked and set aside his empty plate. Then he took up the gun. "I will, won't I?" he said, and with that the levity vanished.

Across the room, the fake Helen dropped her plate to the floor. "Now what?" she said.

"We wait."

Ubell leaned back into the chair. His shoulders slouched and the hint of a paunch swelled below his ribs. For a moment, he closed his eyes. Then he opened them and poked at his teeth.

"He better be here, soon. This deputy of yours," he said and opened another beer.

"He will."

"No tricks."

Cubiak shook his head. "No tricks." Bathard would have alerted Rowe to the seriousness of the situation, and the sheriff trusted his deputy to act accordingly.

"So as I said, we wait. And while we wait I would like you to tell me your theory about how Payette got away with the yellow viol."

"You're sure it was him, then."

Ubell snickered. "Oh, I know it was him, but you already surmised that. So, yes, for the sake of the story . . ."

Cubiak's legs were cramped, and an uncomfortable tightness was building in his shoulders. He wanted to stretch but settled for shifting his weight and rocking slightly back and forth on the hard floor. "You've heard the expression 'hidden in plain sight'?" he said.

"I have. Go on."

Even Helen-Marlene leaned forward, listening carefully. Cate hadn't shifted position but Cubiak sensed that she was paying close attention.

"Very well then. Time and location were on Payette's side. He was traveling and recording with the GAR group and didn't live in Door County full time back then, but he'd spent much of the previous summer on the peninsula teaching at Birch Creek and playing at different venues. Being around as much as he was, he could go back and forth to Washington Island without drawing attention to himself. And as a musician, it wouldn't seem unusual for him to bring an instrument. It's just a theory, as you say, but I think he used his presence here in the months leading up to Dixan I as cover to transport several old viols to the island."

"Why would he do that?" the fake Helen asked.

"He needed them for his scheme to work. The extra instruments had to be on the island, hidden away."

"Where?"

"I don't know, but it really doesn't matter. He could have stashed one under the stairs of the old dance hall and another two or three in a deserted barn. There are plenty of out-of-the way spots where he could hide the extra viols. Places he could access quickly but where no one else had any reason to look."

"And how many of these did he secret away?" Ubell picked at his teeth again.

"I think he would have needed four or five."

The German smiled, as if in agreement.

"Everything Payette—the alleged thief—did was in preparation for the final step, the moment when he could finally get hold of the yellow viol. I'm guessing that he planned to snatch it the night of the last concert, perhaps after the final performance when everyone was celebrating the success of the festival. Under normal circumstances, this would have been a difficult and risky heist to pull off, but there were no other opportunities. Then, fortunately for him, the circumstances changed. Your mother unexpectedly went into labor, and between the medical emergency surrounding her situation and the approaching storm, the yellow viol was left unattended for a full day. Instead of minutes, Payette had twenty-four hours to nab the viol."

"But surely it was under lock and key," Helen-Marlene said.

"The viol was locked inside a summer cottage. The protection was flimsy at best," Cubiak said.

She gestured impatiently. "Yes, yes, perhaps it was. But then what? What did he do after he got it?"

"He disassembled it."

The fake Helen gasped. "No. That is impossible."

"It is very possible."

"How?" Cate said.

The three of them looked at her. She ignored the two captors and spoke directly to him.

"How could he take apart the yellow viol without destroying or seriously damaging it?"

"I wondered about that for a long time. So did Dutch."

"Who is Dutch?" Ubell demanded.

"Dutch Schumacher was the sheriff at the time the viol disappeared. He knew that these instruments—viols, violins, or whatever—were pieced together, and like most people who are unfamiliar with the craft, he assumed that it would be nearly impossible to separate the components without destroying them. Given how delicate the instruments are, it's a logical conclusion. I made the same mistake, but then I got curious and looked into the process. As it turns out, the people who make string instruments don't use wood glue to hold the pieces together. They use a water-based glue."

"Which is water soluble," Cate said.

"Did you know that?" Helen-Marlene asked her colleague.

He waved away the question. "Let our guest tell his story."

"I talked to a luthier who said he could take apart a stringed instrument like a violin or cello in less than an hour using a slim spatula, a small handsaw, and a dab of water."

The German slapped his knee. "Yes! By God, you are right, Sheriff. But to dare and try such a thing with the yellow viol."

"The traditional viols were made of very thin wood, which would require very careful handling. And because the yellow viol was especially old, the wood would be brittle, making it even more challenging. But the principle remains the same. With time and care, it could be done."

"Are you suggesting Payette disassembled my father's yellow viol and then smuggled the pieces off the island by slipping them inside the instruments he'd previously hidden on the island?" Ubell spoke up again.

"It's an interesting idea, but I don't think that's what happened. If my theory is correct, the decoys had been on the island for weeks or even months, giving him plenty of time to take them apart. Once he had the yellow viol, I think he combined the various pieces—some from the relatively worthless viols and some from your father's viol—to create a series of hybrid instruments."

"Frankenstein viols!" Ubell said.

"Something like that. The authorities had photographs of the yellow viol and so they knew what they were searching for: an instrument that looked like the one in the picture. They inspected every case that left the island, went through all the luggage, searched every vehicle, but none of the instruments, nothing that Payette or anyone else transported back to the mainland, matched the missing viol."

The sheriff stood. When Ubell didn't object, he rubbed his arms gingerly and walked to the window. The German reached for the gun but Cubiak pretended not to notice. "It was a carefully laid out plan, expertly executed."

"What about the decoy instruments? If what you are saying is true, there were many leftover pieces that had to be destroyed."

"You're right, but there's an explanation for that as well. Records show that the summer was among the hottest in memory and that the month of August in particular was sweltering. In his case notes, the former sheriff drew attention to an odd fact: The musicians stayed at cottages and vacation houses donated by festival sponsors. The owner of one particular cottage, the Knotty Pine, found ashes in the fireplace when she returned a couple of weeks later. Normally this wouldn't be unusual. Even in summer, evenings on the island can be rather cool. But not that year. So there was no logical explanation for anyone making a fire."

Helen-Marlene scoffed. "The ashes could have been from an old fire."

Cubiak shook his head. "According to the owner, the house had been thoroughly cleaned before the guest musician arrived."

"Is that where Payette stayed?"

"He was assigned to a cottage a half mile up the road, but from what I've learned the musicians often traded accommodations for their own reasons. He may have swapped with someone, claiming that he wanted to be nearer to Richard Mayes and Annabelle Larson, the other members of his trio, who were both assigned cottages near the Knotty Pine."

"And you think that Payette moved in and burned the extra pieces in the fireplace?" Cate spoke once again.

"It's possible," Cubiak said. He hesitated. "Even likely. The house was fairly remote so a small fire would have gone unnoticed, and it gave him a quick, easy way to dispose of the extraneous pieces. If not for the unusually warm weather, there probably would have been fires in any number of the houses and no one would have commented on finding ashes."

"What about the extra music cases he brought to the island?"

"He would have destroyed those as well. Ultimately, the only thing that he had to do was make sure the number of instruments he left with from the island approximated the number he'd brought to the festival. Officially, there was no record, but his colleagues would remember if he had several instruments, and, of course, he did. So he left with several cases. He used one to carry the viol he played at the festival and the others to transport the bastardized instruments."

A long silence followed.

"I think you are correct," Ubell said finally. "It is—was—an ingenious plan."

The fake Helen snorted. "I think the thief came to the island on a boat and left the same way, with the viol intact."

The others ignored her.

"But then what?" Cate said, still addressing Cubiak. "Once Payette got the pieces off the island, what happened next? Do you think he reversed the process and reassembled the yellow viol?"

"He had to."

Cate looked skeptical. "It would take a lot of nerve to reconfigure such a rare instrument and presume it would retain the special quality of sound for which it was known."

"He was willing to take that chance."

"Wouldn't all that meddling alter the viol's intrinsic characteristics, to the point where the sound would be completely different?" she said.

"Perhaps, but if the plan worked, then he'd pulled off one of the biggest heists in musical history," he said.

The German motioned Cubiak back to his place on the floor. "Payette had nothing to lose by failing and everything to gain if the plan worked. The more I consider what you say, the more I am convinced this is what happened. So congratulations, Herr Sheriff, you have solved the mystery of the missing yellow viol."

"But . . ." Helen-Marlene started to protest.

"Silence! It could be done, yes. If the instrument was reassembled correctly, the sound would be similar, not quite the same but close enough. But only if"—he gestured to the ceiling—"the reassembly was completed quickly, within hours or even a few days of the disassembly.

The yellow viol is a very old instrument. The wood is thin and brittle, as you said, and even the slightest warping would make it impossible to rejoin the pieces perfectly. So the work had to have been done *vite, vite*. And if it was, then, yes, what Herr Cubiak suggests is possible. In fact, it may be the only plausible explanation of how my father's precious viol vanished from Washington Island."

"I still don't think . . ."

Ubell went on, as if the fake Helen hadn't spoken. "I knew the sound of the yellow viol like I knew the hum of my own voice, the very murmuring of my thoughts. It was the soundtrack of my life, as they say. My father played his old recordings day and night. Growing up, it was impossible to escape from either the music or his bitterness as he relived the glory days. He drank and listened, drank more and listened more. For a long time, he listened only to his own performances, but later he started listening to new recordings of viola da gamba, playing detective with his ears. You see, he did not believe the authorities who suggested that the yellow viol was at the bottom of the strait. At first, yes, he accepted that theory but when I was around ten he started dreaming about the viol. He said the viol was calling to him, begging to be rediscovered. 'I know my precious instrument is alive,' he would say. He knew, too, that whoever had it could not resist playing it, that eventually the temptation would become too great and they would reintroduce the yellow viol to the world."

Ubell spoke with icy detachment. "For twelve goddamn years he listened. We had no bread and no heat in the house because the little money he earned from teaching went to buy the records and CDs. Every one that he could get hold of. He was like a man driven by madness or strong fever. But nothing came of his mania. He listened for the sweetness of the yellow viol but heard only the squeak of the pretenders. Nothing, nothing like the beauty of the instrument he had been stupid enough to let slip through his fingers. He killed himself, you know. Eventually driven mad from despair and shame."

The German wiped the sweat from his brow. Then he pointed to the empty bottles by the barrel chair and snapped his fingers at his assistant. This time the fake Helen got up without protest and went downstairs.

When she returned with another beer, he grabbed it from her and took a long swallow.

"Payette was a patient man, more patient than my father realized. He waited fifteen years before he dared to make a recording with the yellow viol. It was a studio performance of the third suite from *Pièces de Violle* by Le Sieur de Machy, the very composition my father had made famous. Can you believe the gall or the utter stupidity? Or perhaps he meant it as a kind of twisted homage to the great but now deceased and infamous Franz Acker? The piece was maddeningly close to my father's original work. But why should he care? Who would notice? By then the world would have forgotten all about the yellow viol, no one would pay attention."

"You did," Cubiak said.

Ubell bounced on the balls of his feet. "Not right away. I was in the angry-young-man phase of my life. Ignoring the world of the viola da gamba. Doing anything as long as it didn't involve music. It was merely by chance that I heard Payette's recordings. I was on the other side of the world, working on a merchant marine ship out of Australia. The captain, it turns out, had an affinity for Polish brandy, Cuban cigars, and early music. Such an odd sensation, floating in the middle of the Pacific and hearing the music coming from the captain's quarters as if from heaven, as if my father were serenading the angels."

"You were never in the merchant marine," Cubiak said.

Ubell laughed and saluted the sheriff with the near-empty beer bottle. "Oh, well, it makes a good story."

"Until you came to the States, you never left your homeland. You lived in Cologne, where you were a sound engineer."

Ubell sank back onto the round chair. "Ah, yes, you did your homework. You are correct; I was a sound engineer. I spent my life in isolated rooms, staring at blank walls and listening to music, trotting along in my father's footsteps. How pathetic, eh? As a musician, I was a washout—another disappointment to my dead Papa—but searching for the yellow viol? Well, that was different. I had been trained by the expert, and once I made up my mind to follow his lead, I was determined to succeed where he had failed."

The German stretched his legs. "Father kept copies of the program from Dixan I, so I knew the names of the musicians who were at the festival. To me, each player was a potential suspect. Periodically, I checked up on them to see what they were up to. Some were teaching; one had died of a heart attack; another was killed in a car crash. Several appeared to have abandoned the gamba world. One became a yoga instructor, if you can believe it. With the internet it was easy to keep tabs, and to listen in on the performances and recordings of those who continued to play. Always with an ear for the telltale sound of the yellow viol's own little idiosyncrasy."

He stopped for a moment. "And you know what? The funny part of all this? Despite all my diligent searching, I finally stumbled on it totally by accident. Mere luck really. I was online, buying a Vivaldi CD, when I hit the wrong button and by mere chance purchased one of Payette's recordings, one that I had somehow missed. When the CD came, I realized my mistake immediately but it was hardly worth returning the disc, and since it was probably something I would have bought eventually, I opened the package and played it.

"You can imagine the sensation when I realized what I was hearing. It was the de Machy piece, of course, and at first, I thought it couldn't be right, that like my father I'd gone mad from all those years of listening and imagining just such a moment. Still, I couldn't trust my ear, not completely. I didn't dare. The next day, I took Payette's CD and my father's recording to the studio and compared them. I knew what I was looking for. The yellow viol had a quirky vibration peculiar to the G-sharp, similar to what is now called a wolf tone. Despite the flaw, my father chose to play the instrument because it was so good otherwise. And there the wolf was on Payette's recording, the same exact motherfucking thing. I sat at my console sweating like a pig, listening like I'd never listened before. As this familiar, peculiar sound washed over me, I knew—I knew without a doubt—that George Peter Payette was the man who had stolen the yellow viol."

Ubell lit a cigarette and inhaled deeply. "Bastard!" he said. The word came out low and guttural, and the look on his face put him far away from Door County and Cate's condo. He smoked until he filled the room with the stench of burning tobacco. "Goddamn fucking bastard," he said.

The German dropped the nub of the cigarette into an empty beer bottle. When the sizzle subsided, he pushed to his feet.

"I began stalking Payette. Oh, not in person but online and through whatever means I could find. I started a file and hunted down every performance, recording, and photo I could find of him. Never, not once, did he appear with the yellow viol. Well, of course not. He was too clever to let the instrument be seen in public. Someone might recognize it. And he never played it before a live audience. Never. Only on his recordings. And on every one, the wolf tone appeared. The critics didn't mind. Such rave reviews he received. They drooled over the warm 'golden' sound of Payette's viol. The rarefied delicacy of his touch. The sound of angels, one commentator said. The sound of a thief!" Ubell spat out the word.

"Are you going to tell me crime doesn't pay, Sheriff? George Payette was making a name for himself with the yellow viol. He had destroyed my father and ruined my life and now the thief was rising to the top on the crumbling ruins of my family."

"Why didn't you go to the authorities?" Cubiak said.

"With what, my theory? That's what they would have called my accusation. I had no tangible proof. Yes, yes, I know the sound matched, but there are experts who would dispute my findings. They would say there was something off in the recording or something amiss in my equipment. Without the actual yellow viol, there was no irrefutable proof, just the ranting of a man who wanted to avenge his father. And I would be dismissed as a delusional, sentimental fool. You see my dilemma. I knew Payette was in possession of the yellow viol, but I could not prove it because he kept it well hidden and I did not know where. Even the recordings—how could these be made without someone seeing the stolen instrument?"

"You assumed he had accomplices?"

"Initially, no. I suspected only Payette. But the more I considered the situation, the more it seemed reasonable, necessary even, that he had to have had help."

"The GAR group."

Ubell frowned. "The three rising stars of the gamba world. Why not? They were friends. They had worked together, probably slept together. Trusted each other, as often happens. I assumed their breakup was a ruse, a convenient cover to divert attention from them, but it didn't fool me. I widened my focus to all three and was determined to learn everything I could about them in the years since Dixan I. I wanted to destroy them all."

"You didn't have to worry about Annabelle. She'd done a good job of that herself," Cate said.

Helen-Marlene hissed menacingly and rose to a half-standing and half-sitting position.

"Save your energy," Ubell said.

She sighed and dropped back down on the bed.

"My faithful helper," the German said. "How can I not succeed with such a devoted assistant?"

Helen-Marlene blew him a kiss, and Ubell went on. "I worked another year, saving money and planning. I knew that I had to come to the States to find them. There was no other way." He turned to Cubiak. "I'm sure you have tracked my steps."

"You know I have," the sheriff said. For Cate's sake, he filled in the blanks. "New York, Madison, and, finally, Chicago."

"The Windy City! Big, beautiful. And that magnificent lakefront. So much to celebrate. Except that Annabelle was dead by the time I got there, and that made it a little less enticing. But, of course, there was Lydia. In some ways she was second best, but in others even better. Lydia was an ignorant, pliable girl. She was gullible and hungry, a perfect combination for my purpose. And she had her mother's diary and the box of mementoes. Bonus prize for me."

"You're forgetting about Helen Kulas."

Ubell sneered. "The pesky, mousy friend with the little dog that would sink its teeth into your ankle and not let go no matter how hard you tried to shake it off. Dearest Helen. I went to her, of course. I tried to be nice. I needed to befriend her and make her my ally, but Helen did not like me. She did not trust me. She resented my closeness with Lydia and urged her to ignore me. The old woman was an obstacle in my path, as tenacious as that ugly dog of hers."

"So you killed her."

Ubell ran the barrel of the pistol along his jaw. "I moved her aside. I had to, and not just because she was a nuisance. She knew a man named Eric Fielder, but he no longer exists, and for him to remain a nonperson, there must be no one who can connect him to me or this place. To the people at the festival, I was nothing, another peon, a face in the background. They would not remember me. But Helen Kulas would."

"So would Lydia. Which is why you killed her too."

"What does it matter, Sheriff? People like those two are not missed. Lydia was a lost child, a loony-tune adult. She had no skills, no education, no value in the world. And the same with the old crone. She had no family, no friends other than the deceased Annabelle, nothing beyond that stuffy apartment and her boring job teaching a bunch of *dumme kinder* to read music. They were two people of no consequence. Their lives didn't matter."

"They did to them."

"Oh, Sheriff, what a softie you are. And why? You know as well as I that people like that woman die every day and no one cares. They are forgotten, curled up on park benches or warehoused in nursing homes, talking to the walls. Don't waste your time trying to make me feel any regret for what I did."

Ubell was on his feet again, pacing between them. "My father was the victim. He suffered the great injustice of his life and because of that I, too, suffered injustice. What I did, what I am doing, is simply to even the balance."

He swiped at his face with a dingy handkerchief, and then he threw open the balcony door to a stream of cold night air.

Helen-Marlene shivered and pulled the spread up around her shoulders. "It's freezing," she said.

"It is good to change the air," Ubell said. He breathed in deeply and then turned back to his audience. "Last spring I rented a car and drove to Door County to see firsthand the place where Payette had settled. By then he had become quite famous and prosperous. He had acquired an estate and a collection of rare instruments. I was curious and timed my visit to coincide with his monthly tour. To him I was just another tourist. The man had an enormous ego; he had to show us everything. That's how I learned about the private recording studio. As soon as I saw that room, all became clear. That's where he made the recordings with the yellow viol. In private, where the world could not see."

"But where did he hide the instrument?"

Ubell shrugged. "A secret chamber; a special room. It had to be kept somewhere on the grounds. Perhaps it was secured behind a false wall or at the bottom of a hidden staircase. The place is immense and has several levels that would make it easy to construct a climate-controlled chamber for the viol."

"Eventually you found out, of course."

Ubell snickered.

"What about the GAR group? How involved were they in the scheme?"

"I think that is an aspect I got wrong. Annabelle knew nothing, and thus she got nothing. Left out in the cold, as they say."

Ubell started to say something else but instead he glanced at his watch. His face clouded, and he slammed the door. He's wondering why the boat is taking so long to get here, Cubiak thought.

"And Richard Mayes," the sheriff said, bringing the German back to his story.

"I don't know if he was involved from the beginning. My guess now is that Payette would not have trusted anyone. But Mayes had to find out at some point. The two were too close all those years. Whether Payette told him or Mayes discovered the truth on his own is of no relevance. The fact that Payette kept him on as his assistant indicates that he knew about the yellow viol. Mayes's salary and comfortable lifestyle were his payoff for keeping silent."

"And you threatened to expose him unless he told you the whereabouts of the yellow viol. But he didn't give you what you wanted, and so you poisoned him too."

"If you like."

"With selenium. Tell me, how'd you know about it?"

Ubell grinned. "I had a job once working for an antique dealer who kept the stuff in the back room. He's the one who told me about its magical properties."

The German was being provocative but Cubiak refused to react. "It must have been easy enough for you to slip the poison into the food you gave Lydia, but how did you manage with Mayes?"

"Piece of cake, as you say here. I was in charge of boxing up the lunches for those on special diets, and among them was your Mister Mayes. Vegetarian, gluten free, allergic to nuts and soy. Every day, I laced his food with my own special ingredient."

"He was dead whether he cooperated with you or not."

"Precisely. Everything I did was part of my plan."

Ubell had just confessed to killing three people. His disregard for human life was chilling. He saw himself as strong, but Cubiak suspected that the arrogant façade hid not so much strength as a robotic rigidity. What wouldn't bend could be broken. Small comfort under the circumstances, but the only hope he had.

"What about Lydia's bag? Whatever became of that?"

"Poor Lydia's dying wish was for me to have her mother's precious memoirs. She gave the bag to me."

"Or you took it out of her dead hands."

The German shrugged. "Whatever you wish. It makes no difference to me."

"Where is it?"

Ubell laughed. "I had no more need for that drivel. It's gone, sunk to the bottom of the deep, blue lake."

Cubiak arched his stiff shoulders in a pretense of nonchalance. "And now what? You have the yellow viol, but you can't do anything with it. You certainly can't sell it."

"Not publicly, but privately there are always possibilities. Big possibilities. Don't play the naïve innocent with me. You know as well as I that there are fantastically wealthy people who would give a fortune for the pleasure of owning something so rare and beautiful. They are connoisseurs, people of impeccable taste who are more interested in possessing a coveted treasure than in knowing how it came to them."

Cubiak pointed to the black instrument case behind the barrel chair. "That's assuming the instrument you have with you is the yellow viol," he said.

Ubell's eyes narrowed.

"How do you know that the viol you've stolen from the thief is the authentic instrument? Perhaps it's a copy or just a well-crafted imitation. The original may still be hidden on Payette's estate or sequestered God knows where in Door County or beyond." Cubiak gestured with his hands. "America is a big country."

Ubell approached Helen-Marlene. He pointed the Glock at Cubiak and then aimed it at Cate. The fake Helen was pale and jittery with excitement. She grew more wide-eyed when he held the gun out to her. "Now you have two. One for each hand. If the sheriff moves, shoot his wife first, and then shoot him," he said.

She took the Glock and Ubell pressed his mouth to the top of her head. "Good girl," he said.

Cubiak's instinct was to leap up and tackle the man but he forced himself to remain still. It would be foolish to try anything now. In his other life, he had held his dying wife as her blood ran onto the cracked pavement of a city street. He had loved Lauren beyond all measure, and now he loved Cate. He would not do anything to cause her harm.

The sheriff slowed his breathing and glanced at the women. Cate was watching Ubell cross the room, and Helen-Marlene was watching Cate. I will protect you, he promised silently, hoping that somehow his wife could hear his thoughts and trust him to keep his word.

A loud click drew Cubiak's attention back to Ubell. The German had laid the black instrument case on the floor and released the first of three latches. Two more clicks followed, and then the hushed squawk of the lid being raised. Ubell stared at the interior.

"At last, the yellow viol is mine," he said.

With a reverence that seemed to belie his nature, the German lifted the mysterious viola da gamba from the case.

In the dim light, Cubiak got his first look at the exquisite object that had driven one man to despair, another to thievery, and a third to murder.

SEVEN STRINGS

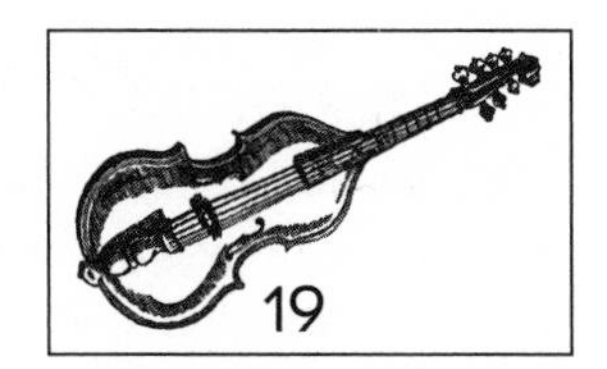

Ubell carried the yellow viol to the barrel chair. Cradling the antique instrument between his knees, he closed his eyes and fingered the strings.

"There are seven strings, which makes it unusual," he said as he tuned the instrument. "Do you know the story behind the name?"

"Augusto Fiorrelli made the viol for his wife's birthday and dyed the strings her favorite color," Cate said.

The German looked up. "How . . . ?" he said and laughed. "Of course, Google."

"History of Early Music one-oh-one," Cate said.

"So even in America, there is an attempt at education," he said derisively.

As Ubell took up the bow, his posture relaxed, his face softened, and the meanness in his eyes vanished. He almost seemed to be smiling.

Cubiak had no music training, but when he was a boy his elderly upstairs neighbor had played the violin, and the few times his parents went out or he was home sick from school, the old man came down to stay with him. The neighbor always brought his violin. He had let young Dave try it out, and after the boy produced a series of painful squawks and wheezes, the old man would take it back and effortlessly draw beautiful sounds from the sleek, almost feminine-shaped instrument.

Compared with the neighbor's violin, the yellow viol seemed primitive. The shoulders drooped dramatically. The two openings cut into the body were not the familiar *f* shapes but outward curving *c*'s. The long, wide neck was lined with frets, like a guitar. To Cubiak, the viol looked like a stunted cello with swollen glands.

Earlier, Ubell said he had failed as a musician. Perhaps by his father's exacting standards, this was true, but to the sheriff's uncultured ear, he played like a pro—his thick fingers racing expertly up and down the neck, the bow sweeping back and forth. In the strange setting, the sheriff was momentarily transformed back to the magical hours of his childhood when, against all reason, strands of horsehair scraped across thin strands of steel ushered a bounty of grace and beauty into the austere surroundings of his parents' tawdry apartment. He had found comfort in the music then, and at first he felt the same as the German played. But the sensation was fleeting.

The longer the performance went on, the more Cubiak realized that the music was not meant as a serenade. It was a warning.

Ubell played to prove that the instrument he had taken from George Payette's estate was the long-lost yellow viol. He performed for the captive audience to establish his claim to the coveted instrument and to signal to the sheriff that he would do whatever was necessary to keep it. He had killed before; he would do so again if he deemed it necessary. The placid façade that he wore was truly the mask of evil.

What about the fake Helen? Cubiak wondered. Was there any hope that a reasonable soul lurked behind her harsh exterior? He looked up and met her cold gaze. The Glock remained firmly in her grasp and pointed at Cate. The other was aimed at him. She was as much a demon as the man she was teamed up with.

The music continued to fill the room, but through it, the sheriff detected a distant murmur coming from the outside. He had lived on the water long enough to recognize the sound as the far-off drone of a motor. Sound carried oddly over the lake. Was it Rowe on the *Speedy Sister* or a distant boat carrying a fisherman toward the ship canal, someone who was tired from hours on the water and eager to get home?

The noise faded. He glanced at his watch. The timing was about right for his deputy to arrive. Moments passed and he heard the boat motor again, only louder this time. Whoever was piloting the boat was moving fast, the way that Rowe liked to drive.

Then Ubell heard it, too. Abruptly, he stopped playing, and in the sudden silence, the thrumming of the engine was clear. One by one they looked toward the balcony. Helen-Marlene started to get up but Ubell signaled her to stay seated. A cruel smile played across his face as he nestled the viol back in the case and snapped the lid shut. The sound of the motor intensified. It seemed to be coming toward them, and Cubiak wasn't sure if he was relieved or alarmed. Ubell had a plan, and when Rowe reached the townhouse the scenario would be put into motion. The German waited another minute and then opened the balcony door to the motor's roar. As they listened, the sound diminished to a faint gurgle and stopped. Once again, an eerie quiet engulfed the room.

Ubell peered into the darkness.

"Your friend perhaps is here," he said.

Cubiak pushed to his feet.

"Sit." Ubell spoke just as the sheriff's phone chirped. The cell lay on a small table between the two men. The German grabbed it. "It's a text from Mike. 'All set,' he says."

"That's Rowe. My deputy."

Ubell typed a short response.

"What did you tell him?"

Ubell gave him a quizzical look. "To wait, of course." He motioned the women to get up. "Time to leave."

"Where are we going?"

"You will find out soon enough."

Cubiak stood. "Leave her. Let her stay here," he said, indicating Cate. "There's not enough room on the boat for all of us. It'll be faster with one less onboard."

Ubell shook his head. "We will make room. She goes. You go. We all go," he said, pointing around the room. He retrieved his gun from Helen-Marlene.

"I need the black bag."

Almost gleefully, the fake Helen hurried out of the room and thumped downstairs. A few minutes later she returned carrying a small duffel. "Here," she said and pulled out a handful of long leather strips, which she gave to Ubell in exchange for the gun.

"The slightest misstep and I shoot," she said, leveling the barrel at Cate and Cubiak.

Ubell worked on the sheriff first. Letting his arms hang loosely at his sides—"in case anyone is watching," he said—the German tied the cord to one wrist, threaded the rope through a back belt loop, and knotted it around his other hand. It was a clever ploy. Cubiak knew that with his arms free to swing a few inches as he walked, no one would suspect he was being held captive. At the same time, he had no chance to break free. Ubell did the same to Cate and unshackled her ankles.

When he finished he pushed them against the wall.

"You have extra jackets here?" he asked Cate.

"Down the hall, in the closet of the guest bedroom."

Helen-Marlene left again and reappeared with an armload of jackets and sweaters. Ubell stuffed the clothes into one of the packs and hoisted it onto her back. He swung the other over his shoulder, and then he picked up the canvas bag and the case with the yellow viol.

"We will go ladies first," Ubell said as he escorted Cate to the door. "You will lead, and then my love will go next. Our honored guest and I will follow, but not too close."

He draped a scarf over Helen-Marlene's gun hand. "Don't hesitate to use it," he said. She sniggered and prodded Cate with the concealed weapon.

Cubiak watched the fake Helen carefully. Each time she was given more responsibility, her ego inflated and she grew more willful. A dangerous combination, he thought, although having Ubell guard Cate would be even worse. The fact that the German was staying with him meant he felt threatened by the sheriff. Good, he thought.

"Now?" Helen-Marlene said.

Ubell turned off the lights. "Yes, now."

The fake Helen shoved Cate toward the hall. "Go," she said.

Cate stayed her ground. Helen-Marlene kicked her shin and sent her staggering from the jolt.

Cubiak moved to intervene and felt the sharp jab of the gun barrel between his shoulders. He recoiled as best he could. "Cate, do as she tells you. We'll be OK," he said. He kept his voice level, hoping to reassure his wife. But Cate was no fool, and like him she probably understood that every step they took from the condo put them in greater peril. Once they left land, they would be in the greatest danger. Where were they headed? How far would they get in Rowe's speedboat?

The sheriff knew that Ubell didn't care what happened to him or Cate and suspected that he wouldn't hesitate to sacrifice his willing assistant if he was forced to choose between her and the yellow viol. The German was determined to get away from Door County with the valuable instrument. How well did he know American geography? the sheriff wondered. Wisconsin was in the Midwest but it was far from landlocked. Did Ubell realize how much water surrounded them?

The state of Michigan sat some fifty miles away, due east across the lake, but there were no towns of any size along the northern shoreline. Milwaukee was the nearest big city and it was nearly two hundred miles south. Going there would take the German deeper into the heart of the country. If Ubell wanted to reach the city of Green Bay by boat he had two options: he could go the long way around the peninsula or take the shortcut through the ship canal. They would save time via the canal, but they would have to go by the coast guard station at the entrance to the channel and then pass under the three bridges that his deputies had under surveillance. The deputies would take notice of a pleasure boat going through at that time, and there was a good chance they would recognize the *Speedy Sister II* and try to get Rowe's attention.

The only real option was to head north toward the Upper Peninsula and then cut across Lake Michigan to the Straits of Mackinac. And then what? Try to reach Sault Sainte Marie and Canada? They would need good maps to navigate that stretch of unfamiliar territory and plenty of fuel to cover that distance, probably more than Rowe had onboard. There's only wilderness and more water there. It would be insane to head in that direction, Cubiak thought.

Ubell gave the order to start. They walked single file out the door, through the hall, and down the stairs to the first floor.

"Go that way," he said, motioning toward the patio.

He unlocked the sliding door and pushed Cate toward it.

"Careful," Cubiak said as she started forward. Cate looked down in time to step around the chair he had put in the way.

The cool night air was tainted with a faint fishy odor. Heavy cloud cover hid the stars, and the wind washed waves of surf over the sand. As they crossed the damp lawn, separate streaks of lightning slashed the dark sky to the north—a summer storm, maybe two. There was no thunder, which meant the storm was more than ten miles away, but it was impossible to know which way it was moving. The wind might be blowing the rain out over the lake or steering it inland toward them. A burst of laughter came from the restaurant, but the outdoor tables were deserted and the paucity of cars in the lot meant few people were still dining.

Cate knew the path well, but she took her time leading them along the brick walkway that ran from the edge of the lawn to the pier. Of the two dozen townhomes that fronted the beach, only three had windows that were lit, and in these the curtains were pulled tight. Anyone glancing out would see a party of four on their way to the vessel at the dock.

Until that night, Cubiak had not seen Rowe's new boat. He knew it was a thirty-two-footer, not that much longer than the original *Sister*, but it seemed substantially taller and bigger. How seaworthy it was, he had no idea. Rowe had bragged about it having twin inboard engines, but Cubiak wasn't sure what that meant. He hoped they were big engines. He hoped there were life jackets onboard as well. Even in August, the lake was cold.

If seeing the quartet alarmed Mike Rowe, the deputy didn't display any concern. He stood in the cockpit of the *Speedy Sister II* and rode the gentle rocking of the boat like a man accustomed to water and late-night rendezvous. Rowe wore a black jacket and a dark watch cap pulled down over his ears. Two years' working with Cubiak had taught him to look first and ask questions after, and so he waited, mute as a rock, until the entourage reached the dock.

"What's going on?" he said.

"No questions. No talking," Ubell said. He took in the *Sister* and then glared at Cubiak. "I thought you said it was a fast boat. This is some kind of party boat."

Rowe bristled. "She'll do forty-five on the open water. That's as fast as you want to go out there, unless you've got a cigarette boat or a sixty-footer. Right now, it's this or nothing."

"How much fuel?"

"Enough to get us a hundred miles or more, depending on what we run into."

The German grunted and tossed his backpack over the gunwale. He signaled Helen-Marlene to do the same with hers.

"They go in the cabin," Ubell told Rowe.

The deputy left the bags at his feet. He wouldn't do anything until the sheriff gave the order.

"Do as he says," Cubiak said.

Rowe threw the backpacks below. The German gave the canvas bag to Helen-Marlene and then helped her climb aboard.

"Frisk him," he said, indicating Rowe.

It was an odd sight, but the boat was in the shadows and probably no one could see the goth woman patting down the clean-shaven young man. Helen-Marlene finished and then gave an extra swipe to the deputy's inner thigh. "He's clean," she said.

"You, next," Ubell said, shoving Cate forward. Cate was a seasoned sailor but with her hands bound, she lost her footing and fell against the side bench. Cubiak stumbled in and nearly landed on top of her.

Rowe moved to help them but Cubiak warned him off. "We're good," he said.

Ubell remained on the dock. "Sit, both of you," he ordered the sheriff and his wife. "You, give me your mobile," he told Rowe. The deputy hesitated, but at a signal from Cubiak, he complied. The German flung the phone into the lake and then told the fake Helen to check the boat.

She seemed to know exactly what to do. Moving around the three in the cockpit, she swept her hands under the cushions and the instrument panel. Then she knelt and ran her hands across the deck and along the base of the rear and side benches. Radio chatter occasionally broke the silence until she went below and switched it off. They heard cabinet doors open and slam shut.

A few minutes later she appeared in the gangway. "Nothing," she said.

All this time, Ubell had been holding the yellow viol. Given the all clear, he finally stepped onboard with the precious cargo. For a moment he seemed uncertain what to do with it. Almost reluctantly he gave it to the fake Helen.

"Put this below, somewhere safe," he said.

Ubell eyed Cubiak and Rowe. "No secret tracking devices, I assume. Because if there are—if we are being followed—one of you will die. If I discover weapons on board, someone will pay. And explosives?" More lightning exploded in the distance, and he laughed. "If you are that foolish, then you drown with us. We are in this together, don't forget."

Cubiak pushed up to his feet. "There's no reason for my deputy to go with us. You have two hostages. That's enough. Leave him here. There'll be less weight on board and . . ."

Helen-Marlene was halfway up the stairs. "'We'll make better time.' Is that what you were going to say, Sheriff? Of course we will leave your friend behind—so he can call for help," she said.

"You can tie him up in the condo. He won't be able to do anything," Cubiak said.

"Don't listen to him," Rowe said. "You need me out there. I know this boat. I can pilot it with my eyes closed, which is about what it's like trying to go anywhere on the water at night."

Rowe was right. Bathard had taught the sheriff to sail but he was little more than a seasoned novice. Cate was a veteran on the water, but he doubted that Ubell would trust her at the wheel, and besides, running a powerboat was different from operating a sailboat. It pained Cubiak to realize he was putting his deputy in jeopardy, but without Rowe at the helm they were all in danger. Beyond that, he figured that the two of them might have a chance of overpowering their captor. Better than any he had on his own. And if they ran into rough weather, they would need Rowe to get them through.

"He stays with us," Ubell said.

"Then trade him for Cate."

As he spoke, Cubiak looked at his deputy. He had to try to negotiate; they both knew that.

"I'll go in her place," Rowe said.

Ubell snorted. "We all go."

He pushed Rowe to the front of the cockpit and pointed to where he wanted the others. The fake Helen and Cate were on the starboard side facing in. Cubiak was in the stern.

When he had them all seated, Ubell undid the mooring lines and pushed the boat away from the dock. The wind had come up and the *Speedy Sister* pitched gently on the water.

"Now. It is time," he said.

The deputy started the engines.

"Go gently. Do nothing to attract attention," Ubell said. "Soon, we will go fast, the way you like."

AWAY FROM EVERYTHING FAMILIAR

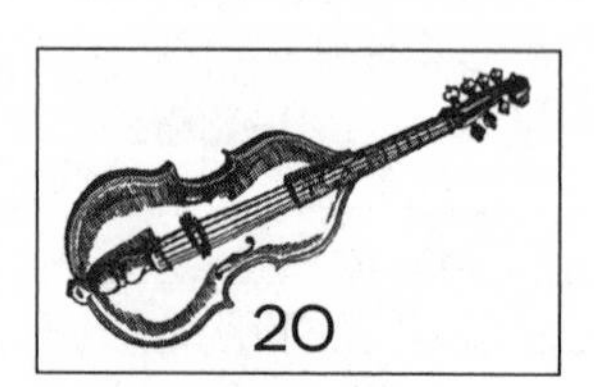

As the *Speedy Sister* slipped away from the pier, an elderly couple in jaunty resort attire emerged from the restaurant. "Have a good trip," the man called out and both waved. Ubell raised a hand in a show of false cheer as the boat motored through the shallow scallop of a harbor.

Within minutes they passed the breakwater and churned toward the deeper depths of the lake. Since Cubiak had learned to sail, his fear of water had lessened, but as they sped farther from land the familiar, childhood terror rose up again. Why was he so damned frightened by deep water? Sitting with his hands tied, he remembered. It went back to a hot summer day, not long after his sixth birthday. He was a scrawny kid, on a picnic with his parents and a gathering of boisterous relatives he barely knew. They had gathered at a small lake in Indiana, and all the kids except him were diving and splashing in the water.

"What's the matter, are you afraid of a little water? Scared you'll melt?" his uncle had said.

When young Dave said he couldn't swim, the man grabbed him and carried him kicking and yelling to the end of the dock. No matter how hard the boy protested, his uncle wouldn't put him down. Onshore, the adults watched the show.

"Best way to learn to swim," his uncle said, and with a roar, he tossed Dave into the murky lake.

The water burned his nostrils and closed over his head. The mossy carpet cloyed at his feet. His eyes stung. Desperate and half blind, he groped for the dock. If he reached a post, he could pull himself up, but there was only water, more water. Panicked, he lost all sense of direction. When there was nothing left in his lungs, when he was sure he would die, a hand grabbed his wrist and an arm swung around his thin shoulders, and he was dragged back into the air and shoved onto the splintered pier, where he struggled to his hands and knees and vomited up his lunch of hot dogs and the lake's green sludge.

That evening a cousin told him that he had been rescued by a neighbor boy who had come down to the lake to catch turtles. Cubiak's father, it turned out, had been too drunk to save him, and the cruel uncle had refused to go in after him, insisting he would do fine on his own.

"Where to?" Rowe said glancing back at Ubell.

"North."

North. The word snapped the sheriff back to the moment and prompted a different fear. North was away from everything familiar. What the hell was the man up to?

"North where?" Rowe said.

"There." The German pointed into the great maw of darkness that stretched before them.

"I need more than that," the deputy said.

"In due time," Ubell replied. He sat equidistant between the two men.

"Do you want me to turn off the running lights?" Rowe said.

"And draw attention to us? Clever lad, huh? We obey the laws. The lights stay on," Ubell said.

After a few minutes, he stood. "Now, go fast," he told Rowe.

The deputy hit the throttle and the *Sister*'s two engines roared. As the boat leapt forward, Ubell lost his balance and tripped over the fake Helen's foot. When he caught himself he was down on one knee just inches from the sheriff. Their eyes locked.

"You would cut my throat if you could, wouldn't you?" Ubell said quietly.

"Yes."

The German laughed and righted himself. "We understand each other, then."

Cubiak had suspected no less. Ubell was not the kind of man to show mercy. The sheriff had seen evidence of his ruthlessness. The German meant for only one of them to live to see the dawn, and the sheriff knew the odds were not in his favor. But that would change. He looked toward Cate. It has to, he thought.

The fake Helen sneezed. "It's fucking freezing out here," she said, shivering under a double layer of jackets.

Ubell gave her a flashlight and pointed to the galley. "Go below then. And take her with you." He pulled Cate to her feet and pushed her toward the stairs. "If she tries anything, you know what to do."

Helen-Marlene flaunted the silver pistol. "Aye, Captain, "she said.

They were still far enough in that the water was calm, and they made good time. Here and there a light broke the monotony of the inland coast, but along the Whitefish Dunes, the shore was dark. Past that an occasional solitary light glimmered from an isolated house or a summer cottage. When the sheriff least expected it, a cluster of pinpricks blinked out of the void.

Ubell noticed the lights, too. "Where are we?"

"Baileys Harbor." There was a melancholy longing in the way Rowe named the town. He had been standing until then and he sat down.

"You OK?" Cubiak said.

"Yeah. You?"

"No talking," Ubell said. "You want to say something, you say it to me."

Muttering under his breath, Rowe gunned the motor and steered away from shore.

"What are you doing? Where are you going?" the German said.

"We have to head out a couple miles. There are some small islands up ahead and a cluster of unmarked shoals. I can't chance it in the dark."

As they crossed into deeper water, the darkness swallowed the last flickering village lights and the wind picked up speed. A sharp chop pummeled the hull of the *Speedy Sister*. At three miles, the lake depth dropped to nearly two hundred feet. Cubiak wondered if they were that far out yet, as he imagined the lake bottom falling away beneath them.

The water grew rougher. The boat bucked up and down as it rode the crest of each new wave, dropped into the trough, and then went up again. The sheriff felt queasy. He knew the ride was worse for Cate down below. Be safe, he prayed.

They were heading north again when the sky ahead lit up and a three-pronged fork of lightning knifed into the water. Cubiak shuddered. Jesus, that was close. Since moving to Door County, he had learned how quickly storms could come up on Lake Michigan and how unpredictably they moved across the water. Once on the *Parlando*, he and Bathard had been caught in a squall that dropped out of a bright blue sky. Lightning was his greatest fear, even though the coroner had explained that on a sailboat the mast acted as a lightning rod. If they were unlucky enough to be hit, the electrical force would travel down the pole, through the keel, and into the water.

There wasn't anything on the *Speedy Sister* that looked like a lightning rod. The boat was little more than an oversized fiberglass tub, a flea on the water, he thought. What the hell will happen to us if we're hit?

Another strike speared the lake.

"You see that, Mike?" Cubiak said.

"On it, Chief."

Cubiak was intent on tracking the storm and nearly missed the splash of light that swung over the water from the west.

"What's that?" Ubell said.

"The lighthouse at Plum Island. We'll be passing through Death's Door soon."

"Porte des Morts." Ubell seemed to take perverse pleasure in saying the name out loud.

Cubiak hoped it didn't portend their fate. Earlier that week, he had crossed the strait with young Kevin Norling at the helm of a small motorboat. As ominous as that had appeared, he felt safer with the boy piloting the miniature craft than he did on Rowe's powerboat with the madman holding them hostage.

Ubell checked his watch. "Good. On time," he said.

More lightning blazed along the horizon.

"We need to slow down and let the weather pass," Rowe said.

"The storm is moving away from us. You keep going fast," Ubell said.

Rowe cut the throttle and kept the engines at a simmer. "I gotta use the head."

"Go over the side. Man's prerogative," the German said and laughed.

"My hands are frozen so bad I can barely grip the wheel. If you want me to keep steering this boat, you've got to give me a break. It's warmer down there. I need a few minutes to thaw."

Ubell looked at his watch again. "Five minutes. If you're not back, I shoot your boss."

"We can keep going at a couple knots. The sheriff can handle the wheel while I'm gone," Rowe said.

The German roared. "And have two of you with hands untied. You think I'm stupid? Cut the engine and go. You will make up for lost time when you get back."

Rowe disappeared down the stairs. Cubiak heard a muffled shout from Helen-Marlene and a sharp retort from his deputy. Ubell yelled at them both to be silent, but Rowe ignored him and said something to Cate.

"I'm good," she said.

"Be quiet." It was Helen-Marlene again.

"Go to hell," Cate said. Her voice was strong and strident. Cubiak knew that she was both taunting the fake Helen and letting him know that she had not given up.

He called out to her. "Cate, stay calm and we'll be OK." Uncharacteristically he added: "I love you."

Ubell snickered. "I love you." His tone was mocking and harsh. He leaned toward the open hatchway. "You hear that, lady. Your hero loves you." Then he turned toward the sheriff. "You sentimental Americans make me want to vomit."

The German turned sideways and swept his hand up along his neck just as a rogue wave smacked the boat. Cold water flew up into his face and he jumped to his feet. "Goddamn, fucking shit," he said, shaking his head and arms.

Another wave hit the stern and drenched Cubiak. Thunder followed each lightning strike. He estimated the time in-between at about thirty seconds, which put them within six miles of the gale. Ubell was wrong; the storm was closing in. The wind whistled over the lake, roiling the surface. In the next flash of light, he saw whitecaps foaming against the black water. The *Speedy Sister* rose and fell with the swells. They were spinning off course.

"Deputy Rowe!" Ubell shouted down to the cabin.

Rolling thunder announced Rowe's return. He had put on gloves and a fleece vest and carried an extra jacket. "Here," he said and tossed the coat to Cubiak. The stairs were wet and as the deputy reached for the wheel, he slipped and slid down into the galley. Helen-Marlene yelped.

"Keep him away from the viol," Ubell shouted to her.

For an unguarded moment, the German's back was turned, and the sheriff pushed to his feet. Struggling to stay balanced on the undulating deck, he stepped forward. If he was quick, he could take Ubell by surprise. But with his hands tied, he couldn't do anything more than shove him toward Rowe, who was coming up the stairs again. Caught off guard, the deputy would tumble into the galley. The idea was a fiasco. Reluctantly, Cubiak fell back. It was too dangerous to try to outmaneuver their captor on the open water. Ubell needed Rowe to pilot the *Speedy Sister*. He might take a chance on wounding the deputy but he wouldn't hesitate to kill the sheriff. He had to stay alive until they reached their destination. On land, he and Rowe might have a chance to fight back.

Rubbing his elbow, Rowe retook his place behind the wheel.

"Are you hurt?" Cubiak said.

The German raised his voice. "No talking."

The deputy answered anyway. "I'm all right," he said as he scanned the dials. Then he restarted the engines and reoriented the boat north. "I'm not going back to full speed until we're clear of the storm," he said.

Ubell grunted but this time he didn't protest.

They moved beyond the reach of the beacon from Plum Island and plunged back into complete darkness.

Rowe spoke up. "Washington Island's coming up. You'll see the lights at Detroit Harbor soon."

"Washington Island, the scene of the crime," Ubell said.

"The first one, you mean."

The German ignored Cubiak's comment.

Ubell wore only a light windbreaker but he seemed oblivious to the cold. Cubiak tried to sit on his hands. He had managed to get the extra jacket over his shoulders, but despite the additional layer, he was cold. He tried conjuring up the warm weather at Dixan V, but thinking about it only made him feel worse. At least Cate was out of the wind and would be warmer in the cabin. It was a small thing for which to be grateful, but it was all he had at the moment.

"Where are we?" he asked his deputy.

"We should be near Rock Island. After that we'll go through the Rock Island Passage and cross the state line into Michigan."

"Between the forty-fifth and forty-sixth degrees of latitude," Ubell said, as if he were their schoolmaster.

He had done his homework, Cubiak thought, chagrined that their captor knew more than he did about the region.

"What's up there, anything?" the sheriff said.

"Ultimately we'll run into the Upper Peninsula," said Rowe. "But before that, there's an archipelago of deserted islands. Saint Martin. Poverty. Summer. Little Summer. The chain starts with Washington Island and runs pretty much in a straight line to the UP. There used to be a few fishing villages and summer resorts scattered around there, even a couple old hunting camps. In the really old days, the Indians used the islands as staging grounds for their hunting forays. They'd come down from up north looking for deer and bear and whatever else they could shoot with a bow and arrow. Now the land's been converted to bird sanctuaries and wildlife refuges."

Ubell cut in again. "There's nobody there, gentlemen. No one to hear your cries of distress. Only ghosts and peeping birds."

He swept his arms out toward the water. "That's what I love about your country. All this spectacular wilderness. The great open spaces. In Europe, we're crammed together, everyone knowing everybody else's business. But here in America, there's plenty of room where a man can get lost."

Or dump the bodies of those he kills, Cubiak thought.

A tremor shook the *Sister*. When the boat stopped vibrating, a sharp grinding sound churned below the floorboards, and they began to slow down. Rowe pumped the fuel line, but there was no response. "We're losing power," he said.

Within minutes, they were dead in the water.

"Shit," he said.

"What's wrong?" Ubell jumped to his side.

"I don't know. Something with the engines."

"You fucker!" He raised a fist at Rowe and then whirled toward Cubiak. "You tricked me. You told me it was a good boat."

"It is a good boat," Rowe said. "But it's a used boat, OK? And we've given it a real beating tonight. I own it with my friends. We had the engines overhauled when we bought it. No guarantees, the guy said, but we trusted him."

"Fools." Ubell looked around. "Can you fix it?"

"I can try."

Rowe pushed Ubell to the wheel. "Keep heading into the waves," he said.

Without power, it was impossible to steer the boat. Cubiak knew that much and waited for Ubell to object. Instead he grabbed the wheel and peered intently over the bow while the deputy knelt on the cockpit floor and raised a panel.

Rowe leaned into the underbelly of the boat. When he pulled back up, his hands were black with grease. "It's a loose bolt. I have to tighten it but I can't do it myself."

Ubell said something in German that sounded like a curse. He waved Cubiak forward and untied his left hand.

"I'm right-handed," the sheriff said.

"I know." Ubell gave him a hard look. "Any funny business, Cate dies," he said, and then he pushed him down toward Rowe.

Cubiak didn't know what his deputy was up to, but he followed his lead. If they were in mechanical trouble he hoped Rowe knew what to do; if this was a ruse, he hoped there was a good reason for it.

Rowe gave Cubiak a small flashlight. "Hold it. There." He pointed to the rear of the engine compartment. "No, no. there." The deputy moved the sheriff's arm back, and Cubiak felt the small knife that Rowe had taped to the wall.

"Got it?" the deputy said.

"Yeah."

Ubell leaned over them and watched. A wave hit them broadside and Rowe landed on his chin. Another wave hit, and the boat tilted again.

"Jesus. I told you to head into the waves. You want this done or not?" With a youthful daring, the deputy yelled at the German.

Ubell swore. As he turned and tried to correct their course, Rowe pulled the knife free and slipped it into the sheriff's right pocket. Cubiak didn't dare look up. If the German suspected anything, it was over for them.

The *Sister* shifted erratically.

"Turn harder, to the left. More." The deputy looked up and gave the order. Then he fiddled with the engines again.

The first time he tried to restart them, they didn't respond. But on the second try, they kicked in. Rowe took over at the wheel and Cubiak went back to the stern. He kept his face blank and struggled to slow the pounding in his heart.

"On your knees," Ubell said as the sheriff was about to sit down.

"You think you put something over on me?" he said as he pulled the knife from Cubiak's pocket. Shouting something incomprehensible, he pressed his boot to the sheriff's neck and pushed him down to the deck. Cubiak waited. A bullet to the head meant pain and death in the same instant. A shot to the leg or shoulder would hurt like hell and render him helpless. Instead of rescuing the others he would be a burden to them. But what if Ubell shot Rowe?

The German put more weight into his foot and then, unexpectedly, he backed off. "Get up."

Cubiak stumbled to the rear bench, pain spiking his neck and chin. The fucker still needs us, he thought. That's all it is.

When he trusted himself to be able to talk, the sheriff picked up the thread of conversation as if nothing had happened.

"Where are we going? You can at least tell us that much," he said.

"You'll find out soon enough."

Within minutes, the wind began to die. The storm was moving away from them toward the east. Spears of lightning slashed into the water but at so great a distance that the thunder no longer reached them. As the mist cleared, a solitary star appeared and then another. Soon a small chorus of flickering dots emerged and closed ranks with the nearly full moon to play hide-and-seek with the scuttling clouds.

Ubell lit a cigarette. With the first inhale, he blew a cloud of smoke at Cubiak.

For a fleeting second, it almost made him feel warm.

When the German got down to the filter, he flicked the butt over the side and pulled an electronic device from his pocket. From where Cubiak sat, he could see a glowing green screen but nothing else. The device looked too large for a cell phone. What was it? he wondered. Ubell's mouth twitched as if he were talking to himself.

Abruptly, he stood and moved toward Rowe. "Slow down," he said.

The deputy cut the speed several knots.

"More."

Rowe eased the throttle and reduced the *Speedy Sister* to a crawl. An errant swell rocked the boat, and Ubell grabbed the gunwale to keep from tipping over.

"Are we there?" the fake Helen yelled from below.

"Quiet," Ubell said. Regaining his balance, he checked the handheld screen again.

"Head northwest," he said and pointed to the compass.

Rowe held the wheel steady. "There's nothing out there."

"You do as I say. Now."

Rowe looked back at Cubiak, and the sheriff nodded.

The deputy turned the wheel and nudged the *Speedy Sister* through the undulating water. "I don't know this area. There might be shoals or hidden rocks," Rowe said.

Ubell ignored him. A wave slapped them portside. It was followed by two more in quick succession.

"Lake Michigan's three sisters," Rowe said.

"Dangerous?"

"They can be."

But only to sailors far out on the lake. Cubiak had learned this much from Bathard. Rowe was again deliberately misleading Ubell.

"More slow," the German said.

The clouds moved in again. With the stars and moon shut off, the night sky became a thick overhead shroud. As they crept forward, Cubiak strained to hear past the hum of the motor, hoping to catch a sound that might indicate what lay ahead. Were they nearing land, or heading to a rendezvous with another vessel?

"You have searchlights?" Ubell said.

Rowe pointed to a lamp mounted on the prow.

"Turn it on."

The yellow beam streamed over the bow and split the dark. Ubell swept the headlamp back and forth in careful, slow arcs. What's he looking for? Cubiak wondered as he followed the rotating light. They had slowed to trolling speed and seemed to barely move against the current. It was impossible to calculate distance. They might have traveled fifty feet or fifty yards.

Another five minutes passed, and a low ribbon of land skimmed the horizon. The patch of earth was maybe a half mile out, maybe less or more, and even blacker than the night sky.

"Keep going," Ubell said.

As they drew closer, Cubiak heard the rush of surf. They were near one of the islands. In another sweep of the light, he glimpsed the skeletal remains of a dock. Rowe said the archipelago was uninhabited but someone had lived there once, as evidenced by the pier they had left behind.

The fake Helen appeared in the stairway. "What's going on?" Her tone demanded a response.

"We have made it. We are late, but still within the parameters," Ubell told her. His voice was heavy with relief and satisfaction.

It was just past midnight by the sheriff's watch. The witching hour.

They were here to meet someone, Cubiak realized. But who?

ANCIENT WEAPONS

They motored forward with the searchlight trained on the rendezvous point. The island looked like a jagged pencil stroke drawn across the black miasma of water and sky, but slowly the features came into focus: First, the rickety dock that extended out into the water. Then the ring of gray boulders that lined the shore. Finally, the thick forest of wind-wrecked fir trees that formed the serrated horizon. Taken together, they formed a forlorn and uninviting habitat.

The pier had been badly neglected for years. Cycles of wind, sun, rain, and ice had stripped the paint and weathered the wood to a dull noncolor. Some of the boards had rotted through, leaving gaping holes in the surface. Ubell swore quietly.

"Shut everything down," he told Rowe.

The deputy hit a series of switches, and they were plunged again into darkness. Cubiak felt the quivering underfoot as the *Speedy Sister* went numb. The only sounds were the wind and the restless surf lapping the hull.

In the dark, the boat thumped against the dock.

"I have to put out the bumpers," Rowe said.

"Forget it." Ubell kept the gun on the deputy as he tossed the mooring lines around the dock posts and secured the boat.

They had landed on one of the islands, but which one? Cubiak wondered. Did it matter? Was someone waiting onshore? Perhaps a black-market viol buyer? Although it hardly seemed like the kind of venue for a sales transaction. Or someone paid to transport Ubell and his precious cargo out of the US?

"Dave?" Cate sounded frightened.

"Keep her quiet," Ubell told his colleague.

Cubiak shouted over him. "I'm here. We're OK."

"Shut up, everyone." Ubell seemed tense. He pulled Rowe away from the wheel and lashed the deputy's hands behind his back. "Sit," he said and shoved him down on the side bench. Then to Cubiak, he said, "Stand up. Go there."

"Where? I can't see anything."

"To the dock. We are getting off."

Ubell let the sheriff pass and then he nudged him from behind. "Go," he said.

"What about Cate and Helen-Marlene?"

"Never mind them. Go."

Cubiak inched forward. As long as he did as he was told, the fake Helen wouldn't hurt Cate, but he feared that if she was left on her own with her captive, she could turn reckless. The woman was unpredictable. She envied and resented Cate, and her enmity could make her act irrationally.

"Stay calm, Cate," he said.

The German prodded him again.

Cubiak hesitated. For years, he had been uncomfortable around boats and fearful of deep water. But that night, he dreaded the thought of trading the security of the *Speedy Sister* for the unknown dangers that lay ahead on land.

In the dark, he couldn't see the island, but he sensed its menacing presence. The lake had been terrifying but alive. In contrast, the land exuded a morbid stillness, as if the ground and everything growing from it was trapped in a stagnant limbo. He took a breath. The air was damp and seemed colder than it had been on the lake. Worse was the fetid smell that perfumed the atmosphere.

Ubell pushed him a third time. "Now," he said.

With his hands secured behind him, the sheriff clambered over the side and onto the dock. He had miscalculated. The pier was low and slick with moss. Thrown off balance, he toppled forward and fell to his knees. He struggled to his feet and then nearly fell again when Rowe tumbled after him.

"What stinks?" the deputy said.

"Rotten wood."

Cubiak slid his foot forward and pressed down with the toe of his boot. The board yielded to the pressure like a wet sponge.

Ubell appeared out of the dark. Holding the tan canvas bag and a flashlight, he panned the pier. The shore end of the dock was wedged between two clusters of rocks. From there a narrow path led to a small clearing that looked large enough for a couple of tents but not much else. Beyond that, there were more stunted firs. Cubiak couldn't tell what they were, white pine perhaps or tamaracks. Like the trees along the shore, they grew so close together that their branches interlocked into a solid black wall.

"Go," Ubell said again, pointing the feeble beam down the length of the rotting pier.

Cubiak stepped over a gaping hole.

"Careful," he said to Rowe.

The sheriff didn't trust the dock to hold the combined weight of the three of them, and he moved slowly. He was already cold; he didn't want to get soaked again. He also wasn't eager to find out what Ubell had planned for them onshore.

"Faster," the German said.

"This is as fast as I can go."

When Cubiak finally stepped onto solid ground, he turned around to see how far he had gone. By his reckoning the *Speedy Sister* lay some fifty feet away and was all but invisible, save for a faint flickering glow, probably a candle in the cabin. He grimaced thinking of Cate, trapped in the cramped space with Helen-Marlene. But he knew that as long as the yellow viol was onboard, Ubell would do nothing to endanger the boat and Cate was probably safe. That thought gave him small comfort.

If Ubell sold the viol on the island, he would have no further need for her or either of the men. If he was transferring to a larger vessel, he would still need a hostage and would take Cate along. He would kill Rowe and Cubiak before departing, and then he would murder Cate when she was no longer useful to him.

"Sir," Rowe said as he stepped off the pier and took his place alongside the sheriff. It was an expression of respect, a single word spoken with confidence.

The burden of the office was on Cubiak's shoulders. He was in charge; he was the person responsible.

"Keep calm. Stay ready," he said quietly. He needed a plan.

Safe on solid ground, Ubell grew cocky again. He was nearly jovial as he pulled a dented, red metal can from the canvas bag. It was the kind used to transport gasoline. The German set the can down and shoved Rowe to his knees. Then he untied the sheriff's hands.

Cubiak rubbed his wrists and waited.

"We need firewood. Lots of it. You go first to look. Start piling it up over there." With the flashlight Ubell drew a circle on a patch of dirt near the water. "Any funny business and I shoot the deputy. If my compatriot hears my gun, she shoots your wife."

"Everything is wet from the storm," Cubiak said. He was stalling. Ubell was going to use the gasoline to light a bonfire, a signal that would bring his accomplices to shore.

"Go. We need a few pieces to start."

"I won't be able to find my way back in the dark."

"Call when you are ready to return. I will guide you here."

Cubiak plunged into the forest. Branches lashed his face and hands. He kept his head down to protect his eyes and kicked at the ground as he searched for twigs and fallen branches. Drops of cold rainwater fell from the branches and slid down his neck. The work made him sweat, and soon the perspiration ran cold as well.

As he gathered wood, Cubiak thought about what lay ahead. Once Ubell was satisfied that there was enough wood for the fire, he would kill the sheriff. Maybe Rowe as well. Unless he still needed the deputy to pilot the *Speedy Sister*. But at some point, he meant to shoot him too.

For Cubiak the threat of death came with the job. He knew the same was true for Rowe, although he also knew that he would not let the deputy die if there was any way to save him. But Cate? His strong, brave Cate, who had forgiven him so much already. Could she ever see past this? She was at risk because of him. And not just her, but the baby, too. Hours earlier when they had climbed aboard the *Speedy Sister*, she had looked at him with a mixture of fear and calm assurance. There was no question that she understood the danger they were in but had complete faith in him to save them all. How? Rowe had been clever in hiding and then retrieving the knife on the boat, but Ubell had thwarted the attempt. With a weapon, Cubiak stood a chance, but he was unarmed. If both he and Rowe were ever free together, they could attack Ubell, but their captor made sure that one of them was always bound and under guard.

Cubiak couldn't chance a mistake. A simple misstep and Ubell would shoot the deputy—a signal for the fake Helen to shoot Cate. Clever bastard, that one. The world was full of men like him. Though unknown to each other, they formed a brotherhood of conniving fiends. There were others, wild and drunk bastards, who killed as easily and with as little remorse. These men destroyed by sheer happenstance. Ubell killed by intent. There were three known victims along his trail of dead bodies: Helen Kulas. Lydia Larson. Richard Mayes. How many before them? How many more to come?

The sheriff had to get back. He had to keep Ubell in sight.

Cubiak had been circling in the dark. Too late he realized that he was unsure how to retrace his steps to the clearing. With his arms full of firewood, he called out. When he heard Ubell's shout, he started toward it. After a while, he stopped and called out again and reoriented himself by the response.

The forest fought his every step. He staggered up a sharp rise and then on the way down, he caught his foot on a tree root. Cubiak fell and the branches he had collected tumbled from his arms. On his knees, he scrambled to retrieve the scattered pieces of wood.

The stony ground was layered with moss and pine needles. He had recovered half the firewood when he made one more pass with his hand

and felt a sharp sliver of rock jutting up from the surface, probably the top of a boulder. He started to move on, but then he slid his hand back over it again. The exposed rock was the size of a half dollar and rippled with minute bumps and hollows. Cubiak dug away the surrounding detritus and worked the piece free. When he had it in his palm, he traced the outline with the tip of his finger. The piece was triangular, and despite having been buried in dirt for decades, the point and edges were sharp. He had stumbled on an arrowhead, a relic of one of the Native American tribes that had once inhabited the islands. Rowe said they had used the islands as staging grounds for hunting. Maybe there were more of the ancient weapons buried in the ground. Cubiak tore at the patch of lichens desperate to find another. Instead of an arrowhead he uncovered part of a broken knife blade, probably a remnant from one of the white settlers' early fishing camps. The blade was short and dull; the arrowhead hard as steel. Both were thin enough to slip into the back pocket of his jeans.

"Where the fuck are you?" Ubell yelled, and Cubiak realized that the German had been shouting at him for several minutes.

He started back. On the boat, he had felt a surge of hope when Rowe slipped the knife to him, but that had been quickly shattered. Now hope was resurrected.

"What the hell were you doing out there?" Ubell said when the sheriff stepped into the clearing.

"I fell," Cubiak said. He dumped the wood and held out his scraped hands as proof.

"Idiot."

"It's dark out there."

Cubiak started to sit down.

"You go again," the German said.

"I'm tired."

"Fuck tired. Go."

The sheriff made two more forays before Ubell retied his wrists and made him sit on a tree stump by the stack. The pile of twigs and branches was nearly three feet high, but the German wasn't satisfied. He sent Rowe to scavenge for more wood. How long before there was enough and their time was up? Cubiak wondered.

"You're going to let the women onshore when you light the fire, aren't you? They must be half-frozen on the boat," he said.

Ubell splashed the flashlight into the sheriff's eyes. "None of your business what I do."

"It's awfully quiet out there. How do you know my wife hasn't gotten the better of Helen-Marlene?"

Ubell scowled, and then he turned toward the dock and shouted in German. The fake Helen answered. She was long winded and whiny. While the two went back and forth, Cubiak worked the arrowhead toward the top of his pocket. When the flat stone was partially out, he pinched it between the tips of his fingers and pulled it free.

"Patience," Ubell called out over the black water. Then to Cubiak, he said, "Everything is fine."

"I don't know if Cate is OK. I won't go for more wood until I do. You can shoot me in the foot, I don't care," Cubiak said. As he spoke he pulled his shoulders back and twisted his wrist to get at the rope that bound his hands.

Ubell yelled again. After a moment, Cate spoke. Her voice was strained but strong.

"Dave. I'm OK. Are you there? Are you all right?"

He slashed at the ligature but missed. "Yes. I'm here. Try not to worry."

Ubell laughed. Cate started to say more but he cut her short. "Enough," he said and mocked the sheriff with his own words. "Worry? I do not worry," he said as he rearranged the pile of logs and branches.

Rowe crashed through the trees with an armload of wood. Ubell sent him back out and stacked the pile higher. While the German was occupied, Cubiak sawed at the taut cord. He felt it loosen, or was that his imagination? There was little circulation in his hands, and his fingers were numb. The arrowhead was thin, and hard to hold. He hit the rope at an odd angle and the flinty rock slipped. He tightened his grip and took a slow breath. Willing the tension from his shoulders, he again jabbed the arrowhead toward his wrist. The first stab connected but the second slashed into his arm. The pain was sharp and sudden. Blood trickled over his hand, and the arrowhead fell to the ground. He leaned back but he couldn't reach down far enough to get it. He swore silently. Sweat burned his eyes. His hands tingled. He had one more try. Like the man with the last match in the short story he had read when he was a kid.

Rowe reappeared and tossed his load onto the stack. The pile gained another foot.

"Enough for now," Ubell said.

He bound the deputy again and sat him down opposite the sheriff.

Cubiak began working the knife blade from his pocket. This is for Cate and for you, he thought, focusing on Rowe. I won't let the two of you down.

The blade had lodged deep in his pocket. He rocked forward to get at it. Please, God, he said as he slowly eased the piece free.

Finally, he had it.

He worked on the rope as Ubell uncapped the gasoline can and danced around sprinkling the fuel on the wood.

The German seemed to enjoy putting on a show for his captives. He waited for the fuel to soak in, and then with a dramatic sweep he tossed a lit match onto the stack. Whoosh! The timber went up. Orange flames darted high into the air. The heat scorched Cubiak's face. Cold as he was, he turned from it.

When he looked back, Ubell stood at the foot of the dock and stared out over the water.

Cubiak slashed the blade again, and a strand of rope snapped.

"You're waiting for a bigger boat, something that will take you across the border to Canada and then down the Saint Lawrence. For that you need something faster than the *Speedy Sister*," he said.

"Shut up." Ubell didn't bother to turn around.

"A friend is coming. Someone with a very big boat."

Ubell laughed.

"How many did you book passage for?" Cubiak talked as loud as he dared. He wanted the fake Helen to hear. "He's not taking you with him, Helen-Marlene. You know that, don't you? Why share the spoils when he can have it all to himself?"

"Shut up, I said."

"You won't have time to bury all of us, and it's too risky to leave bodies on the shore. A party of fishermen might show up in the early morning and make the grisly discovery. You'll dump us in the lake. A feast for the big fish."

Ubell picked up a flaming branch from the fire and tossed it at Cubiak. The sheriff ducked, and the metal shard slipped from his fingers. He swore again. The rope was loose but not loose enough. He had to retrieve the blade and quickly.

The German was reaching for another torch when Helen-Marlene appeared on the deck. She held a lantern aloft, and in the cone of bright white light that enveloped her, she looked weak and ghostly pale. But when she spoke, her words were fueled with fierce determination. "You don't know what you're talking about. Ubell will never desert me. We are married. I am his wife."

"Husbands kill their wives," Cubiak said. He leaned back as far as he dared and groped for the blade. On his second attempt, he snagged it between his fingers.

The fake Helen clambered out of the boat and picked her way down the dock, talking as she advanced toward the shore. "No. Tell him, Ubell. Tell him you love me."

The German met her at the foot of the pier. When she was within reach, he clutched her around the waist and kissed her fiercely. Then he stepped away. The fake Helen was still gloating when Ubell grabbed her hair and wrenched her head back. "Enough of this silly nonsense. Go back to the boat and babysit that bitch," he said. He shoved her toward the *Speedy Sister*. Helen-Marlene staggered several feet and then turned and stared at him. She seemed confused and hurt.

"Don't listen to him," Ubell said, gesturing toward the sheriff. "He's desperate. He has nothing but words. Empty words. We have a plan. Remember that."

The fake Helen looked at the roaring fire. "A plan," she said, smiling and echoing the words. Then she pivoted and started back toward the boat.

As the two put on their show, Cubiak sawed at the rope.

"He kills anyone who knew him as Eric Fielder. He said so himself."

The fake Helen hesitated.

"Get to the boat," Ubell yelled.

"He doesn't need you. He's mad, Helen-Marlene. Don't trust him."

The fake Helen let out a loud sob. Then she clamped her hands to her ears and scurried toward the boat.

Ubell kicked into the fire and sprayed fiery embers at the sheriff. "I told you to shut up."

Enveloped in smoke and hot ash, Cubiak coughed and nearly dropped the blade.

"Chief, you OK?" Rowe said.

Ubell spun around. His face was red, either from the fire or rage. "Shut up," he said and stood glaring at the two men.

The sheriff returned his hard stare.

"Your father must have been a mean son-of-a-bitch. I know mine was," he said quietly. "Is that where you get it from?"

Ubell sneered.

"Mine beat me when he got drunk. Did your father beat you?"

The German sniggered but meanness seemed to etch deeper into his face.

Cubiak rubbed the knife shard against the rope. Almost there. How to taunt Ubell further? "Maybe it's a good thing you never knew your mother. Mine was no prize, and perhaps yours wasn't either."

Ubell grabbed a burning log from the fire and was turning to swing it at Cubiak when the sound of a motor floated across the water. The roar was distant but steady. Ubell lowered the stick and listened.

Helen-Marlene emerged from the cabin.

"Go back," Ubell ordered. "Now."

She disappeared below deck.

Who was out there? Cubiak wondered. No lights shone through the blackness. Only the steady, low hum gave away the boat's presence. At this point, the sound was neutral, indicating neither friend nor foe. But it had to be one or the other. Had Ubell's contact seen the fire, or had the light attracted someone else? Anyone could be out there: fishermen, a boatful of tourists. Just what he didn't need now was a group of over-eager and even liquored-up men trying to play hero. Had Rowe notified the coast guard and hidden a tracking device on the boat, something that the fake Helen hadn't found? Would a rescue squad make such a bold approach? Cubiak looked to Rowe for a sign, but the young man was intent on the water. So he didn't know who was coming either.

The sound from the lake persisted. Ubell tossed the burning stick on the fire and checked his watch.

"My friends are here," he said. He rubbed his hands together and grinned like a little boy about to get the biggest toy at Christmas.

Forgetting his captives, Ubell moved past the fire and started toward the shore. It was the moment Cubiak had been waiting for. With a final slash, the dull blade severed the last strand of fiber, and the cord dropped away from his wrists. He was stiff and sore, and he staggered getting up. Rowe watched incredulously as the sheriff regained his balance and slipped toward his deputy.

"How?"

"Shh."

Cubiak cut the ropes and rubbed Rowe's numb hands. "Ready?"

"Yeah."

Rowe grabbed the cord that had been around his wrists while the sheriff lifted a log from the stack of firewood.

Cubiak motioned toward the dock, and the two men crouched down and crept forward.

They were less than a yard from the water when Ubell turned around. But he was too late.

Cubiak swung the log at his head, and with a single *ooph*, the German crumpled to the ground.

THE FALL OF EVIL

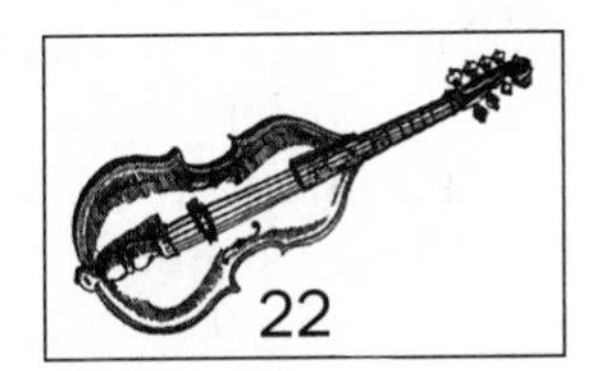
22

Cubiak had his man, but the moment of triumph was fleeting. The approaching vessel was churning up the water and gaining on them. They had to secure Ubell and hide the *Speedy Sister* before the mystery boat reached the island.

"Here, tie his hands," Cubiak said. While the deputy worked, the sheriff pulled the German's gun and phone from his pockets. Then he pulled a jacket over his head and secured the sleeves around his chin and mouth. Even if he revived and tried to shout, his voice wouldn't carry far.

On the water, the hum of the boat engine swelled to a roar. Cubiak looked up. A small green light danced in the darkness. Green signified starboard. The boat was coming from the north, so it wasn't the coast guard, which would approach from the opposite direction.

To the north there was only the Upper Peninsula with its sparse population and more of the turbulent waters of Lake Michigan. Given the lateness of the hour and the threat of more bad weather, the most likely people onboard were Ubell's contacts, and they were headed to the island to meet him.

"There's more line on the boat for his legs and feet," the deputy said when he finished lashing Ubell's hands.

"Not yet."

Cubiak checked the lake again. The light was still green but the boat seemed to be moving faster. Judging from the fierce scream of the engine it had to be a very big boat, he thought, and he saw the worry in Rowe's eyes.

"Sounds like a cigarette boat."

"We have to get away before they see us," the sheriff said.

"We don't have much time."

"I know. Wait here."

"What about the fire?"

"Let it be. If it dies, that's in our favor. When you hear my signal, bring him onboard."

Cubiak started toward the dock. He didn't dare use the flashlight, and in the dark, each step on the decrepit pier was a gamble. The sheriff kept Ubell's gun in his pocket. He would try to entice the fake Helen out of the cabin. If he had to go below, he would draw the Glock only if she had laid down her silver pistol. If she had her gun aimed at Cate, the weapon would do him no good.

When he reached the boat, he crouched low and thumped his fist against the side wall.

For a moment, there was no reaction. Then Helen-Marlene spoke. "Ubell, is that you?"

In response Cubiak undid a mooring line and noisily tossed it onboard.

"What's going on? Who's there?" The fake Helen sounded excited and scared.

The sheriff slipped over the gunwale and ducked behind the wheel. Seconds passed and the cabin door cracked open.

The sound from the mystery boat filled the night air. He knew the fake Helen heard it. He waited. She had to be listening. Either she knew what the plan was or could guess at it.

"Ah, the boat comes," she said.

The fake Helen started up the stairs. Midway, she stopped.

Come on, Cubiak urged silently. He imagined her squinting into the darkness, uncertain what to do and fearful of making a mistake.

Then she gambled and came up into the cockpit.

"Ubell, where are you?"

The fake Helen looked toward the pier. As she turned toward him, Cubiak stepped out and slapped a hand over her mouth. Startled, she jerked and dropped her pistol. He pinned her arms behind her back and threw his other arm around her shoulders. She clawed and kicked. She was strong and fierce, and she fought hard. But he held tight.

A muted sound rose up from below.

"Cate, it's me. I've come for you," Cubiak said.

Helen-Marlene squirmed.

The sheriff tightened his grip. "Ubell is my prisoner and no good to you anymore. You'd do well to cooperate," he said.

The fake Helen tried to shake her head and twist her shoulders.

"Whoever is on that boat isn't coming for you," he said.

She tensed.

"Do you want to live or not?"

Helen-Marlene squirmed again.

"I'll keep you safe, but he won't."

She made a noise and tried to pull free, but then he felt her resolve fade. He grabbed the silver handgun and pushed her toward the hatch.

"Go," he said, sounding much like Ubell had earlier, as he propelled her down the stairs.

The cabin curtains were pulled, and in the dim light Cubiak saw Cate in the corner, behind the table. The cloth around her mouth was loosened but her hands were tied. He held a finger to his lips.

After he immobilized the fake Helen and gagged her with a rag, he turned to Cate. She was on her feet. Her gaze was steady and calm. "Thank God, you're safe," he said and pulled her into his arms. He wanted to hold her forever. He wanted to tell her again that he loved her. Instead he kissed her forehead, undid her bindings, and put the silver pistol in her cold hands. "You know what to do. We don't have much time."

Topside, Cubiak looked out at the black lake. There were two lights visible now, one red and one green. The mystery boat had turned and was on a straight line toward the island, Boats have distinct sounds, and the vessel that barreled toward them out of the darkness roared like a monster biting its way through the water.

The sheriff cupped his mouth and whistled. He had never been very good at it and the sound came out flat and weak. Would Rowe hear the signal over the scream of the engine? The sheriff waited. Then he whistled again. After a moment, he heard the clear chirp of a bird. Rowe had signaled back.

The sheriff met his deputy midway down the pier and helped him drag Ubell to the *Speedy Sister*. The German was still unconscious.

"Start the motor and head that way." Cubiak pointed away from the pier. "Keep it low, just trolling speed."

"Got it."

Rowe switched on the ignition and the engines came to life. Cubiak felt the hull shiver as they started to move. The boat slid through the water like snow falling in the night, soft and quiet. Neither man spoke. Cubiak kept his eyes on the shore. The bonfire had shrunk but wood was still burning. They had to pass in front of the flaming logs, and as they did they would be visible to anyone on the boat looking toward land.

"Quickly now," Cubiak said.

For a precious moment Rowe let the *Sister* race forward. Then he cut the engines again and brought the boat back to a crawl.

The sheriff knew the deputy was worried about ramming into rocks or running aground.

"You're doing fine. We're good," Cubiak said.

Despite the heavy cloud cover, his eyes slowly adjusted to the dark. He had no idea how large the island was. As best he could, he followed the faint outline of the shore, searching for an inlet or cove where they could hide.

They rounded a point and the shoreline dipped inward toward a solid black wall. More trees, Cubiak realized. Then he spotted the dock. It was short and probably as old as the first pier they had moored at. "There," he said.

Rowe saw the dock, too. "We must be on Summer. It's one of the larger islands." He aimed the *Sister* toward the shore and cut the engines. The boat drifted forward.

From out on the lake behind them, the scream of the mystery vessel softened to a throaty murmur.

"They're heading in," Rowe said as Cubiak tied the *Sister* to the decrepit pier. "Should I radio for help?"

"We can't chance it. If they intercept the message, they'll know we're here."

Suddenly a powerful searchlight swept over the island, illuminating the tops of the trees. Loud voices erupted from the other side of the forest. Two men argued in a mishmash of languages: part English, part French, part something else. One voice was high pitched and the other low and guttural.

In the onslaught of light and noise, Ubell's cell phone dinged. A text message appeared on the bright screen: *Where r u?*

Cubiak replied, *on island hurt neede help*.

"You got any fishing line onboard?" he asked his deputy.

"Yes."

"Get it."

Ubell moaned and slowly worked himself up to a sitting position. His expression gave away nothing but there was hate in his eyes. Cubiak pulled him to his feet and prodded him down the stairs. The fake Helen blanched as the sheriff pushed him into the opposite corner and re-tightened his restraints.

Bundled in a thick wool blanket, Cate sat holding the silver pistol.

"If either of them tries anything, shoot to kill. Him first. Her second," Cubiak said, pointing to the German and his accomplice. Then he leaned down and whispered. "Are you OK?"

She moved her head up and down.

He went on so only she could hear. "Rowe and I have to go. But we'll be back."

"Right." She didn't ask for an explanation.

On deck, Rowe waited with two rolls of fishing line.

"It's not strong enough to stop anyone," he said.

"That's OK. We just need to trip them up."

"We're going back?"

"It's our only option." Plan C, he thought.

The sheriff led the way along the edge of the dock. When he reached the end, he leapt past the boulders and onto the ground.

"We'll follow the shore back the way we came. We'd make better time on the rocks but we can't chance being seen, so we'll keep to the trees."

In a few steps, the dense forest closed over the two men.

"Stay close," Cubiak said.

He held up his hands and began to claw through the weblike netting of the pine branches. The searchlight had stopped rotating back and forth.

"They're showing us the way," Rowe said.

"That's either good or bad."

The sheriff guessed that they were about a quarter mile from the clearing and that it would take them ten minutes to get there. But in the trees, he lost all sense of time and distance.

The searchlight snapped off, and the men on the water went silent.

"We have to reach the clearing before they do," Cubiak said.

"You think they'll come ashore?"

"If they want what Ubell has, they will."

When they had gone another ten feet, the man with the high-pitched voice began ranting. His tirade was followed by a menacing silence. Finally, the second man, the one Cubiak pegged as the boss, responded with a curt two-word reply that sounded like *Fuck off* or *Fuck you*, or something similar.

"You catch any of that?"

"Nope, sorry."

"Me neither."

Abruptly, Cubiak stopped.

"Look," he said.

Through the dense underbrush, they saw the clearing. The fire was still burning and gave them enough light to see past the pier to the open water where the mystery boat was anchored some hundred yards offshore. Rowe was right: Ubell's cohorts had driven a cigarette boat to the rendezvous.

Cubiak crouched down. Rowe did the same.

"Think you can get to the other side and secure the line to one of those trees?" he said, pointing across the clearing. "And then bring it back to this side and tie it to another tree."

"How high?"

"Two feet off the ground. I'll cover you."

"Got it."

"Be careful. Stay in the trees," Cubiak said.

Rowe grunted and crept forward.

As the deputy inched around the opening, the men on the cigarette boat started up again.

"I don't like the looks of this," the frightened man said.

"We came too far to go back empty-handed."

Seconds passed and Ubell's mobile vibrated. Another text: *Boat?*

Sunk prize safe, Cubiak replied.

Had Ubell told them about the priceless viol? Probably not, but he would have had to guarantee a big haul to lure them into the scheme.

"Come and get it, you bastards," Cubiak said in a whisper.

The sheriff watched for Rowe. There was no hint of the deputy, no subtle movement in the brush. He had lost track of him.

"Damn." Cubiak flattened and low-crawled closer. The ground was cold and smelled of old pine and mildew. He was as far as he could go and still be undercover when Rowe rolled out from behind a thick stump.

"Jesus, you scared the life out of me."

"Sir. Sorry. It's all done. Now what?"

"We wait."

A wind gust blew smoke from the fire toward them, and Cubiak struggled not to cough. Then a log popped, and a shower of sparks sequined the darkness. As the sparks withered, he felt the ground vibrate with the steady thrum of the cigarette boat's engines. Ubell's accomplices were on the move. Were they leaving or heading in?

The searchlight popped on again, and the island lit up under the blistering glow.

They were coming ashore.

"Don't move, and don't look at the light or you'll be blinded," Cubiak said.

Head down, he listened as the vessel churned closer. A few minutes passed and it thumped against the dock. He heard the whoosh of the lines being thrown around the same tilting posts where hours earlier they had tied up the *Speedy Sister*.

"Let's go," the boss man said, and boots thudded on the pier.

The newcomers left the searchlight on and advanced on foot. Lying prone on the damp earth, Cubiak shaded his eyes and peered through the flickering flames of the dying signal fire. The men were formidable against the backlighting. The first was tall and gangly. The second was even taller and had the swagger and build of a wrestler. Their features were blotted out, but he saw that both wore black and both were heavily armed. Their guns looked like Uzis, which made the Glock in his hand feel like a water pistol.

The lead man had reached the end of the dock when his partner broke through a rotted board. The jagged planks stopped the muscular assailant from falling all the way through and left him suspended in midair. With his upper torso above the pier and his feet and legs dangling in the water, he twisted and cursed in a language the sheriff didn't understand.

The first man swung around. "Fucking asshole," he said, and Cubiak recognized the voice of the man he thought of as the boss.

"Chief . . . ," Rowe said.

"Not yet."

The trapped man struggled to get free. Leaving him, the boss plowed ahead. He was nearly on top of the lawmen when he tripped over the fishing line. As he toppled forward, he lost hold of the Uzi, and it skittered toward the fire.

"Now," the sheriff said, pointing his deputy toward the pier.

As Rowe hurtled toward the lake, Cubiak threw himself at the man on the ground. The boss was young and strong. He punched the sheriff's jaw and broke his hold. As the intruder went for the weapon, Cubiak scrambled up and kicked the Uzi into the glowing embers.

A sudden fusillade of gunfire tore across the clearing. The trapped man was firing at the commotion onshore.

Cubiak dove behind the fire.

"Stop, you idiot," the boss yelled, but the sickly staccato of the semi-automatic swallowed his words. The bombardment continued for several more seconds before the bullets stopped hammering the clearing and started pinging at the pier and the surrounding water. This second outburst was followed by a loud splash, then a surprised cry and silence.

Cubiak didn't dare look toward the lake. But he imagined what had happened. Rowe had waded out beneath the pier toward the trapped man. When he reached him, he grabbed him from below and yanked him through the gap.

The sheriff was about to call out to his deputy when his assailant emerged from behind the tree. The boss had a knife.

Cubiak grabbed a flaming branch and advanced.

The young man stared at Cubiak with dead blue eyes and didn't move.

"Where is Ubell?"

"He's my prisoner."

"Ah, you have the prize as well?"

"Of course."

The man grinned and the dragon tattoo on his cheek puckered. "We make a deal."

"No deal."

"Be reasonable." The boss gestured toward the dock with the knife. "Your friend has taken out my friend. That's one down. We kill Ubell and your friend, and then we share. Sixty-forty."

"Fifty-fifty." The branch was burning down toward Cubiak's hand.

"The fuck. You have no way off this place. You need me."

"But I have the prize. So you need me more."

The boss sneered. He leapt forward and with a powerful karate kick knocked the burning stick to the ground. The sheriff ducked to grab it, and the young assailant darted forward. He held the knife high and thrust his arm down, plunging the long, serrated blade toward Cubiak.

A shot rang out. The man yelped and staggered backward. The knife dropped into the dirt as blood streamed down his sleeve. His wrist was shattered. Cubiak grabbed his other arm and rammed it up behind his back.

Rowe must have pulled a handgun off the man on the dock. That was the only explanation. Expecting to find his deputy on the other side of the clearing, the sheriff spun around.

And saw Cate. She had fired the shot.

She stood across from him, tall and impervious. Holding the silver pistol steady, she kept it aimed at the bleeding man.

The boss snarled with rage and contempt. "A goddamn woman," he said.

Yes, and thank God for her, Cubiak thought.

With the injured man subdued, they moved quickly. Cate devised a tourniquet from her sweater to stanch his bleeding, while Cubiak helped Rowe drag the other shooter from the lake.

"You OK? You're not hurt?" he asked his deputy as they pulled the protesting lump out from under the dock.

"Just fucking cold. Water's like ice," he said.

Rowe was limping, and when they got to shore, Cubiak saw the blood on his shirt. "You've been hit," he said.

The bullet had grazed the deputy just above his belt.

"Lucky for you it's just a flesh wound," the sheriff said, knowing it could have been much worse.

Onboard the cigarette boat, Cubiak found a first aid kit with gauze and tape that Cate used to patch up Rowe. When he was satisfied that his deputy was OK, he made Rowe and the man who had crashed through the pier strip to their skivvies and sit down by the fire. Then he went back to the boat for dry clothes and the assailants' passports.

They were from Tunisia, if the documents were authentic. The boss was Zied; the other man, Pierre.

"Tell me about your arrangement with Ubell," Cubiak said, back at the clearing.

Zied refused to say anything, but Pierre held his hands to the fire and talked freely. As the sheriff suspected, Ubell had hired them to transport him and his companion along with the unidentified prize to Michigan's Sault Sainte Marie and then across the border to Canada.

"That's enough. Shut up," the boss said.

The big man ignored him. "I don't hafta take no orders from you no more. The German guy said there'd be a third passenger, too, but only for as long as needed. Kinda like protection if we were stopped or something."

They didn't know who the third person was, but it had to be Cate.

"And then?" Cubiak said.

Pierre shrugged, as if to say *You know*.

Without the Uzi, the man looked a little lost and almost harmless. "You kill us?" he said, staring into the fire.

"What do you mean?"

"You got this guy, Ubell, right? You got his prize, whatever it is. You kill us all and get rich. That's the plan, ain't it?"

"Not exactly," Cubiak said. He felt inside his pocket for his badge.

"Oh," Pierre said.

Zied kicked at an ember. "Shit." He spoke as if he would rather be shot dead than face what was coming.

Cubiak radioed the coast guard from the *Speedy Sister* and then brought it around and tied it up behind the monster boat.

"Coast guard's already on the way. They'll meet us at Washington Island and escort us the rest of the way in," he said. The sheriff looked at his deputy. "It seems that Bathard got instructions from you to contact them if he didn't hear from you within an hour. Is that right?"

"Yeah. I hope . . ."

"That you did the right thing?" Cubiak clapped his deputy's shoulder. "Absolutely. Good call, Mike."

They took both boats back. Rowe insisted he was fit to pilot the monster boat with the fake Helen and Pierre onboard. The others followed in the *Speedy Sister*. The sheriff took the helm and sent Cate below with the Glock to guard Ubell, Zied, and the yellow viol.

Cubiak held the wheel steady and followed the white stern light of the cigarette boat. Rowe was traveling fast, and he was glad. The sooner they reached Sturgeon Bay, the sooner Rowe would get to the ER for a thorough exam and he would get through the usual red tape of processing the prisoners. Mostly, however, he thought about Cate and getting her home safely. What if she lost the baby after what she had been through that day? Would their marriage dissolve into vague emptiness? Would she leave him? The possible consequences left him numb.

After a while, she came up top.

"Aren't you cold?" he asked. The question seemed banal but he could think of no other.

Cate shook her head. She was bundled in sweaters and coats and had pulled a red wool cap over her ears.

"Ubell and that guy creep me out. I'm done looking at them. I'd rather be looking at this." She pointed to the vista ahead.

The clouds had fallen away from each other like tatters of lace. As they drifted apart, they created a pathway overhead. Moonlight cascaded through the opening and formed a long, straight silver line that paved their way across the black water.

"How do you feel?" Cubiak said, although he was almost afraid to ask.

"I'm fine." She slipped her hand into his jacket pocket. "At some point you're going to have to stop asking me that."

He felt his fears start to slip away. "In about seven months maybe, but not before then."

Cate rested her head against his shoulder. "Fair enough."

They were quiet for a moment, and then Cubiak spoke again. "You saved my life back there. You risked everything for me. If anything happens . . ."

"Shhh. I only did what needed to be done. I did what you do every day."

"What made you come to the clearing?"

"I heard the gunfire. You had Ubell's Glock, and I knew Rowe was unarmed. That left me holding the only other weapon for our side. I thought it might help even the odds."

"You're a brave woman." Cubiak wrapped an arm around his wife.

Just then a shooting star plummeted toward the earth. "There's something that I have to ask," he said when the flash of light disappeared.

"Yes?"

"Where the hell did you learn to shoot like that?"

Cate laughed. "Uncle Dutch taught me. I used to go camping when I was a teenager, and he said he couldn't rest unless he was sure that I knew how to protect myself from wild animals."

"I guess I owe a lot to Dutch."

"You know that wasn't his real name, don't you?"

"It wasn't?"

"No." Cate looked up and smiled. "It was Dave."

MUSIC FOR THE GODS

The calendar had flipped to October, the month when summer retreated into memory and Door County settled into the welcome leisurely pace of autumn. With the number of tourists dwindling as quickly as the vivid fall leaves faded, the routine job demands at the justice center eased as well, giving Cubiak time to catch up on paperwork. That morning, he had two reports to read.

The first document summarized the events surrounding the Viola da Gamba Music Festival. Nearly seven weeks had passed since he had locked Ubell Acker, Helen-Marlene, and the two Tunisians behind bars. After their night in the Door County jail, he had remanded them into FBI custody. Within days, the four were arraigned on charges that included murder, attempted murder, kidnapping, theft, and assault. The report spelled out the details of the subsequent findings. Most interesting to him was the fact that all of the suspects' names were aliases, even that of the man who had claimed he was Ubell Acker. According to the German police, the real Ubell, the son of gambist Franz Acker, had been missing for more than two years and was presumed dead.

"Well, isn't life strange," Cubiak said when he came to that bit of information.

For him, the second report, which Rowe had just brought in, carried more immediate import. It detailed the investigation of the shoplifting ring led by Meryl Gregory, the woman the sheriff had encountered at the Washington Island gift shop during the festival.

"She ran a group of nine people. All of them were married to musicians who traveled around the country performing at different festivals and summer concerts. While the musicians worked at their gigs, the spouses 'shopped.' In two summers, they swiped more than a hundred grand worth of merchandise. Most of which they sold on eBay," Rowe said.

"Were they all women?"

"Mostly, but there were two or three men as well."

"And the spouses—the musicians—knew nothing about the scheme?"

"That's what they all claim."

Cubiak shook his head. He was about to say *Well, isn't life strange* but realized he would be repeating himself and wasn't that a bad sign? Instead he looked at his deputy. "How're you doing?"

Rowe patted his left side. "Good as new," he said.

"I still regret letting you pilot the Tunisians' cigarette boat back to Sturgeon Bay."

"Too much adrenalin. I didn't feel a thing."

"Or you just wanted to drive a monster down the lake."

Rowe laughed and stepped back toward the door, where he nearly collided with the sheriff's assistant.

Lisa was unusually animated. "There's a gentleman here to see you," she told her boss.

"Who is he?"

"He wouldn't give his name, but you'll want to see him. Trust me."

The last time Lisa had said something similar, the devious fake Helen Kulas had sat down across from his desk.

"You're sure?"

"Positive."

Cubiak glanced out the window. The view opened to the pasture across the road, where a herd of Holsteins grazed. Earlier the cows were scattered over the grass, but now they had moved out of sight, leaving the empty meadow to shimmer in the brilliant October light. The glow was almost otherworldly. A sign, perhaps.

"OK, send him in," he said.

A pale, sandy-haired man wrapped in a monk's cassock floated through the doorway bearing a massive bouquet of yellow roses. The visitor was slight of build, and with his tonsured hair, he looked like an apparition of Saint Francis of Assisi. A wide cowl encircled his throat, and his shoulders stooped under the weight of the coarse, brown fabric that cascaded to the floor. He wore sandals and no socks. A mendicant. As soon as he saw him, Cubiak regretted his decision.

What the hell is this? the sheriff thought as he stood to greet the visitor.

"I am Ubell Acker," the monk said. With an unabashed smile, he presented the flowers to Cubiak.

The sheriff was dumbfounded. "Ubell Acker is presumed dead."

"Dead to the world, yes. And, indeed, for a while that was true. But as you see, I am very much alive."

Cubiak didn't know what to say and was saved by Lisa, who had followed the visitor in.

"May I?" she said as she reached for the roses. "I'll put them in water. Coffee, sir?"

"Please."

"Father?"

The visitor bowed his head. "I am Brother Franz, named in memory of my father, not a priest, but thank you for the use of the honorific. And tea, not coffee, if it's not too much trouble."

The sheriff seated Brother Franz at the small table near the door. For a moment, the monk busied himself studying the trappings of the office. He seemed content not to speak, so Cubiak waited.

When Lisa returned with the vase of flowers and mugs of tea and coffee, the sheriff signaled for her to close the door.

"Two months ago, I arrested a man who called himself Ubell Acker. According to the FBI, his real name is Karl Jager. Have you ever heard of him?"

"Sadly, yes. Karl Jager was my former longtime friend, pretending to be me."

"You know him, then?"

Brother Franz gave a woeful smile. "Karl and I grew up together." The monk sipped the tea and then launched into the sad story of his childhood. Some of the information was already familiar to Cubiak: After the theft of the yellow viol, Franz Acker returned to Germany with his infant son and tried to take up his old life in Hamburg. Emotionally distraught, he was unable to perform in public and ended up giving private lessons to make a living. But much of what the monk revealed was new.

"Many of the neighbors also were not kind to my father. There were whispers and sniggers, sometimes behind his back and sometimes to his face. He had been a famous man and now he was reduced to a joke in their eyes. Eventually their vitriol drove him away from our home. I was three or so when we moved to a small farm in Bavaria, where my father meant to start over. No one paid much attention to us, except for old ladies who baked him cakes and tried to win his favor for their unmarried daughters."

The monk paused, as if remembering. "And that was where I met Karl," he said. "We started together in kindergarten and remained classmates all the way through gymnasium, which is like your high school. I was a shy child and Karl became my best friend, my only friend, really. It was from me that he learned so much about the yellow viol."

Brother Franz looked at the sheriff with sad eyes. "You must realize that my father remained tortured by the events of that terrible night. He blamed himself for everything that happened and never ceased talking about it—the storm, the arduous journey to the hospital, my mother's death, the theft of the viol. And I, though sworn to secrecy, complained endlessly to Karl."

"You must have had great trust in him," Cubiak said.

"We were both farm kids without many playmates. He shared secrets with me, and I did the same with him. There didn't seem to be any harm in it." The monk made a small sound like a laugh. "Ironically, of the two of us, Karl was the one with the talent for music."

"Your father taught him to play the viol?"

"He did. And Karl was quite good."

"What happened then?"

"My father died and Karl and I grew up. He went to study in Cologne and I in Berlin. He had family in Bavaria and probably went back but I had no reason to return. Over time we lost track of each other."

Brother Franz reached for the tea again. "I endured much hardship growing up, and in Berlin I became acquainted with people who had been lavished with wealth and ease. Getting to know them, I realized how different my life would have been if my father had not lost the yellow viol. I would have enjoyed luxury instead of deprivation. I became very angry."

He gave Cubiak a meaningful look. "It is easy to be angry in Berlin. There are many outlets for one's rage."

"Drugs? Alcohol?"

"That, and more."

The monk fell silent, and the wall clock ticked off several minutes before he returned to his story.

"I hadn't thought about Karl in nearly two decades, until a few years ago when he emailed me and suggested we get together. 'For old times' sake,' he said. I hardly recognized him—not just physically because, of course, so much time had elapsed, but in his personality. He'd been a modest, unassuming kid, but as a man he was full of braggadocio. He told me he was a freelance journalist who traveled the world on assignment. Near the end of our conversation, he said that he wanted to write a book about the yellow viol. He hoped that we could sit down and talk more about it, possibly even collaborate on the project. 'Share a byline,' he said."

"Did you?"

Brother Franz dipped his head. "I admit that it was tempting. There was a moment when I almost agreed to his suggestion. It was only later that I realized that he assumed I'd been searching for the viol and wanted to know what I'd learned. But, no, I didn't accept his offer."

"Why not?"

"For one, I'd worked hard to put my past behind me, but also, I couldn't. I was about to enter the monastery and commit to a long period of isolation. It seemed misguided to immerse myself in old worldly concerns just as I was about to embark on this new path of spiritual growth."

"I see, and what did this entail, this period of isolation?"

"There was to be no communication with the outside world for twenty-four months."

"Two years?"

The visitor nodded. "Unwittingly, I gave my former friend both carte blanche to abscond with my identity and ample time to do his evil deeds."

"You know that he wasn't a journalist."

"I know that now. He was a sound engineer. With the skills he acquired from his work and the information I'd given him about the viol, he was convinced he could find it."

"There's no reason to blame yourself. It was a common enough story, wasn't it? As I understand, there were many articles written about the theft."

"Yes, but I told him things that no one else ever knew. How my father became fixated with finding the yellow viol and how he systematically listened to every gambist recording he could find, convinced that he would know the yellow viol by its sound."

"You mean the wolf tone?"

Brother Franz looked surprised.

"The man pretending to be you told me about it."

"Ah, so there it is. Don't you understand, Sheriff? I told Karl what to do; I drew the blueprint for him to follow. And then he succeeded where my father had failed."

"You can't blame your father. By the time Payette began to release recordings made with the yellow viol, your father had already died."

"That is very true. As it was, my father eventually gave up his quest and accepted the theory that the thief had fled by boat, and that both the robber and the viol sank in the storm. I think that my father lost so much that night, he could survive only by believing that the thief had been punished as well."

The phone on the desk rang. Cubiak ignored it.

"Whatever became of him, George Payette, the thief?" Brother Franz said when the ringing ceased.

"Ultimately he was punished, as your father assumed. The statute of limitations on the theft expired over three decades ago, but once the story came out, Payette's reputation was destroyed. After he recovered from the beating that Ubell—sorry, Jager—gave him, he left Door County. His house is up for sale, so it's probably safe to say we'll never see him here again."

"Poetic justice," the monk said.

"Something like that. But what of the yellow viol, now that it has been recovered?" Cubiak said.

"As you can imagine, there were many doubts about its legitimacy, but the International Viola da Gamba Association has authenticated the instrument, and it has been returned to the Guttenberg heirs."

"You have no claim on it?"

Brother Franz shook his head. "None at all. But the family has agreed that it will allow the yellow viol to be featured annually in a series of concerts and that a portion of the proceeds will be donated to the clinics and schools that my order operates in areas of need around the world. It is what you Americans call a win-win situation."

"You've come a long way to tell me this."

The monk touched the cross that hung on his chest. "I came to thank you for recovering the treasured yellow viol that was stolen from my unfortunate father so many years ago. It is a great debt that I owe you, and one that I needed to pay in person."

From the hall came the sounds of the staff leaving for the day. Brother Franz had talked for more than two hours. But he wasn't finished. "I regret the deaths of the innocent people," he said, his voice soft but hoarse.

"You were not responsible for that."

"No? Perhaps if years ago, I had done what this devious fiend did, I could have discovered the viol and prevented this second tragedy."

"Perhaps, but probably not." Cubiak leaned forward. "You seem to be a humble man. And isn't it a sign of humility to acknowledge that which is outside our control?"

The visitor was quiet a moment. "Thank you, Sheriff. That is very kind of you to say that. You are a man of faith, are you not?" he said finally.

"I was once."

Brother Franz smiled. "Faith withers, but I believe that it never completely disappears. I have a gift for you that perhaps will help the seed to germinate again."

The monk reached into the folds of his robe. Cubiak expected him to fish out a Bible or a prayer book from a hidden pocket. Instead Brother Franz pulled out a single CD. "This is the last recording my father made with his beloved yellow viol. It is music that speaks to the soul," he said as he handed the slim plastic case to the sheriff.

As the visit drew to a close, Cubiak invited Brother Franz to come for dinner and to stay the night, but the monk declined.

"Thank you, but I have made arrangements to go to Washington Island. It is a place that has shaped my life, and I would like to spend a little time there. I've heard that it is very beautiful."

"It is."

"I think that I should see it before I die, don't you?" he said.

Cubiak nodded.

After a moment, the monk stood. "May I give you a blessing?"

Cubiak hesitated. He had long ago stopped participating in religious rituals, but the man was so sincere he didn't think it right to refuse. "Of course," he said and closed his eyes.

Brother Franz placed his hand on the sheriff's head. For a moment, the monk seemed lost in silent prayer but then he spoke. "You have known sorrow, but you will know joy again. My prayer for you is that when joy comes, you will embrace it."

I will try, Cubiak thought.

After the visitor left, Cubiak removed two roses from the bouquet. He put one flower on Lisa's desk and the other on Rowe's. The rest he took home for Cate.

"You shouldn't have," she said.

"Yes, I should have, but I didn't."

Over dinner, he told her about Brother Franz. "The flowers were his way of showing his gratitude for the recovery of the yellow viol, but given what you did that night, I say you deserve them more than I do."

Cate smiled. "I wanted to make sure this baby had a father."

While Cubiak cleared the table, she moved to the couch and pulled her feet up on a pillow. Now that she was past the first trimester, she was sleeping better and had relaxed into what the doctor called the "golden period."

Ever since that night on the island, Cubiak had worried about Cate and their unborn child. Sitting with her that evening, he realized that his anxieties had eased as well. They were going to be fine.

"The baby's moving," Cate said.

He rested his hand on her abdomen. Earlier, when Brother Franz said that he would know joy, the monk hadn't qualified the prediction. Feeling the sure, quick thrust of life, Cubiak realized that the joy would come from the baby and his new family.

Thank you for that gift, Brother, he thought.

The house was quiet. The lake had pummeled the shore for days, but that morning it had changed its mood and by evening the water lay flat and still.

Cubiak dimmed the lights and put on the CD the monk had given him. He had seen the photo of Franz Acker with the yellow viol and pictured the gambist bent over the venerable instrument. As the master performed, the room filled with the pure, sweet sound of his music.

Brother Franz called it music that spoke to the soul. As he listened, Cubiak understood what the holy man meant. It was almost as if, like his son, Acker understood the heart's longing and through his music paid homage to humanity's hopes and dreams.

Cubiak settled next to Cate again. If the revered gambist played with such grace on earth, what beauty would he create in heaven? Surely, the sheriff thought, it would be music worthy of the saints and angels. Music worthy of all the world's children waiting to be born.

ACKNOWLEDGMENTS

Writing can be akin to jumping off a high ledge with a closed umbrella firmly in hand. The umbrella is the idea that inspired the work, and as you plummet downward, you pray it will open. If the parasol remains shut, you're out of luck. But if it unfurls, you stand a chance of landing on your feet.

As I worked on this book, I asked many people to help open the umbrella. I am humbled that they all stepped up and embraced the task. My deepest gratitude to Susan Rozendaal, who introduced me to and explained the finer points of the viola da gamba and early music.

My thanks as well to David Baldwin, Peter Jang, Hoyt Purinton, Julianne Hill, and Monica Haley Heenan, who provided much-needed information and guidance on various plot points.

To B. E. Pinkham, Jeanne Mellet, and Esther Spodek, the talented and devoted women in my writers group, who read and critiqued the manuscript as it progressed through the stages of development and then read it all over again at the end. To Norm Rowland, whose carefully considered comments made me rethink important elemnets of the story. To Barbara Bolsen for her vigilant reading of the final (not quite!) draft. To Max Edinburgh, who read the completed manuscript out loud to me not once, but twice. His was a gift that all those who write will understand and appreciate.

Finally, to my daughter and creative mapmaker Julia Padvoiskis, who suggested using the ferry as a locale as we made the crossing from Washington Island to the Door County peninsula one sunny day. And to my daughter Carla Padvoiskis, whose keen insight and suggestions challenged me to look at aspects of the story in a different way. Thank you both for your unwavering support.

Since the publication of the first book in the Dave Cubiak Door County Mystery series, the University of Wisconsin Press has proved to be outstanding. My sincere appreciation to Director Dennis Lloyd and his exemplary staff, including Raphael Kadushin, Sheila Leary, Sheila McMahon, Andrea Christofferson, Anne McKenna, Lindsey Meier, Adam Mehring, Terry Emmrich, Scott Lenz, and Amber Rose. Thanks as well to copyeditor Diana Cook, for her vital review of my work, and to graphic designer Sara DeHaan, for another enticing book cover.

I remain humbled and inspired by the support from readers, librarians, and booksellers. Thank you all.